‘I

‘To bring you this.’ He reached down to the floor beside the settee, bringing up the umbrella she had lost in Sydney Gardens. ‘I thought you might need it in such a rainy place as Bath.’

‘That is kind of you,’ she said slowly. ‘But surely you could have sent a servant?’

‘I could not entrust a servant with the rest of my errand.’

‘The rest of your errand?’

‘This.’ Marco reached out to gently cup her cheek in his palm, cradling it softly like the most delicate porcelain. Slowly, as if to give her time to draw away, he lowered his lips to hers.

But Thalia had absolutely no desire to turn away. Indeed, she could think of nothing at all—nothing but the feel of his mouth on hers, the slide of his caress along her cheek.

...Amanda McCabe's sumptuous Renaissance trilogy coming soon from Mills & Boon®

A NOTORIOUS WOMAN

'Court intrigue, poison and murders fill this Renaissance romance. The setting is beautiful…'
—*Romantic Times BOOKreviews*

A SINFUL ALLIANCE

'Scandal, seduction, spies, counter-spies, murder, love and loyalty are skilfully woven into the tapestry of the Tudor court. Richly detailed and brimming with historical events and personages, McCabe's tale weaves together history and passion perfectly.'
—*Romantic Times BOOKreviews*

HIGH SEAS STOWAWAY

'Smell the salt spray, feel the deck beneath your feet and hoist the Jolly Roger as McCabe takes you on an entertaining, romantic ride.'
—*Romantic Times BOOKreviews*

TO KISS A COUNT

Amanda McCabe

First published in Great Britain 2009
Paperback edition 2009
Harlequin Mills & Boon Limited,
Eton House, 18-24 Paradise Road, Richmond, Surrey TW9 1SR

ISBN: 978 0 263 86808 1

Set in Times Roman 10½ on 12¾ pt
04-1109-67078

Harlequin Mills & Boon policy is to use papers that are natural, renewable and recyclable products and made from wood grown in sustainable forests. The logging and manufacturing process conform to the legal environmental regulations of the country of origin.

Printed and bound in Spain
by Litografia Rosés, S.A., Barcelona

Amanda McCabe wrote her first romance at the age of sixteen—a vast epic, starring all her friends as the characters, written secretly during algebra class. She's never since used algebra, but her books have been nominated for many awards, including the RITA®, *Romantic Times BOOKreviews* Reviewers' Choice Award, the Booksellers Best, the National Readers' Choice Award, and the Holt Medallion. She lives in Oklahoma, with a menagerie of two cats, a pug and a bossy miniature poodle, and loves dance classes, collecting cheesy travel souvenirs, and watching the Food Network—even though she doesn't cook. Visit her at http://ammandamccabe.tripod.com and http://www.riskyregencies.blogspot.com

Previous novels by the same author:

TO CATCH A ROGUE*
TO DECEIVE A DUKE*

*Linked to TO KISS A COUNT

Prologue

Sicily

'Oh, Miss Thalia! We'll never be able to leave tomorrow, there's still ever so much to do.'

Thalia looked up from the books and papers she was packing away to see her maid Mary dashing around the chamber, her arms filled with gowns. Open trunks dotted the floor, half-full. Clothes and shoes spilled from the armoire and drawers.

'Really, Mary,' Thalia said with a laugh, 'we have been moving about so much of late, I'm surprised you don't have the packing down to an exact science.'

'Well, we've never left in such a hurry before, either. There is no time to do things properly!'

Thalia agreed with her there. Her father, Sir Walter Chase, was not usually one to rush his travels. They had moved leisurely through Italy, seeing all the sites and meeting all Sir Walter's scholarly correspondents before coming to rest in Sicily. But now his work here was nearly done. His ancient town site was thoroughly excavated, studied, and turned over to local antiquarians. Thalia's older sister Clio was married to her true love, the Duke of Averton, and off on her honeymoon to lands east.

Sir Walter himself was now married again, to his longtime companion Lady Rushworth, and ready to see new places. They were headed to Geneva for the summer, along with Thalia's younger sister Terpsichore, called Cory. It had been assumed that Thalia, too, would go with them. But after all that had happened in the last weeks, all that she had seen and felt and done, she was weary of new places. So, she was for home. England.

Her eldest sister, Calliope, Lady Westwood, was expecting her first child, and her recent letters were uncharacteristically plaintive. She asked when they would return home, when she would see them again. Thalia suspected Calliope would prefer Clio's company. As the two oldest of the Chase Muses, they were very close. And no one was stronger, more capable than Clio.

But Clio was gone, and Calliope would have to make do with Thalia. Thalia, the one they all thought of as so flighty and dramatic. Perfectly adequate for visits to the modiste or amateur theatricals, but not for delivering babies.

Not for catching villainous thieves.

Thalia caught sight of herself in the dressing-table

mirror. The Sicilian sunlight poured from the windows, turning her loose hair to the buttery shade of summer jonquils. Her heart-shaped face and wide blue eyes, her roses-and-cream skin, were pretty enough, she supposed. They certainly gained her admirers, silly, brainless suitors who wrote her bad poetry. Who compared her to porcelain shepherdesses and springtime days.

Her own family seemed to share that view. They praised her prettiness, smiled at her, indulged her, yet they seemed to think there was nothing behind her blue eyes. Nothing but ribbons and novels. Cal and Clio were the scholars, the heirs to their father's work; Cory was a budding great artist, a serious painter. Thalia was an amusement, the one their mother used to call her 'belle fleur'.

Oh, they never *said* that to her, of course. They applauded her theatricals, indulged her writing. But she saw it there when they looked at her, heard it in the tone of their words.

She was different. She was not quite a Chase.

Thalia turned away from the mirror, tugging her shawl closer around her shoulders, as if the thin cashmere offered some armour. Some protection against disappointment.

She had hoped that the strange events of the last weeks would change their minds. Would show them her true strength, what she was really capable of. When Clio had come to her and asked for her help in catching Lady Riverton, who had stolen a rare and sacred cache of Hellenistic temple silver, Thalia was overjoyed. Here at last was something *useful* she could do!

Something that would prove she was a Chase.

Her play had seemed to work, drawing out Lady Riverton's accomplice, but then it had all gone wrong. Lady Riverton had escaped, presumably with the silver, and now Clio and her husband had to try to find her. A pursuit in which Thalia had no part. She had not helped her sister, or her father.

Or the one person she found she most wanted to impress. Count Marco di Fabrizzi. Her partner in the theatricals—and in quarrelling. The Italian antiquarian and aristocrat. The most handsome man she had ever met. The man she was certain must be hopelessly in love with Clio.

Her sisters teased her for rejecting all her suitors. But none of them had ever been at all like Marco. It was entirely her luck that when she *did* find a passionate, attractive man, he would love her sister!

Thalia took up the books and papers again, going back to packing them in her trunk. One manuscript slipped from her hands, fluttering pages onto the carpet. As she knelt to retrieve them, the title page caught her eyes. *The Dark Castle of Count Orlando—* An Italian Romance in Three Acts.

Her play, the one she had started writing when she met Marco and the adventure of the silver unfolded. A great story of Renaissance Italy, full of love found and lost, vile villains, ghosts and curses. Passion that transcended all else. She had been so excited about it. Now, it seemed rather pointless.

She straightened the pages and bound them up with string, tucking them into the trunk. Perhaps one day she would take it out again and laugh at it, at her silly fantasies of adventure and true love. Right now, she needed to help Mary finish the packing. England, real life, waited.

The breeze outside the window was turning brisker, rustling the leaves of the lemon tree. Thalia went to pull the window shut, and stopped to gaze down at the garden, and the cobblestone street beyond the gate. It was truly beautiful, the dusty, sun-soaked old town of Santa Lucia. Beautiful, and full of secrets. Would she miss its sleepy heat, its blasted-blue sky and rocky hills, when she was in cool, green England?

As the church bells tolled, marking the hour, their servants went on carrying out trunks and cases, piling them up by the garden fountain. She leaned out over the windowsill, watching as the hillocks of luggage grew higher and her time here grew ever shorter.

The breeze caught at her hair, tugging the golden strands over her brow. As she impatiently brushed them back, she saw him—Marco. Walking slowly past their gate.

She had heard he had left Santa Lucia after Clio's wedding, but here he was now. He leaned on the locked gate, watching the commotion around their house with no expression on his dark, gorgeous face.

The sun gleamed on his wavy, blue-black hair, turning it as glossy and fathomless as midnight.

Before she could think, Thalia whirled around and dashed from the room, running down the stairs and out the front door. She dodged around footmen carrying out more trunks, and at last came to rest before Marco. The low, wrought-iron gate was between them, just narrow-spaced bars their hands could touch between. But it might as well have been an ocean.

Marco straightened, smiling down at her. He *was* so very handsome, she thought as she stared at him. His bronzed skin over his high, sharp-edged cheekbones, his Italian nose and gleaming dark brown eyes, rich as fine chocolate. The classical beauty only slightly roughened by the dark whiskers along his jaw. Like a Greek god in his temple, a Roman emperor on a coin. Like her own Count Orlando in his dark castle.

But Thalia had met many handsome men in her life. Her sisters' husbands, many of her own suitors. There was more to Marco than his fine looks. There was a fiery passion, only thinly veiled by flirtatious good manners. A fierce intelligence. And secrets. Many secrets, which Thalia longed to uncover.

She doubted she ever *could* excavate his hidden soul, even given the famed Chase tenacity. He was too skilled at disguises, too consummate an actor. Being good at masquerades herself, she could spot a fellow thespian. No, she could not read his true self, even if she had ten years for the deciphering. And she did not have ten years now; she doubted she even had ten minutes.

Yet she recalled the hours they had spent together in the ancient amphitheatre. Arguing, laughing—feigning love as they rehearsed their play. They were golden hours indeed, and she knew she would never forget them.

Never forget *him*.

'I thought you left Santa Lucia,' she said.

'I thought *you* had, Signorina Thalia,' he answered, giving her a smile. That heartbreaking smile of his, with the one perfect dimple.

Her Renaissance prince. Who just happened to love her sister.

Thalia glanced away, calling on all her well-honed acting skills, everything she had learned in the last few topsy-turvy weeks, to hide her true feelings from him. She remembered the solemn, sad look on his face at Clio's wedding, and it gave her the strength to give a careless laugh.

It would be too, too mortifying for him to know how she really felt. To be yet again in her sister's shadow.

'We had far too much packing to do to make a hasty departure, as you see,' she said, gesturing to the trunks. 'My sister Cory's sketchbooks, my father's copious notes on his work…'

'Your *Antigone* costumes?'

'And those.' She finally looked at him again, turning to find Marco watching her closely with his vast dark eyes. She could read nothing there, not a flicker of the strange friendship they had formed on that ancient stage. No past, no future. Just this one moment to be together again.

'I am sorry we never got to perform Sophocles's play,' he said.

'So am I. But we had a dramatic scene of a different sort, did we not?'

Marco laughed, a wondrously warm, sunny sound that made her want to laugh, too. Made her want to throw her arms around his neck, and never, ever let go. Once he was gone, once this time was gone, her life would go back to grey, mundane reality again. She would be pretty, useless, flighty Thalia, and her adventures here would be a dream. A warm memory for cold nights.

'You are surely the most fearsome ghost Sicily has ever beheld,' he said.

'A compliment indeed! I think I have never seen such a haunted place as this. Perhaps…' Her voice faded, and she glanced away again.

'Perhaps what?'

'It will sound odd, but I wonder if I will become a ghost here,' she said, all in a rush. Her heart teetered on a precipice with him; she should just push it over and be done with it.

After all, she was known in her family as headstrong. Fearless. Yet something, some hidden kernel of caution, held her back just a bit. Even as she watched little pebbles skitter into the emotional void below her.

'I wonder if I will leave my true self here,' she murmured, 'wandering around the old agora, all lost.'

Marco gently touched her hand. His caress was feather-light, the brush of his fingertips on her skin, yet the contact felt like a quick flash of fire. A heat she craved, even as she knew it would consume her and leave her that pale ghost she feared.

'What is your true self, Thalia?' he said, all his sunny Italian humour turned to frightening intensity. She wondered if he could indeed see inside her. 'You are a fine actress indeed, yet I think I see—'

'Thalia!' she heard her father call from the doorway. 'Who are you talking to there?'

Thalia was deeply grateful for the interruption, even as her heart sank at the tearing of their solitary moment. The abyss still waited, but she would not tumble over just yet. 'It is Count di Fabrizzi, Father,' she called, still staring at Marco's hand on hers.

But he drew it away, and that shimmering instant was truly gone.

'Invite him in!' her father said. 'I want to ask his opinion on something to do with those coins Clio found.'

'Of course.' Thalia gave Marco a quick smile. 'You see all there is to see,' she whispered to him. 'I am an open book.'

'I have heard many falsehoods in my life, *signorina*,' he said. 'But few, I think, as great as that. Your sister Clio, now *she* is an open book. You are like the Sicilian skies—stormy one moment, shining the next, but never, ever predictable.'

Did he really think that of her? If so, no one had ever paid her a finer compliment. Yet it made clear that he still did not really see, did not understand. Not entirely. 'You have only known me in highly unusual circumstances, Marco. At home, in my real life, I am as predictable as the moon.'

Marco laughed. 'Yet another falsehood, I suspect. Perhaps one day I will see you in this "real life", and judge the true Thalia Chase for myself.'

Thalia smiled at him wistfully. If only that could be so! If only they *could* meet again, and she could show him that Clio could never be the one for him. Show him how she really felt, and what knowing him had meant to her.

Yet that was just one more hopeless dream. When she left Sicily, when she set sail for England and he went back to his home in Florence, they would surely never meet again.

And she would live on her memories of him for years to come.

Chapter One

Bath

Is it possible that only months ago I was in Sicily? Thalia wrote in her journal, balancing the leather-bound book carefully on her lap desk as the carriage jolted along. *It must have been a dream indeed, for when I look out of the window now I know I have truly woken up.*

The gently rolling lane, surrounded on all sides by the lush, fresh green of hedgerows, the expanse of fields and villages, could not have been more different than the sun-blasted Sicilian plains. Thalia closed her eyes, and for an instant she could swear she smelled the hot scent of lemons on the air. Could feel the warm breeze brush her sleeve against her arm, like the most fleeting caress.

But then the carriage bounced over another rut in the English road, pushing her out of her memories.

She opened her eyes, and smiled at her sister Calliope de Vere, Lady Westwood, who sat across from her. Calliope smiled back, but Thalia could see that it was an effort. Despite the cushions and blankets piled around her, despite the quantities of tea and calves' foot jelly Thalia kept pressing on her, Calliope was still pale. Her brown eyes seemed enormous in her white face.

That pallor was one of the reasons for this journey to Bath. Calliope had not yet recovered from baby Psyche's long and difficult birth, had indeed just become thinner and more tired as the days went on. Her appetite was not good, and she had no energy for her usual organising and taking care of everyone.

Thalia knew it was time to worry when her eldest sister had no interest in ordering her around. She hoped that her brother-in-law Cameron's idea, that Calliope should take the waters and rest for a few weeks, would do the trick. He had gone ahead to find a suitable house, and Thalia had organised the journey.

In the flurry of engaging nurses and maids, packing and closing up the London house, she had almost forgotten Sicily and Marco. Almost.

'What are you writing?' Calliope asked, checking the basket where Psyche slept amid satin blankets. The baby had blessedly fallen asleep after miles spent wailing. 'A new play?'

'Just a few notes in my journal,' Thalia answered. She tucked the little volume away. 'I haven't yet begun a new play.'

Calliope sighed. 'I fear that is my fault. I have kept you so very busy you've scarcely had time to breathe since you returned from Italy!'

'I don't mind in the least. What are sisters for, if not to help in times of need?'

'Then we are fortunate indeed to be so peculiarly rich in sisters!' Calliope said with a laugh. 'And now nieces and stepmothers.'

'We are a family of females to be sure.' Thalia peered down at Psyche, so deceptively angelic in her pink satin and lace, black hair like her mother's curling softly on her pretty head. Her little nose wrinkled as Thalia smoothed back a strand. 'Psyche has proved herself to be a Chase through and through already.'

Calliope gave her sleeping daughter a soft smile. 'She does have a will of iron.'

'And lungs to match.'

'She will never refrain from expressing herself, I fear.'

'Will she turn out like her Aunt Clio?'

'A duchess? She just might.' Calliope eased the coverlets around Psyche's shoulders, and settled herself carefully back on her seat. 'I do confess I was utterly astonished to hear of Clio's marriage. She and Averton despised each other! After what happened in Yorkshire…'

Thalia remembered Clio's wedding in the Protestant chapel in Santa Lucia, how very radiant she was as she had taken her Duke's hand and repeated her vows. How he had raised the veil on her bonnet and kissed her, the two of them seemingly bound in their own little sunlit world. 'Magical things can happen in Italy.'

'So I understand.' Calliope peered closely at Thalia from beneath the narrow brim of her hat, making Thalia squirm just a bit. When they were children, Calliope always knew when Thalia had done something naughty, and she could elicit guilty confessions in no time. It was no different now.

'What of you, then, Thalia dear?' Calliope said. 'Did magical things happen to *you* there?'

Thalia shook her head, memories of Clio's wedding shifting into a starlit night. A masked ball, a dance. 'Not at all, I'm afraid. I'm exactly the same as I was before I went.'

Thalia could see that Calliope did not believe her, but she seemed too tired to pry. Yet. 'Poor Thalia. You must play nurse to me after such a grand holiday! And now I am dragging you off to fusty old Bath. I fear the Upper Rooms can hold no charms like ancient ruins. Or Italian men and their dark eyes!'

Thalia glanced sharply at Calliope, trying to see if there was anything behind that 'dark eyes' remark. If she *knew*, and was teasing about it. Calliope just gave her an innocent smile.

'Oh, I have hopes of Bath, never fear,' Thalia said lightly. 'The theatre, the parks, the old Roman sites. The wealthy men seeking cures for their gout *and* young wives to wheel their chairs about. Perhaps there will be some overfed German prince there, and

I will outrank even Clio! Princess Thalia. Sounds nice, don't you think, Cal?'

Calliope laughed, her pale cheeks taking on a hint of pink at last. 'It will sound nice until you find yourself in some drafty Hessian castle! I suspect that would not suit you at all.'

'I dare say you are right. I haven't the temperament for cold winters *or* draughty castles.'

'Not after Italy?'

'Exactly so. But Bath will have its charms, not the least of which will be seeing you well and strong again. The waters will do you good.'

'I hope so. I am so tired of being *tired*,' Calliope said wearily, the first hint of any complaint Thalia had heard from her.

Thalia leaned forwards in concern, tucking a blanket closer around Calliope's knees. 'Are you in pain, Cal? Should we stop for a rest? This infernal jostling…'

'No, no.' Calliope caught Thalia's hand, stilling her fussing. 'Bath is not far, I'm sure. I want to try to make it before nightfall. I long to see Cameron.'

'As I'm sure he longs to see you.' Calliope and her husband had hardly been parted since their marriage. Thalia didn't know how they could stand it, they were so very devoted.

'He says he has found a fine house right on the Royal Crescent, where we can be near everything,' Calliope said. 'I do want you to have some fun while we're there, not spend all your time at my sickbed.'

Thalia laughed, even more worried now and trying

to hide it. 'What sickbed? You will be too busy promenading around the Pump Room for that! And I am happy just to be with you and little Psyche. We have been too long parted.'

'Yes. If only Clio were here!' Calliope squeezed Thalia's hand. 'Our little trio would be complete again.'

Psyche chose that moment to wake up, letting out a lusty shout that shook the carriage to its silk-lined walls.

'It appears we would be a quartet now,' Calliope said, lifting her daughter from the basket.

Thalia gazed out the window again. The rolling lanes, the hedgerows, had at last given way, and the carriage turned onto one of the bridges leading over the Avon into Bath itself. Five elegant arches rose over the bridge, forming a new view of the town and the hills beyond.

Even after the dramatic landscapes of Italy, Thalia had to admit Bath was quite pretty. It looked like the rising layers of a fancy wedding cake fashioned in pale gold stone, sweeping up along the hill slopes. As a Chase, the daughter and granddaughter of classical scholars, Thalia approved of the city's classical lines, all neat rows of columns and clean-cut corners.

At this distance, the dirt and noise all towns produced could not yet be seen or heard. It seemed a doll's city, built for pleasure. Built for gentle strolls and polite conversations, for good health and conviviality. For new dreams—if she could only find them.

As Psyche cried on, they rolled off the bridge into the city, the carriage jolting along the stone streets with the endless flow of traffic. Thalia studied the well-dressed families in their barouches, the dashing couples perched high on their phaeton seats. The pedestrians on the walkways, showing off their fashionable clothes as maids scurried behind them laden with packages.

The shop windows displayed a variety of fine wares—lengths of muslins and silks, bonnets, books and prints, china, glistening pyramids of sweets. Thalia remembered dusty little Santa Lucia, its ancient markets and little shops.

She lowered the window and inhaled deeply of the mingled scents of dirt and horses, sugary cinnamon from a bakery, the faint metallic tang of the waters that hung over everything. She was far from Sicily indeed. And none of the men they passed were in the least like Marco di Fabrizzi.

Calliope peered over her shoulder, rocking Psyche in her arms. Even the baby seemed fascinated by the town, as she ceased to scream and gazed about with wide brown eyes.

'You see, Thalia,' Calliope said. 'Bath is not so very bad, even Psyche thinks so. Look, there is a sign for the Theatre Royal, they're performing *Romeo and Juliet* next week! We must go. A little bit of Italy right here.'

Thalia smiled at her sister, and at Psyche, who had popped her tiny fingers into her mouth as she watched the sunlight gleam on the mellow Bath stone. 'I always do enjoy the theatre, of course. But you must not tire yourself, Cal. We can always go later.'

'Pah! Sitting in the theatre is hardly likely to do me harm, unless someone chucks an orange at my head. I don't want to be a poor invalid,' Calliope said stubbornly.

They quickly left the more crowded lanes behind, making their way to the comforts and quiet of the Royal Crescent.

The neighbourhood Cameron had chosen for their holiday was an elegant sweep of thirty houses, built in deceptively simple Palladian style for Bath's most exclusive occupants. How very perturbed those snobby builders would be, Thalia thought, to see the arrival of two bluestockings and a squalling infant! Even if Cal *was* a countess. The Chase girls had never been much for stuffiness. It was too time consuming.

But she had to admit it was very pretty, and suited to their classical studies. The carriage swayed slowly along the gentle curve of the crescent, past immaculately scrubbed front steps and austere columns. The houses exuded a quiet, prosperous serenity, the perfect place for Calliope to rest.

'We can take walks here in the mornings,' Calliope said, pointing toward the walkway around a large, open, grassy space across from the curve of houses. 'There in Crescent Fields.'

'Only if it is early enough! We would not want to be run over by fashionable promenaders.' Thalia watched a couple stroll past, the lady in an embroidered yellow spencer and large feathered bonnet, the lead of a prancing pug dog in her hand. The wide brim of her hat hid her face, and even half-obscured her tall escort.

Yet even in a fleeting glimpse there seemed something so strangely familiar in that male figure. Those lean shoulders in dark blue superfine. Was he someone she knew?

But she had little time to speculate on the man's identity, as their carriage at last jolted to a halt before a house near the end of the crescent curve. A footman hurried down the front stoop to open the carriage door, and right behind him was Calliope's husband.

Cameron de Vere, the Earl of Westwood, was a very good match for her sister, Thalia always thought. They were both darkly beautiful, kind-hearted, and devoted to the study of ancient history. Yet he was full of humour and light, where Calliope could be intense, and they balanced each other. No two people had surely ever made a happier life together than they.

Cam's face, usually so smiling and handsome, looked worried today as he took his wife's hand and gently helped her down from the carriage.

Thalia took Psyche, cradling her close as they watched Calliope and Cameron embrace in full view of the Crescent's passers-by. Cam held her so very close, as if she was a precious piece of ancient alabaster, and Calliope arched into him as if she was home at last, her head on his shoulder.

Thalia felt a wistful pang as she observed them together, a quick flash of loneliness. How very *right* they were together! Like two halves of a Roman coin.

And how solitary *she* was.

Yet there was not time for self-pity. It was not Thalia's way, either, to waste time wishing for what she did not have! Not when there was so much she did have, so much she needed to do.

The footman helped her to the pavement, and she handed Psyche to the waiting nurse, who had followed in a second carriage with the other servants. She carried the baby into the house just as a great squall went up.

'Thalia!' Cameron said, kissing her cheek. 'How well and pretty you look, sister. The Bath air agrees with you already.'

Thalia laughed as Calliope playfully slapped her husband's arm. '*She* is blooming and pretty, while I, your poor wife, am a pale invalid?'

'I never said you were poor…' Cameron protested teasingly.

'Just pale, then?'

'Never! You are my Grecian rose, always. And now, fair rose, let me show you to your new bower.'

He swept Calliope into his arms, carrying her up the shallow steps, beneath the classical pediment into the house. Cal protested, yet Thalia could see she was tired and glad of the help. Thalia scooped up a bandbox a footman had left on the pavement and hurried after them.

The entrance hall was cool and dim after the sunny day, smelling of fresh flowers and lemon polish, with a flagstone floor and pale marbled wallpaper.

Cameron led them through an archway to the tall inner hall, where a staircase curved to the upper floors. Psyche was already up there somewhere, shouting her protests at the new surroundings.

Cameron carried his wife into a drawing room off the hall, a fine room with gold damask walls and draperies. Coral-coloured silk couches and chairs were grouped around a tea table, already set with refreshments.

Next to the windows were a pianoforte and a harp. As Cameron settled Calliope on the couch, Thalia wandered over to examine the instruments.

'These are very fine,' she said, picking out a little tune on the keys. 'I can play for you in the evenings, Cal! I learned lots of new songs in Italy.'

'I always love to hear you play, Thalia dear,' Calliope answered. She accepted a cup of tea from her husband, but swatted him away as he tried to tuck a blanket around her. 'But you deserve a much larger audience for your talents! This is a very pretty room. We must have a card party or a musicale, as soon as we find new acquaintances here in Bath.'

'Cal, you must rest!' Thalia and Cameron said at the same time. They all laughed, and Cam went on, 'Remember what the doctors said. Plenty of rest and quiet, and taking the waters every day.'

Calliope waved her hand impatiently. 'By Jove, but you two fuss as if I had just announced I meant to cross the Channel in a rowboat! A small card party will be as nothing. Thalia must have *some* fun, or she will surely desert us for Italy again.'

'I will not desert you, Calliope. I am here to help make sure you get completely well again.' Thalia took off her bonnet, gazing out of the window at the fields beyond. More people strolled past, but not the tall man in the blue coat. The man with that dashing air of familiarity.

He must have been yet another figment of her imagination.

Chapter Two

Marco tossed his hat onto the nearest table and fell back into the room's one chair, scowling as he watched the shadows lengthen on the polished floor. The White Hart Inn was quiet at this hour; everyone was tucked away in their own rooms, readying themselves for that night's concerts and assemblies. Even the corridors and sitting rooms were free of the usual coming-and-going clatter.

But Marco's thoughts were far from quiet. They whirled around in a scarlet-and-black maelstrom, caught in a labyrinth from which there seemed no escape. It had been thus ever since he arrived in Bath. Bath, the white, hilly town everyone said was so very respectable and dull! It was nothing of the sort. Philosophical lectures and Pump Room promenades hid dark depths.

Or rather, they hid dark people, people with secrets and hidden agendas. He had been here over a week, trying to befriend Lady Riverton, to gain her trust—or at least gain access to her papers and safe, so carefully guarded in her villa on the outskirts of town. Trying to discover where she had hidden the temple silver hoard from Santa Lucia. All he had got for his troubles thus far was a headache from her pug's squealing.

And the silver, those ancient, invaluable relics, were farther away than ever.

'Maledetto,' Marco muttered. Perhaps he had been a fool to think charm and flattery would be more effective, more unexpected than brute force in this vital errand. Lady Riverton was used to dealing with rough *tombaroli,* after all; flirtation would be unsuspected.

And indeed Lady Riverton *did* seem to like him, seemed more than happy to have him escort her around Bath. But if he came no closer to finding the silver very soon, he would have to find a new plan. Quickly.

Because he felt like the veriest fool. Not to mention whorish, dancing court on a giggling woman he despised!

Sometimes, when Lady Riverton took his arm and simpered up at him, he saw not her brown ringlet-framed face, but the blue, teasing eyes of Thalia Chase. That clear, bright blue that could darken in a stormy instant as she squabbled with him. Or could turn a pale, misty grey in the candlelight.

He had not been so fascinated by a lady since he was a young man, infatuated with Maria. Poor Maria, so lovely—so unlucky in love.

He had only spent a brief time with Thalia in Sicily, but a woman like Thalia Chase, so beautiful, intelligent, creative, and as forceful as a summer rainstorm, left a great impression indeed. If she knew what he was up to now, surely those eyes would flash with contempt. Running full-tilt into battle, roaring with fury, was more her style.

And perhaps she was right. Perhaps his cause was too great to be won except in pitched battle, with bloodshed. His old friends in Florence and Naples, who shared those dreams of Italian independence, of glories regained, would say so. But he, fool that he was, still stubbornly hoped otherwise.

That was why it was so very important to find that silver.

Marco pushed himself out of the chair, and went to the desk set in a small alcove of the room. It was stacked with books and papers, with the blotted pages of the pamphlet he was writing. The subject was what he had learned in Santa Lucia, of the peaceful, prosperous Greek town and farms that were once on that site. A beautiful site, where a great agora and amphitheatre rose, where farmers grew barley, olives, grapes, and wealthy families built their fine holiday villas. There was culture, contentment, a thriving worship of Demeter and her daughter Persephone.

It was that worship that had given birth to an elaborate set of temple silver. Beautifully decorated cups, libation bowls, ladles and incense burners, sacred to the earth goddess who gave the valley its riches. Until that peaceful community had been destroyed by invading Romans and their mercenaries, who looted, burned and killed, enslaving any who survived. One pious man had snatched the silver from the temple, just ahead of the invading army, and had hastily buried it in his farmhouse cellar.

There it had stayed until the *tombaroli* hired by Lady Riverton dug it up for her own selfish pleasure, her own hidden collection of precious, stolen antiquities. Complete sets of temple silver from the Hellenistic period were rare indeed, and these pieces and their story had high symbolic value. A heritage of beauty and culture, smashed by an invading army. Yet another piece of Italy's past, lost.

He sat down at the desk, reaching for his inkwell. It was a tale that had to be told. Yet how very much more powerful it would be to have the silver itself! It would inspire others to join their cause.

Marco had spent nearly all his adult life dedicated to the glorious past, and to Italy's future. To retrieving lost artefacts, lost history. He would find the silver, too, no matter what it took.

And if only the memory of Thalia Chase's all-seeing eyes would cease to haunt him!

Chapter Three

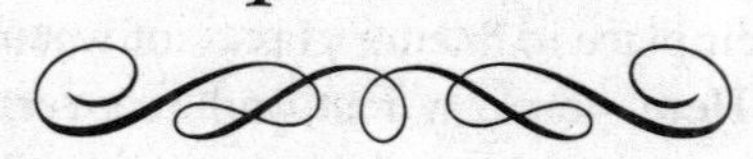

It was the crowded hour for the Pump Room, ten o'clock in the morning, when Thalia and Calliope stepped from the Abbey churchyard under the pillared colonnade and into the throngs of people.

The vast white space, bathed in pale grey light from the cloudy day outside, echoed with laughter and animated conversation. Snatches of words floated to the ceiling and dispersed. *That hat—the height of vulgarity! Could hardly breathe in the assembly, it was absurd. The doctor says I must...*

'And this is supposed to be conducive to reviving one's health and spirits?' Calliope said doubtfully, dodging a dowager's Bath chair as it rolled past. 'All these crowds with their nonsensical chatter? We might as well have stayed in London!'

Thalia took her sister's arm, drawing her close as Calliope leaned on her. Cameron had gone to sign the book, agreeing to meet them by the pump itself. If they could safely cross the room.

Thalia was not tall, but she did know how to get her way when needed. She edged the gossiping hordes aside with her blue silk-clad arm, giving any who stood in her way a calm stare until they hastened to clear a path.

'The air in London was not good for you,' she said, taking their place in line for glasses of water. 'Nor for Psyche. Here you can rest and recover, with no demands on your time at all. No Antiquities Society, no Ladies Artistic Society, all those unending societies…'

'Lady Westwood? Miss Chase?' a voice said, and Thalia and Calliope turned to see Lord Grimsby, a friend of their father's from the Antiquities Society, standing behind them, leaning heavily on his walking stick.

'Lord Grimsby!' Calliope said. 'What a delightful surprise to see you here.'

'You cannot possibly be as surprised as we were to hear of your father's marriage to Lady Rushworth!' he said, chortling. 'But Sir Walter wrote to us that you might be visiting Bath soon. My wife and daughter will be so pleased to hear you have arrived. Society has been so sparse in Bath.'

Thalia glanced around at the jostling crowds. 'I can see that!'

'You must come to the next meeting of the Classical Society, of course. We are not as numerous as the Antiquities Society in London, but we do have lectures and debates quite often, as well as excursions to see the Roman artefacts. There are so many Roman sites to be seen around Bath, y'know!'

'It all sounds most delightful, Lord Grimsby,' Calliope said. 'We were just wondering what we should do without our various societies.'

'We must keep up standards, Lady Westwood, even in Bath. Such a treat to have some of the Chase gels in our midst. You will come to our meeting next week?'

'We would enjoy that,' said Thalia. 'But I fear my sister is under very strict orders to rest.'

Lord Grimsby chortled again, his old-fashioned wig trembling. 'Aren't we all, Miss Chase? What else is Bath for but to rest? That doesn't mean we should rest our *minds*, as I'm sure your father would agree. Our meetings are very quiet, pleasant affairs. I will have Lady Grimsby call on you tomorrow. Until then!'

As Lord Grimsby limped away, Calliope gave their coins to the attendant and accepted two glasses of the water. 'No demands on our time, eh?' she whispered.

Thalia laughed. 'I forgot Father has friends everywhere. We could probably set up camp on a mountaintop and someone would come along with an invitation to a lecture.'

'Well, since Cam has joined forces with the blasted doctors and forbidden dancing, I must take my amusement where I can find it,' Calliope said. She took a sip of water, and wrinkled her nose.

'Drink it all, Cal,' Thalia said, taking a suspicious sniff of her own glass. 'Sulphur and iron, delicious!'

Calliope laughed, too. 'Not exactly French champagne, is it?'

'It is Bath champagne, and will make you strong again.'

Calliope raised her glass. 'Here is a toast. May we all be well enough to travel to Italy next year.'

'I will certainly drink to that.' As Thalia clicked her glass with her sister's, she couldn't help remembering a pair of dark eyes, a wide, merry grin. A man who seemed a very part of the warmth and freedom of Italy. Part of the exhilaration of life, of *real* life, messy and complicated and beautiful.

Not this pallid reflection of existence. Not the constant hollow loneliness of feeling adrift in the world.

She took a drink of her water, and it was just as flat and stale as everything else had been since she had left Sicily and Count Marco di Fabrizzi. Grey. She gazed over the glass rim at the room beyond, at the constantly shifting crowd.

And suddenly she was tired. Tired of herself, her moping ways ever since she had returned to England. Moping never got anyone anywhere, she knew that well.

'You know, Cal,' she said, 'if we cannot get to Italy now, we must make Italy come to us.'

Calliope, who had been frowning into her glass, brightened. 'How so, sister?'

'We shall have a party, just as you wanted. Our own Venetian ridotto.'

'In our little drawing room?' Calliope said with a laugh.

'A miniature ridotto, then. With music, wine, games. You can wear a fine new gown, and preside over the festivities from a regal chaise. That should make the doctors happy. And I will perform scenes from—from *The Merchant of Venice*! And *Venice Preserved*.'

'How delightful! I do want a new gown to show off the fact that I once again have a waist. Who shall we invite?'

Thalia surveyed the room again. 'Oh, dear. I fear it shall be a rather sedate ridotto. We must be some of the very few people under the age of fifty here!'

'No matter. A party is a party.' Calliope set about doing what she did best—organising.

By the time Cameron joined them, bearing yet more water, they had the plans well in hand.

'You see, my dearest,' he said happily, 'you have roses in your cheeks already.'

'That is because she has me to order around,' Thalia said. 'Like the perfect older sister she is.'

Calliope made a face at her. 'I never order people around. I am as agreeable as a summer's day.'

Thalia and Cameron exchanged a wry glance past Calliope's bonnet brim.

'Who is in the book today?' Thalia asked.

'Not very many names as of yet,' he answered.

'None of our acquaintances, anyway. Just a woman named Lady Riverton. Would she be the widow of old Viscount Riverton, the antiquarian? I never met him, but my father said his collection of Greek coins was very fine.'

Thalia froze, her fingers tightening on her glass. 'Did you say Lady Riverton?' she said hoarsely.

Calliope gave her a puzzled glance. 'Do you know her, Thalia?'

Calliope did not know the complete story of the events in Sicily. Thalia simply hadn't known how to tell her. How did one explain stolen silver caches, ghosts and breaking into a man's house in the middle of the night? It all sounded bacon-brained in the extreme. So Calliope did not know what Lady Riverton had done, hiring ruthless thieves to help her steal the silver altar set, and then double-crossing even them to escape with her ill-gotten treasure.

And now she was in Bath, of all places! How could that possibly be? Showing up and brazenly signing the book. She must feel rather secure, knowing Marco, Clio and the Duke of Averton were far away, and no one among the invalids and retired clergymen would know her bad deeds. Had she come to hide the silver? Or chase some other treasure? Lord Grimsby was correct, there were many Roman sites nearby.

Well, Lady Riverton had obviously *not* counted on Thalia. That would be her undoing. Thalia was accustomed to being underestimated. Her blonde curls and blue eyes fooled many into thinking her merely fluffy and empty-headed. She knew now how to work such low expectations to her advantage.

Lady Riverton would be very sorry she ever came to Bath.

'Thalia?' Calliope said. 'Do you know this Lady Riverton?'

'There was a Lady Riverton in Sicily,' Thalia answered lightly. 'A ridiculous lady with far too many hats, and a fawning *cicisbeo* named Mr Frobisher who followed her everywhere.' Frobisher—one of Lady Riverton's greedy dupes. He was paying the price now. But Thalia saw no need to mention that.

'I take it you were not exactly bosom bows,' Cameron said wryly.

'You could say that.'

'Well, perhaps this is a different Lady Riverton,' Calliope said. 'I should hate to meet such a creature just now. The combination of ridiculous bonnets with all this water would be too much for my constitution.'

Thalia handed her empty glass to a passing attendant. 'Excuse me for a moment, Cal,' she said. 'I see someone I must speak to.'

She strolled away, keeping to the edges of the room where the crowds were thinner. Though she walked slowly, smiling and nodding at acquaintances as if she hadn't a care in the world and no place to be, she carefully scanned each face. Each overly adorned bonnet. If Lady Riverton was indeed here, Thalia would find her. She could not hide.

Thalia felt more excited than she had since leaving

Santa Lucia. She had a purpose again, an errand! A way to do something useful. Oh, if only Clio were here, so they could work together again as they had on the ghost play that had flushed out Mr Frobisher and the true villain, Lady Riverton. If only…

If only Marco were here. Despite their bickering, they had proved to be a fine team when united in a scheme.

But she was alone as she circled the Pump Room, dodging walking sticks and offers of yet more water. It was all up to her now.

There was no sign of Lady Riverton, and Thalia had begun to despair of her errand when at last she caught a glimpse of a tall-crowned brown satin hat trimmed with bright blue and yellow feathers. They waved above the crowd like a gaudy beacon.

Thalia stretched up on tiptoe, straining for a better glimpse. Not for the first time, she wished she were taller, more like Clio. All she could see were backs, blocking her view! Using her elbow again, she forced her way through at last to a somewhat clearer space near the counter.

The woman with the feathers was just taking a glass of water. Her brown satin pelisse and a cameo earring, a chestnut ringlet, was all Thalia could see. But then she laughed, that dreadful high-pitched giggle Thalia well remembered. It was Lady Riverton, without a doubt.

Thalia's first, fiery instinct was to dash forward, snatch that terrible hat off the woman's head—along with a handful of hair!—and demand to know where the silver was. But even she, with all her Chase impulsiveness, knew that causing a scene in the Pump Room would avail her nothing. It would cause a scandal, and worse would tip her hand to Lady Riverton, making it all too easy for her to escape again.

No, she had to bide her time. Plan her next move carefully. She wouldn't fail again.

She slid closer to Lady Riverton, who was chattering away as if she was in no way guilty of anything but crimes of fashion. '…must procure theatre tickets *tout suite*, my dear! There is no finer way to meet people in Bath, I am sure. The Upper Rooms can be such a squeeze, but only the very best people are in the theatre boxes.'

Thalia nearly laughed aloud, wondering what Lady Riverton's idea of the 'best people' could possibly be. And who was the poor man being forced to listen to such faradiddle? He was too tall to be Mr Frobisher, who as far as Thalia knew was still in the Santa Lucia gaol. As she watched, Lady Riverton took her escort's arm and the pair of them turned to stroll away into the crowd.

Thalia hurried in the direction of their path, nearly tripping over the front wheel of yet another Bath chair. By Jove, but those things were a menace! At last she came face to face with Lady Riverton, and saw that her escort was…

Marco. The Count di Fabrizzi himself, in all his Roman-god handsome splendour.

For an instant, all she could do was gape at him in utter astonishment. Surely it could not be! Perhaps he had a twin. An evil twin, who paraded around the spa towns of Europe with silly females, and stole their jewels when they were not looking. She had read about such men.

But even as the absurd thought flitted through her mind, she knew that it really was Marco who stood there. No one else could have eyes like that.

As he glimpsed her, those dark eyes widened in surprise, and a smile touched his lips. A mere flash of the dimple set deep in his smooth olive cheek. Then it was as if he suddenly remembered their true situation, and that smile vanished. The spark deep in his eyes went out, and he watched her warily.

As if he did remember—remember that night she had broken into his house, and had no idea what unpredictable thing she might do now.

Thalia smiled politely, sweetly, and said in her brightest voice, 'Lady Riverton! Count di Fabrizzi. What a great surprise to see you here in Bath. It has been far too long since we last met.'

Lady Riverton smiled and nodded, those feathers bobbing maniacally. Marco bowed, still wary and serious. As well he might be, for Thalia was determined to discover what his game was here.

'Why, if it is not Miss Thalia Chase!' Lady Riverton said gaily. 'And looking just the same as when we parted in dear Santa Lucia. How is your lovely sister, the new Duchess?'

'Clio and her husband are both well, thank you,' Thalia said, giving the bizarre couple her sweetest smile. 'They are still travelling on the Continent.'

'I was so very sorry to miss their wedding, but I had to travel in haste to Naples to visit an ill friend,' Lady Riverton said. 'That is where I met Count di Fabrizzi again! He has been such an attentive escort.' She simpered up at Marco, her gloved hand tight on his arm.

Marco gave her an indulgent smile, his eyes soft as he gazed down at her. As if he could not watch her enough, get enough of her presence.

Thalia remembered how just such a look from him could make her feel, back in Santa Lucia. How his teasing smiles made her feel all hot and chilled, weak and invincible, light and unbearably serious, all at the same time.

She wished she still had a glass of the vile water, so she could throw it at him. First Clio, now Lady Riverton! The—the bounder.

'How fortunate, Lady Riverton, that you possess the happy talent of making friends wherever you go,' Thalia said.

'Indeed I do! My dear husband, the late Viscount Riverton, said it was my greatest gift. Or one of them, anyway!' Lady Riverton giggled, leaning on Marco's arm even more. He seemed to have no objections, though Thalia noticed they were beginning to attract interested attention from the passers-by.

'Speaking of friends, Miss Chase,' Lady Riverton continued, 'never say you are here on your own!

Your sister's great marriage must have caused such a lowering of spirits for you. I hope the waters will soon restore your bloom.'

Thalia felt her 'blooming' cheeks grow warm. 'On the contrary, Lady Riverton. We are all most happy that Clio has found someone who loves and values her as much as we do. And I am here with my eldest sister, Lady Westwood, who has recently had a child.'

'Indeed?' Lady Riverton said. 'Well, I am glad you are here with someone to see to the proprieties. If I recall from Santa Lucia, you yourself are often too *busy* to worry about such things.'

Proprieties like stealing? Destroying history? Thalia again felt that burning urge to throw something. At Lady Riverton, whose smugly smiling countenance said she knew Thalia could do nothing in such a public place. At Marco, who seemed to fawn over Lady Riverton like a simpleton, like a new Marco di Fabrizzi. He was obviously playing some game, and it was maddening that she could not decipher it!

'Thalia? Will you introduce us to your friends?' she heard Calliope say, and she turned gratefully to her sister. Calliope had always been the sensible one, the one that drew the rest of them down to earth when their wild Chase-ian schemes sent them flying off.

But Calliope was staring at Marco with wide eyes, as if she could not account for his presence here. Yet how could she know him? She had not been in Sicily. She knew nothing of the silver fiasco there.

Cameron came to her side, taking her hand. The two of them exchanged a long glance.

If Thalia thought she was confused before, now she felt she had tumbled down into an abyss. An upside-down world where nothing made sense.

'May I introduce Viscountess Riverton,' Thalia said, automatically mouthing the polite words. 'And the Count di Fabrizzi. This is my eldest sister and her husband, Lord and Lady Westwood.'

There were bows and curtsies all around, perfectly polite and conventional. But Thalia still felt that strange tension in the air, that taut sensation, as if all the good manners would suddenly snap and send them into chaos.

'We are always happy to meet friends of Thalia's,' Calliope said. 'I hope we will see more of you around Bath.'

'Oh, indeed!' Lady Riverton trilled. 'We are to attend the assembly on Tuesday, and I want to organize a card party soon at my villa. I will send you a card!'

'We look forward to it,' Calliope said.

'But now I fear you must excuse us,' Cameron added. 'My wife has an appointment at the Hot Bath this afternoon.'

'How delightful,' Lady Riverton said. 'Nothing like taking the waters! We shall see you very soon, I'm sure.'

Not if I can help it, Thalia thought. Calliope took her arm in a firm clasp and led her past the still-simpering Lady Riverton, the inscrutable Marco.

At Marco's shoulder, Cal suddenly paused and hissed, 'Don't think I don't remember you, *Marco*. I hope you left your crowbar at home this time, because I will not let you cause trouble for another of my sisters.'

'Lady Westwood, I would not—' Marco began. But Calliope had already marched onwards, drawing Cameron and Thalia with her.

Even as the crowd closed behind them, Thalia could swear she felt Marco's stare on the back of her neck, a warm tingle against her skin.

She rubbed at her nape, just under the edge of her bonnet. 'You already knew Marco?' she whispered.

Calliope gave her a sharp glance. 'You are on a Christian-name basis with him?'

'I—well…' Thalia stammered. How could she even begin to explain all that had happened to Calliope? She couldn't, not here, not now.

But it seemed Calliope had explanations of her own to make. She stared straight ahead, always smiling. She tightened her grip on Thalia's arm until she had no choice but to smile, too.

'We can't speak of this here,' Calliope whispered. 'Wait until this afternoon, when we are at home.'

Cameron thrust another glass of water into Thalia's hand. She stared down at it, wishing it was something a bit stronger. Homemade Sicilian grappa, perhaps—forgetfulness in a glass.

Yes, she could certainly use some of that now. Instead, she just gulped down the water, and cringed.

Chapter Four

'La, but I have seldom seen anyone so altered as Miss Thalia Chase!' Lady Riverton said, clutching Marco's arm as they made their way through the Pump Room. 'I don't remember her being so pale and wan, do you?'

Marco felt his jaw tighten, even as he fought to maintain a careless smile. A fun-loving façade, which was everything in this tightrope game he played. *Wan* was the last word he would use to describe Thalia. He feared the fiery sparks from her blue eyes would set him ablaze.

He was still a bit unsettled by her sudden appearance there before him. Her presence could so easily send this house of cards tumbling, and then where would he be? Without the silver, without justice for Lady Riverton and her minions. And assuredly without Thalia.

He suppressed the urge to glance back, to see if

Thalia still watched him with that contemptuous glare. He kept walking with Lady Riverton, nodding and smiling at everyone as if he had nothing more than pleasure in mind.

That was all they expected of Italians, after all. Sunny, hedonistic pleasure. And those romantic, preconceived notions of theirs served his purpose most admirably. It was easier to get on with his work when no one watched too closely, expected too much.

Yet, somehow, the thought of Thalia Chase's disapproval pained him.

'But then, of course Miss Chase would be out of sorts,' Lady Riverton went on. 'Her elder sisters are married now, so advantageously! Even her eccentric old father has remarried. Yet she, poor thing, has no prospects.'

'I hardly think someone who looks like Miss Chase could be entirely without prospects,' Marco couldn't resist saying.

Lady Riverton shot him a frown from under her silly hat. 'You find her pretty, then?'

He shrugged carelessly, and gave her one of those grins he was coming to loathe. But ladies had often told him his smile was well-nigh irresistible; he might as well make us of it.

Indeed, Lady Riverton did relax her hard clasp on his sleeve, smiling at him in return.

'I am a man,' he said. 'Therefore I cannot help but find Miss Chase pretty. That would be enough for many men, but not for me.'

'No?'

'No. I prefer more substance to a lady. Intelligence. Experience.' He gave her arm a surreptitious touch. 'Hidden depths.'

Lady Riverton giggled. 'Count di Fabrizzi, you are far too amusing.'

'I seek only to please.'

'That, I think, you could not help but do.' She surveyed the crowd around them, giving a deep sigh of satisfaction when she saw that they, too, were observed. 'I am the envy of every lady here, to have your companionship.'

And that was what Marco had wanted, of course, when he had sought Lady Riverton's renewed acquaintance. He had had no luck finding the whereabouts of the silver any other way, and her own abodes proved to be surprisingly well guarded. She was no fool, though she liked so much to play one.

But she *was* a woman, and receptive to a handsome man's flirtations. He had almost gained her trust, was so close. He was sure of it.

Then Thalia appeared.

Lady Riverton excused herself to go and speak to an acquaintance, leaving Marco at last able to slip away. Even his acting skills, honed over years in service to his cause until he could play a gypsy, a king, or a careless flirt to perfection, felt strained in the glasshouse atmosphere of Bath. Under all its pretty gentility, its endless pursuit of diversion, lurked a deep vein of tension. The sense that everyone was just watching, waiting, for something to explode.

Like his head.

Marco slipped out of the doors into the Abbey churchyard. It was just as crowded there, but at least there was fresh air, the open expanse of pearl-grey sky overhead. It had not yet begun to rain, as it always seemed to do in this blasted town, which made everyone linger outside just a bit longer.

Across the yard, past the edifice of the church and the swirl of the milling crowds, Marco caught a glimpse of a bright blue silk pelisse. Thalia had paused to gaze into a shop window, with no sign nearby of her sister and brother-in-law.

Without thinking, without even considering the indisputable fact that he was better off staying far away from her, Marco hurried toward her. He was irresistibly drawn to her, as if her golden hair was a beacon of light and truth in the grey day. A ray of bright honesty in a sordid world.

He remembered how she had portrayed Antigone in that ancient amphitheatre in Santa Lucia, so solemn and certain. He had thought then how Sophocles's doomed princess suited her, both of them women set on their own course. Determined to do what was right no matter the consequence.

He loved that about her, and hated it, too. Her sister Clio had been his partner in the cause of preserving ancient history for a long time. Clio understood him, for they were alike in their belief that subterfuge and deceit were sometimes required when dealing with their dangerous foes. But Thalia had no deceit in her. She was a warrior of the battlefield. She would happily skewer her enemy, yet she would look them in the eye while she did it.

And he feared he was the one about to be skewered.

She saw his reflection in the shop window, her gaze rising to meet his, but she did not turn around.

'I'm surprised your friend has let you off the leading strings,' she said.

Marco laughed despite himself. 'She is not exactly my friend.'

'No, I suppose not. It is quite obvious she considers herself to be more than that. I imagine she required a replacement for poor Mr Frobisher.'

That stung. He remembered Frobisher, scurrying around Santa Lucia to do Lady Riverton's every bidding—until she betrayed him.

Marco longed to tell Thalia what was really going on. They had worked so well together in Sicily, once they had joined forces. Yet the thought of her innocent enthusiasm for the play, of that shining integrity, stopped him. Clio had warned him to keep Thalia out of danger.

And he never wanted to see her in danger again. Not Thalia. Even if the price was her contempt. He had sworn after Maria died that no woman would suffer because of his work again.

'She is useful in introducing me to your English society,' he said cautiously.

'And I must ask myself, why would an Italian nobleman, a count, need an entrée to English society?' she said. She turned away from the window to face him, gazing up at him steadily from beneath her white straw bonnet.

There was certainly nothing *wan* about her. Her smooth cheeks were pink, her eyes a shining sky-blue. 'Why are you here?' she demanded. 'Really?'

He summoned up every ounce of those theatrical skills, remembering all too well that she was also an accomplished thespian. 'I heard there was much amusement to be had in Bath. Sicily was too dull after you and your sister left, and Florence is overrun by boring Austrians.'

'So you came to Bath?' she said doubtfully, scowling up at him. Those furrows on her brow only made her more adorable, made him want to catch her up in his arms and kiss those ridiculous wrinkles until she laughed with him again.

'Do you suffer from gout, perchance?' she said, obviously completely oblivious to his lascivious desires. To the way her white lilac perfume drove him insane. 'From digestive complaints? All those tomatoes in the Italian diet…'

Marco laughed. 'Not at all. I wanted a glimpse of your prince's strange Oriental palace.'

'Then you are in entirely the wrong place, Count. The Pavilion is in Brighton.'

He slapped his open palm to his forehead. 'Ah! My terrible English.'

'Well, at least you have Lady Riverton to rescue you.' Thalia stepped closer, so close he could see the silvery flecks in her eyes, the blonde curls that had escaped from her bonnet to brush against her brow.

'We are indeed a long way from Sicily,' she murmured. 'But I remember what happened there. You are up to something in Bath, Count di Fabrizzi, and I will discover what it is.'

Marco was afraid of that. He had been acquainted with the Chase sisters long enough to know they never backed away from a challenge. Now he had two of them on his trail, Thalia and Lady Westwood, who had once met him in his gypsy guise in Yorkshire, trying to steal a statue from the Duke of Averton. Would Clio and that Duke, now her husband, show up next?

That was the last thing he needed. Not when matters were so precariously balanced.

'Miss Chase,' he said coolly, 'I know that this is an impossible task for a Chase female, but I would advise you to mind your own business. You have no call to interfere in my personal affairs.'

Her eyes flashed. 'Your personal affairs, is it? Well, I have no desire to "interfere" with anyone who has the bad taste to associate with Lady Riverton. And I see clearly that there is *nothing* wrong with your English!'

Marco feared he might fall into those angry eyes and drown. Forget about everything but Thalia, her beauty, her wonderful temper, her talent—and the way she had haunted his thoughts ever since Sicily. He forced himself to step away from her, to give her one of his careless grins.

'Then I hope we understand each other, Miss Chase,' he said. 'I bid you good day.'

'And good day to you, sir!' she snapped. She spun around in a flurry of blue-and-white skirts, stalking off into the crowd. She was quickly swallowed up by the throngs of people, vanishing as if she had never been there at all.

It took all Marco's resolve to turn back toward the Pump Room, to not run after her. Not catch her in his arms and tell her everything. The contempt in her eyes cut deeper than any sword.

But she could not know of his real feelings. Not now—not ever.

Chapter Five

'Fool, fool!' Thalia muttered, pacing from one end of her chamber to the other. She didn't know if she meant herself—or Marco di Fabrizzi. Or perhaps they were all fools. It certainly felt like it at that moment.

She reached the carved marble fireplace, and turned to stalk back in the other direction. Even though her room was exceedingly pretty, with cream-coloured wallpaper, and cream-and-blue chintz curtains and hangings, it was not terribly large. It didn't quite allow for satisfactory stalking, so she plopped herself down at the little writing desk instead.

She had begun a letter to Clio that morning, before they left for the Pump Room, and now Thalia didn't know how to go on with it. All the family news, the gossip about Bath, seemed so silly beside what she really longed to write.

Dearest Clio—was the Count di Fabrizzi in love with you, as I suspect he was? Was his heart utterly broken when you married the Duke? And is that now why he has turned to the attentions of Lady Riverton?

Thalia frowned as she stared down at the paper, seeing not the half-finished scribbles but Marco's face at the Pump Room. That handsome, bronzed Italian face, smiling down so flirtatiously at Lady Riverton.

Lady Riverton, of all people! No, she really could not believe it. It had to be a scheme of some sort.

Thalia reached for her pen and ink, hastily adding a long postscript to the letter. Clio would know how to advise her, could tell her the whole truth of what had happened in Santa Lucia. If only Thalia did not suffer agonies of embarrassment that her sister might guess her own feelings!

The Chase sisters were always united against the world, but amongst themselves they could tease unmercifully.

'My dear Clio,' she wrote. 'Since I concluded my missive, a most curious thing occurred. I met with an old acquaintance from Santa Lucia at the Pump Room—and he was not alone…'

She wrote the rest of her tale as fast as she could, and sealed it up before she could change her mind. She also had to write to her father, and to her younger sister Cory. But she found she was too tired after that one letter, and closed up her writing box until later.

As she shut the lid, she glimpsed a bundle of documents tucked away in its depths. Her play, *The Dark Castle of Count Orlando.*

It was only one act at the moment, Thalia thought

wryly, and likely to remain so for some time. The story, full of intrigue, secrets, forbidden romance, and picturesque Italian ruins full of ghosts and curses, had seemed so grand in Santa Lucia. A story of how finding real love could overcome anything at all. Now that she was face to face with its inspiration, though…

She firmly closed the lid, turning the key in the little lock. She had no confidence in her observational skills now. How could she write convincing drama? Convincing romance?

A knock sounded at the chamber door. 'Come in,' Thalia called, dropping the key into her desk drawer.

A housemaid entered, bobbing a curtsy as she announced, 'Lady Westwood is returned, Miss Chase, and asks if you will join her in the drawing room for tea.'

Very glad of the distraction, Thalia hurried downstairs to the gold-and-coral drawing room, where Calliope reclined on the couch. Another maid set out an array of tempting cakes and little sandwiches, but there was no sign of Cameron or little Psyche.

Thalia kissed her sister's cheek, noticing that, aside from a few damp curls at her temples and a slight pinkness in her cheeks, she seemed unaffected by the waters of the Hot Bath. She also didn't seem to want to eat, though she sipped at some tea.

'You weren't at the baths very long,' Thalia said, helping herself to a strawberry tart. Sadly, emotional turmoil always made her feel *more* hungry!

'It is far too warm,' Calliope said. 'I could scarcely breathe.'

'That, my dear, is why they call it the *Hot* Bath! Here, have a cucumber sandwich, it will revive you. Where has Cameron gone?'

Calliope obediently nibbled at the sandwich. 'I sent him to procure some theatre tickets, and to see about the assembly at the Upper Rooms on Tuesday.'

'Are you quite certain you feel up to all that, Cal? Rest, remember. That is why we came to Bath.'

Calliope frowned down at her half-eaten sandwich. 'I am tired of resting! And I told you, I will not have you grow bored and leave us.'

'I would not leave you! And I am not bored. I'm a Chase, remember? We are never bored. There is always reading to do, studying, writing…'

'Indeed. Though I have not noticed you doing much writing lately.'

'I will get back to it soon.' She thought of that Italian play upstairs. Would she ever want to write of the mysteries of love again?

'Perhaps you are the one who should rest, Thalia. You look weary.' Calliope paused, setting aside her plate. 'I have been thinking, perhaps Bath was not the best place to visit. We could leave here, go to Brighton. Or Tunbridge Wells. Maybe even back to Italy! They have spa towns there.'

'You are not yet strong enough to travel to Italy,' Thalia protested. 'And we have just arrived in Bath. What is this urge to leave so suddenly?'

Calliope shrugged. 'Nothing at all.'

'Of course it is not nothing. Is it—is it because of meeting with Count di Fabrizzi this morning?'

'So, you do know this so-called Count.'

'And so do you!' Thalia cried. 'I knew it! But how? I don't understand anything.'

'Not even why he might be here?'

'Especially not that.'

Calliope gave a deep sigh. 'It is true I have met him before, though in a far different guise. He was pretending to be a gypsy.'

'A gypsy!' Thalia gasped. This was turning into a tale far more interesting than any she could ever devise for a play. And Marco just became more and more complex, more incomprehensible to her. 'When was that?'

'Oh, a long time ago, before Cameron and I were married,' Calliope answered. 'You remember when we went to Yorkshire, to visit Emmeline Saunders's family?'

'Of course I remember. Our Ladies Artistic Society was chasing after the Lily Thief then. We went to Averton's castle…' Suddenly, Thalia felt like the greatest of fools. She slumped back in her chair, shaking her head. 'Was Marco the thief? Even back then?'

'No, he wasn't *the* thief,' Calliope answered quietly. 'But I certainly wouldn't put it past him to be *a* thief. Clio tells me he is quite fanatical about Italian history and culture, about retrieving parts of its great heritage that have been scattered. He must feel such contempt for collectors like our father and Averton! That is probably why he and Clio got along so very well.'

A cold wave broke over Thalia, and she covered her eyes with her hands. 'He was in Yorkshire with Clio.' Of course he was. He *did* love Clio. It was probably good that she was reminded of that fact, before she foolishly drowned in those dark eyes of his.

She lowered her hands to find Calliope gazing at her, her expression full of sisterly concern. Dearest Cal—she had protected all of them for so long, had taken her position as the eldest of the Muses so seriously. But she needed to take care of herself now, and Thalia was weary of being protected.

'I don't know what his feelings for Clio might have been then,' Calliope said. 'She is married now, and it seems he has transferred his affections to Lady Riverton. I wouldn't trust appearances, though. Not with a man like that.'

'A man who is a gypsy, a count, and a thief, all in one?' Thalia said with a laugh. 'Not to mention a ladies' man. Please, Cal, do not worry about me. I won't fall prey to his charms, great though they are. I haven't the time or energy for deciphering such vast complexities as the Count di Fabrizzi.'

'You are the most "energetic" person I know, Thalia,' Calliope said. 'And I am sure you could decipher anything you set your mind to. But I would never want to see you hurt by a man who was so entirely unworthy.'

Thalia laughed again, as if she hadn't a care in the world about 'unworthy' men. Yet she turned her face away so Cal could not see her eyes. 'Not when there are so many worthy men beating down my door?'

'You have far more suitors than any other young lady I know! Mr Bramsby, Lord Egreton, young Viscount Moreby—I know they have all made an offer, and they seem quite respectable. Not to mention utterly infatuated.'

Thalia thought of those men, of the avid way they looked at her as they drove in the park, the way they lined up to dance with her at balls. The flowers they sent, the compliments they paid. The way they never even saw past her façade, her prettiness, her connections, into the real her.

For a few moments in Santa Lucia, she had thought someone did see. Saw, and understood, and answered. But that was foolish.

'They are respectable,' she answered, pouring more tea. 'And nice enough. I doubt any infatuation would last more than a few days, though, once they saw what I am really like.'

Calliope sighed. 'It is true that we Chase girls are not quite as other ladies. We were raised to actually use our brains, to speak our minds! But there are men who quite like that, I think.'

Thalia gave her a teasing smile. 'Men like Cameron?'

Calliope laughed. 'I have never held back from expressing my thoughts to him! We have very—lively conversations. And quarrels, from time to time.'

'Cameron is a very fine man, to be sure. But there aren't many like to him to be found in England.'

'Perhaps that is because his mother was Greek. It is true that my husband is quite unique, but I am sure we can find someone just as special for you.'

Thalia doubted that. Her sisters were very fortunate in their marriages. Lightning didn't strike *three* times.

'I am content as I am,' Thalia said. 'I will write my plays, and teach Psyche her music when she is older. I will be the perfect maiden aunt!'

Calliope laughed, but Thalia could see she looked tired again. 'I cannot be selfish enough to keep you with me, though I would dearly love it. Psyche is so very—vivid now, I cannot imagine what will happen when she is walking and talking.'

'Or, heaven forefend, when she is old enough to have suitors of her own! She is a true Chase.' Thalia went to tuck a blanket around Calliope's legs. 'I will leave you now, Cal dear, so you can rest. Please, don't worry about me. I am entirely well and happy.'

'Are you?'

'Yes, indeed,' Thalia said firmly.

'Very well. I will pretend I believe you. Just do one thing for me.'

'Of course.'

'Write to Clio and ask her about the Count. She will know more of him than I, and she can tell you things I have promised not to speak of.'

Promised not to speak of? Thalia positively ached

with curiosity. Ordinarily she would bombard Calliope with questions, but her sister's pale face stopped her. Calliope was weary, and she would never tell her secrets anyway. She had her share of the Chase stubbornness.

'Yes, I will write to Clio,' Thalia said. She went to the pianoforte, running her fingertips over the cool ivory keys. This was no time for the storms of her beloved Beethoven, the one she always turned to when her thoughts were in turmoil. Instead, she played for Calliope a folksong she had learned in Italy, a light, trilling piece to raise the spirits.

It raised hers, too, drawing her into the other world music always created for her. A place where nothing mattered but sound and creation, emotion and freedom. But as she moved into another song, she happened to glance up at the window.

Passing along the curve of the Crescent were Marco and Lady Riverton with her little dog, arm in arm and laughing.

Thalia's fingers fumbled, clashing on a discordant note. She looked hastily to see if Calliope had noticed, but her sister was asleep. And when Thalia turned back to the window, Marco was gone.

Chapter Six

The assembly rooms were lit up like a Chinese lantern, Thalia saw as their carriage rolled to a halt. They could not get too close, as the crowds waiting to go in were so thick, but even from that distance she saw the golden glow spilling from the windows, the ribbons of light curling out of the open doors, around the pillars of the Doric-style portico, and over the ladies' pastel gowns and fine jewels.

Thalia thought she could even hear the faint strains of music, and it made her feet tap in their pink kid slippers.

'Such a great crush,' Calliope murmured, peering past Thalia's shoulder. 'We shall never get inside until midnight.'

'Perhaps we should leave, then,' her husband suggested. 'Come back on a less crowded evening.'

Calliope laughed. 'Are there any less crowded

evenings? I doubt it. We shall just have to press forwards.'

'I don't want you to tire yourself,' Cameron protested.

'I had a nap this afternoon, just like Psyche,' Calliope said. 'Now I want some company! I can't be shut up like an invalid old lady, and poor Thalia should not be shut up with me.'

Thalia gave her a smile. 'It's true that I would love a dance. But not if you feel unwell, Cal. Cameron is right, we can come back—'

Calliope suddenly cracked her fan against the door. 'I have told you two a hundred times to stop fussing over me! We will *all* dance tonight, and that is that.'

With that outburst, she reached for the handle and swung the door open, climbing down before anyone could stop her.

'Hurry up, then,' she called from the pavement, smoothing her white-and-silver silk gown and diamond necklace. 'Or we shall miss all the fine music.'

Thalia and Cameron exchanged a resigned glance. 'Well, she told us what is what,' he said.

'Indeed,' Thalia answered. 'She is *not* an invalid.'

Cameron followed his wife, reaching back to help Thalia alight in a more conventional manner before they made their way to the front doors. Thalia held on to her brother-in-law's left arm as Calliope took his right. She gazed around at the swirl of faces.

Not that she was looking for Marco, of course not.

She was merely interested in who might be newly arrived in Bath, that was all.

She even nearly had herself convinced of that as they made their way past the marble columns of the central vestibule. Until she glimpsed the back of a tall, dark-haired man, and her breath caught on a gasp.

But then he turned around, and she saw he was not Marco at all.

'Are you quite well, Thalia?' Cameron asked.

'Hmm?' Pushing down those annoying pangs of disappointment, Thalia gave him a quick smile. 'Yes, of course. Why do you ask?'

'Your cheeks went pink all of a sudden.'

'It's probably the crowd,' Calliope said, elbowing aside two gawking young dandies blocking the way. 'Everyone thinks they can just stand right here, preventing anyone from getting into the ballroom!'

Yet Cameron was quite tall, and he soon had them at the crossroads where they could go left to the ballroom, right to the tearoom, or straight ahead into the octagon and card room.

'Could you possibly procure us some punch from the tearoom, my love?' Calliope said. 'Thalia and I will find her a suitable dance partner in the ballroom.'

Cameron frowned doubtfully, causing Calliope to laugh. 'Go on, now,' she said, giving him a playful little shove. 'I promise I will sit down at the first opportunity.'

She took Thalia's arm and drew her into the

ballroom. It was just as crowded in there, but the high ceilings and pale-green walls gave an airy feeling. White pillars soared up past a balcony where the musicians played, to an array of sparkling crystal chandeliers high overhead.

Dancers swirled and twirled along the centre of the parquet floor, a kaleidoscope of silks, muslins and superfine, of shining pearls and shimmering diamonds that made Thalia think of the Murano glass she had seen in Venice.

And thinking of Venice made her think of Marco—again.

'Blast it all,' she muttered, wishing she could dash her fan against something, as Calliope had. Why, *why*, had he come into her life again? Reminding her of things she could never have.

Fortunately, Calliope was too preoccupied to hear Thalia's little outburst. 'Ah, here is a chair,' she exclaimed, drawing Thalia with her as she claimed the last open seat along the wall just ahead of one of those dandies.

'Now I have kept my promise to Cameron to sit down,' Calliope said, snapping open that fan. 'Now I must keep mine to you, Thalia dear.'

Thalia laughed. 'I don't recall any promises.'

'The one where I vowed to find you a dancing partner. Do you see anyone who strikes your fancy?'

Thalia scanned the dancers, the people chattering on the side of the room, the strollers. 'Not at all.'

'There must be someone! Look closer. I refuse to

allow you to stay by me all evening, not when I know how you love to dance.'

It was true, Thalia *did* love to dance. Even now her feet itched to skip and spin in time to the music. She had not had a dance since…

Since the masquerade ball in Santa Lucia. When she and Marco had danced tarantellas and waltzes beneath Demeter's harvest moon. The Bath ballroom before her faded, shifting into a warm Sicilian night, a blur of masks and dreams.

She remembered how it had felt when Marco had held her in his arms and she had leaned into his shoulder. How warm and strong his lean body had been through the thin cloth of his shirt, how he had smelled of citrus and ginger. She had just wanted to stay there for ever, wrapped up in him, inhaling that essence of him into herself until they were as one.

In that moment, she had forgotten so much. Forgotten who she was, who *he* was. Forgotten he loved her sister, that he was involved in mysterious schemes she could have no part of. Being in his arms felt right. It felt like what she had been waiting for.

Someone bumped into her, jolting her out of her Italian dreams and back into Bath. Into the cold reality of her dull, English-lady, useless life. Sicily, and the new sense of energised purpose she had once felt there—it was gone. Dancing in Marco's arms was gone.

'No, Cal,' she said. 'I don't see anyone I would want to dance with.'

Calliope gazed up at her intently, searching for something behind this refusal. Thalia gave her a bright smile. She was getting good at that lately, yet it did not seem to fool her sister at all.

'It is early yet,' Calliope said, waving her fan until her black hair stirred. 'Perhaps more of the gentlemen can be coaxed from the card room later.'

'Perhaps,' Thalia said. But she was equally sure there was no one in there she wanted to dance with, either.

Cameron soon found them, giving his wife her punch, and Thalia excused herself. She claimed she sought the ladies' withdrawing room, but in truth she just wanted a moment alone. A moment to suppress those memories again.

In Santa Lucia, for those few days when Clio had asked for help, Thalia had felt useful. Needed. Her talents for the theatre could be used to bring about justice for a thief, to retrieve a treasure of Italian history! No one had ever needed her help before, or found her useful. She was always just the little sister, to be protected and petted. She wanted to help, wanted a mission.

Those days, working with Clio, Averton and Marco, had filled her with energy, a purpose, a passion she had never known before. She was part of a common cause, and that felt wonderful.

The surprised admiration in Marco's eyes wasn't bad, either.

Coming back to England, to her old role of

cosseted, useless beauty, had frozen all of that. It was just a crystalline memory now.

As was the Marco she had known then. She could hardly think what to make of this new Marco, Lady Riverton's flirtatious companion.

Thalia found her way down a flight of stairs behind a cluster of giggling young ladies. As they disappeared through a doorway, she stayed back, halted before a looking glass on the wall.

For an instant, she thought she faced a stranger. Then she realised that the lady standing there in pale pink muslin, blonde curls bound with a pearl diadem, was still her. Memories of Italy had not changed her at all. Outwardly, anyway. She still looked like a blasted porcelain shepherdess.

She stepped close to the glass, reaching up to tuck an errant lock back into her coiffure. Her gloved fingertips trailed over her cheekbone, just beneath one blue eye. If she looked more like Clio, tall, auburn-haired, sun-browned as an Amazon warrior, and not so much as if she belonged in a swing in a Versailles garden, would people take her seriously?

Would Marco love *her* then, as he loved Clio? Or would she just be a distraction, an affair, like Lady Riverton?

'Never say you have found something to displease you there,' a softly accented voice said behind her. 'For truly your face is nothing less than perfection.'

Thalia's heart suddenly pounded in her breast at the sound of that voice. Her gaze shifted in the glass, finding Marco's reflection just over her shoulder. He watched her, and for once he did not smile, there was no teasing gleam in his eyes. He seemed a part of the shadows.

Her hand fell to her side. 'One could say the same about you. All the ladies are just as in love with you here in Bath as they were in Sicily.'

A whisper of a smile just touched the corner of his lips. 'All of them, Thalia *cara*?'

'Most of them.' She turned away from the mirror, facing him. Perhaps that was a mistake, though. Looking into his eyes reminded her too much of that masked ball, of dancing under the dusty-black Sicilian sky. 'And yet you seem to have eyes now for only one.'

Marco gave a low, deep chuckle, that maddening dimple flashing in his cheek. 'Indeed I do.' He took a step towards her, then another and another, until he leaned his palm on the wall just beyond her head, his touch brushing her hair. He leaned in close, so close she could see the shadow of dark whiskers along his sculpted jaw, the flecks of gold in his brown eyes.

That light citrus-ginger smell, blended with clean starch and the dark essence of *him*, reached out to her like a beckoning caress. Tempting her to lean into him, to curl her hands into the soft linen of his shirt and hold him against her. When he gazed at her like that, so solemn and intent, she forgot her name, where she was, everything. Everything but him and the way he made her feel like the only woman in all the world.

She even reached up to graze her fingertips along the satin lapel of his coat, but that last faint thought stopped her touch. He made every female feel like the only one. He caught them within the snare of his beautiful eyes, and they became giggling, silly creatures, just like Lady Riverton.

Feeling that sudden cold tinge of disappointment, of hurt, Thalia turned her head to the side so she could no longer see him. Her hand fell to her skirt. She did not want to be like all the others! She didn't want to lose herself in some silly infatuation. To go helplessly following Marco around Bath with all his other fawning acolytes. She wanted purpose in her life, and that was not it!

Yet he still stood there, his arm inches away from her cheek, gazing down at her as if he could discern all her secrets.

'What would Lady Riverton say if she could see you here with me?' Thalia murmured, peering at him from beneath her lashes.

Marco frowned. 'Lady Riverton?'

'Yes. Are you not here in Bath as her devoted swain? I suppose she was in need of a replacement for poor Mr Frobisher, after they parted so precipitously in Santa Lucia! Though I must say you are far more handsome than he ever was.'

And surely *he* was in need of a replacement for Clio, for his hopeless feelings for her. But Thalia found she could not say that aloud. Once, for a few blissful days in Sicily, she had felt free of all constraints. Free to say and express whatever she liked. Here, everything was different.

He was different, too. No matter how close he was physically, there was a vast gulf between them.

Marco's fingers curled into a fist against the wall. 'Lady Riverton and I are merely, how you say—friends,' he said tightly.

'Friends as you and I were?' Thalia said. 'Or like you and Clio?'

'No one can ever be quite like the Chases, I think. Lady Riverton merely offered to be my tour guide here in Bath, to show me the sites. How could I say no, after my old friendship with her late husband?'

A sudden flare of angry temper made Thalia grow hot again. 'How can you be so casual, Marco?' she muttered. 'After what happened in Santa Lucia? She is not—'

The door to the ladies' withdrawing room suddenly opened, a crowd of laughing females emerging in a cloud of pale muslins and flowery perfumes. They saw Marco, and commenced to giggling behind their fans.

Thalia feared she knew well how they felt. She slid deeper into the shadows, certain they could not see her there. They would take no notice even if they did. Every iota of attention was on Marco.

He straightened away from the wall, giving them a polite bow and smile. The giggles and fan flutterings increased exponentially, and the ladies hurried up the stairs.

'Thalia,' Marco muttered, spinning back to her when they were again alone. The dimpled smile was gone, vanished into a strange, dark urgency. 'I can see we must talk.'

'We are talking.'

'Somewhere we can't be interrupted. Will you walk with me tomorrow in Sydney Gardens?'

Thalia swallowed hard. She certainly did want to talk to him, to express her confusion and anger! But she also had seen tonight how her rational thoughts just flew apart when he was near. How, despite everything, he still had that sensual, forgetful effect on her.

Could she trust herself with him, even in a public park? Only moments ago she had been ready to jump into his arms.

But her curiosity was stronger than her prudence, as always. She gave him a nod.

'My sister is to take the waters in the morning,' she said. 'I will meet you there after breakfast.'

'*Grazie*, Thalia,' he answered. Before she could stop him, he reached for her hand, raising it to his lips. His kiss was warm and alluring, even through the thin silk. She felt his cool breath against her skin, and she shivered.

He smiled up at her, a mischievous grin, as if he felt that small quiver. He turned her hand over, balancing her wrist delicately on his palm.

'I don't suppose I could tempt you to dance with me?' he said teasingly. He placed another soft kiss just where her pulse beat, and she felt the light touch of his tongue between the tiny pearl buttons.

Thalia snatched her hand away. 'I don't intend to dance tonight.'

Marco straightened, still smiling at her so infuriatingly, as if he read her every thought. 'And if you did it would not be with me, *si*?'

'*Si*—I mean, yes,' Thalia answered, with a firmness she was far from feeling.

'Oh, but Thalia *cara*, I am a fine dancer. Do you not remember the masked ball?'

'Of course I remember it. Your technical skills are not in question, Count.'

Marco laughed, his head thrown back as if in sheer, abandoned delight. Thalia lunged forward, pressing her hand to his mouth to still that sound, even as something deep inside her longed to join in.

'Shh!' she whispered. 'Someone will hear.'

He moved her hand away, still holding it as he whispered in return, '*Cara*, I assure you, no one has ever complained of my—technical skills. If you would just give me a chance to demonstrate…'

Thalia yanked away from him, whirling around to dash up the stairs. His deep laughter seemed to follow her, chasing her as she ran away.

Infuriating man! He was so—so *Italian*. Could he take nothing seriously?

And why, oh, why could she never stay angry with him?

Thalia paused at the top of the stairs, her heart

pounding as she watched the tides of people moving past, their conversation even louder after those quiet moments. She felt laughter rise up within her, a bright bubble that could not be denied or forced away.

She pressed her hand to her mouth, fearing that once she laughed aloud she would not stop. She would fall to the marble floor, gasping and wheezing, until everyone knew what a lunatic she really was.

But she could smell him on the silk of the glove, and the warm citrus-ginger scent made her head spin. She was a giddy fool, there was no denying it.

Footsteps echoed on the stairs behind her, and she suddenly feared to encounter Marco again. She would not be able to resist his invitation to dance twice. Not when she remembered how well they moved together, how his touch felt on her hand. When she remembered his—yes, his 'technical skills'.

She hurried away, melding into the crowd and letting that irresistible tide carry her back to the ballroom. Calliope still sat in her chair by the pale green wall, talking animatedly with two other ladies.

'Thalia dear!' she said, reaching out to draw Thalia to her side. 'There you are. I wondered where you had disappeared to.'

'There was quite a crush in the ladies' withdrawing room,' Thalia answered lightly. 'I'm sorry I left you alone.'

'Not at all. As you see, Cameron abandoned me for the card room, but I found Mrs Smythe-Moreland and Lady Billingsfield. We met at the Hot Bath today, and discovered we have so much in common. Ladies, this is my sister, Miss Thalia Chase.'

Polite greetings were made all around, and Lady Billingsfield exclaimed, 'How pretty your sister is, Lady Westwood! She must meet my nephew, Mr Arthur Dashwood, who is just over there. Do you care for dancing, Miss Chase?'

Thalia glanced toward the doorway. Lady Riverton stood there with some of her friends, unmistakable in a bright turquoise-blue feathered turban. She gazed around distractedly, her matching feathered fan fluttering in agitation, but Marco was nowhere to be seen. Had he abandoned his flirtation already?

'I do enjoy a dance, Lady Billingsfield,' Thalia said.

'And so does my Arthur! How pleasant it would be to see the two of you handsome young people together.'

Lady Billingsfield vigorously waved her fan to summon the hapless, though admittedly good-looking, Arthur Dashwood, who duly asked Thalia to dance with him. As they took their places in the set, Thalia at last saw Marco come back into the ballroom.

He paused just past the knots of people in the doorway, his dark gaze scanning the room. Lady Riverton brightened at his appearance, waving at him, but he did not hasten to join her. His attention slid to Thalia in the dance, and he gave her a mocking little bow. His raised brow seemed to dare her to compare her new partner's 'skills' with his own.

She suppressed a fresh urge to laugh, and turned back to Mr Dashwood as the music began. Their walk in Sydney Gardens tomorrow should be interesting indeed!

'Well, Miss Chase,' her dance partner asked as they joined hands, 'how do you like Bath thus far?'

Chapter Seven

Marco watched Thalia as she skipped gracefully through the figures of the dance. She looked like Aurora, the spirit of the dawn, in her pale pink gown, her pretty face lit up with a joyful smile. She was all light, elegant grace, laughing happily with her partner.

Could she possibly be the same solemn woman he had glimpsed in the dim corridor? Studying herself in the mirror as if she had never seen her face before—and didn't approve of it at all. She was certainly not as she was back in Santa Lucia, so fearless in her search for the truth, single-minded in her work. Here she was just the diamond of the assembly, light and pretty, the focus of so much admiration.

Her fortunate dance partner gazed at her raptly, as if he could not quite believe his luck. As well he might. But did he, could he, see even an inch past her lovely façade?

Marco would wager not. He watched, frowning, as she made a curtsy at the end of the dance and her partner took her hand to lead her back to her sister. She smiled up at him as he prattled to her, and Marco found he burned with a sudden flare of jealousy. Why would she not smile so at *him*? Dance with him? Most ladies seemed to like him. Why not Thalia Chase?

He felt a touch on his sleeve, and was harshly reminded of why Thalia would not smile at him. He glanced down to find Lady Riverton at his side, her gloved hand proprietarily on his arm.

Thalia did not understand why he was here with Lady Riverton, and he could not tell her. Not only did he refuse to put her in any danger, but he had promised his friend Clio, before she had left for her honeymoon, that he would be careful with her family.

That vow had seemed easy enough to keep when he had left Santa Lucia, certain he would not see Thalia Chase again. Now that she was here before him, her beautiful, alluring presence all too real, it seemed one of the hardest promises he had ever made.

He had been intrigued by her in Sicily, intrigued by the complex labyrinth of her mind behind that pretty face. By her creativity, her sly humour, her bravery, and the depth of her understanding of human nature. Human flaws and foibles, not often seen by well-bred English ladies.

But it was just that understanding that could make her dangerous now. If she knew what he was really doing in Bath, she would insist on being involved, just as she had in Santa Lucia. And then his vow to Clio, and to himself, would be broken.

He could not do that. Aurora belonged to the light of day, not to the dark masquerade his life had become. The cause that was his real birthright.

And yet—yet he could not take his gaze from her, as she laughingly fended off all the young men besieging her for dances. She drew him like a hapless, hopeless moth to a brilliant flame.

Lady Riverton tugged harder at his sleeve. He reluctantly tore his gaze from Thalia's pink cheeks to smile down at Lady Riverton. She scowled at him, those feathers trembling in her turban.

'I vow you have not heard a word I said,' she said petulantly.

'Ah, dear Lady Riverton, forgive me,' he answered. He summoned up his most charming smile, the one that seldom failed with the ladies—except Thalia, who seemed quite immune.

Lady Riverton, though, was not. She smiled, too, as Marco raised her hand to his lips, kissing the air above her kid glove. He thought of Thalia's hand in his, of the taste of her skin through the silk.

Lady Riverton, unlike Thalia, did not appear to be immune to Italian charm at all. She giggled and smiled.

'It is so very noisy in here,' he said. 'A "great crush", as you English say.'

'Perhaps we should go somewhere a bit quieter,' she answered, her smile growing softer.

Marco's gaze sharpened. Was this it, then? The

way into her well-guarded treasure vault of a villa? The way into her confidences? 'What are you suggesting, my lady?'

'The card room, of course!' she said, tapping him with her feathered fan. Those feathers wafted under his chin, tempting him to sneeze. 'La, sir, but what did you think I meant? I would have you remember that I am a respectable widow, entirely devoted to the memory of my late husband. Who was your friend, yes?'

'I assure you, Lady Riverton, I remember that at all times,' Marco answered, kissing her hand again. 'As much as I might wish it otherwise.'

Lady Riverton laughed. 'And no matter how very tempting *you* might be, my dear Count. Now, shall we have a hand of piquet?' Her gaze slid across the room to Thalia, who was still surrounded by admirers. 'Unless you would prefer to vie for a dance with the lovely Miss Chase. If, of course, you care to battle every other young man in the room.'

'Now, why would I care to *battle* for anything, when I am already having a thoroughly enjoyable evening?' Marco said. He tucked Lady Riverton's hand in the crook of his arm, leading her toward the doorway.

As they passed Thalia and her coterie, her gaze met his for an instant. Her brow arched, as if in a hint of mockery, and just for a flash he thought he saw hurt puzzlement in the depths of her eyes. But then she was concealed by a wall of suitors, and he passed out of the ballroom with Lady Riverton.

Yet that look haunted him. Marco seldom cared

what people thought of him; he could not afford to, not when he did all he had to for his work. Why, then, was the thought of Thalia Chase's contempt, her puzzlement, so hurtful?

Why did he want so much to gain her admiration? To have her smile at him, so sunny and open, as she had with her young dance partner?

That seemed as hopeless as his task here in Bath. Yet, just as he had to do all in his power to retrieve the silver altar set, he knew he had to seek one genuine smile from Thalia's lips.

No matter what the odds against him.

It was quite late when Marco returned to the White Hart. Bath was not like London, with merriment and distractions at all hours, as most people had to be up and about early to take the waters. But Lady Riverton had met some friends in the card room, who had invited them for an informal card party when the assembly rooms closed.

Now it was late indeed, and he was tired, bored and seemingly no closer to his goal.

'I must be losing my touch,' he muttered, dragging off his rumpled cravat. 'And I am certainly too old for this now!' Parties at all hours had been all well and good in his twenties, but now he was thirty they seemed silly.

Or maybe he just longed for a different companion in revels.

He threw himself into the nearest chair, running

his fingers through his hair until the rumpled locks fell over his eyes. He had done a lot of crazy things for Florence, for Italy, before. He had turned thief, soldier, and, God help him, pamphlet writer. Now he had turned flirt as well, and the sad thing was it didn't seem to be getting him where he needed to be. He was no closer to finding the silver than he had been in Santa Lucia.

Maybe what he needed was to take lessons in flirtation from a true master. He closed his eyes and saw Thalia again, laughing, bright-eyed, surrounded by admirers. She surely made everyone, including him, long to give her whatever she wanted. Tell her anything.

But he knew better than to give in to temptation. Even when it came in as luscious a package as Thalia Chase.

He opened his eyes, and for an instant imagined he glimpsed her sitting in the chair across from him. She leaned back against the brocade cushions, one slippered foot swinging from beneath her skirt as she laughed at him.

'You know I can help you, Marco,' she whispered. 'All you have to do is ask. Remember what a good team we were? It can be just like that again…'

Marco shook his head hard, and she vanished. He was alone again, as always.

That was how it had to be.

He pushed himself out of the chair and went to the cluttered desk, looking for the pamphlet he was in the midst of writing. On top of his blotted parchment, his attempts to tie historic Italian glories to future freedoms, lay the afternoon post. Amid the invitations and a scented note from Lady Riverton, there was a creased letter from Naples. It had obviously followed him a long way to arrive in Bath.

Marco tore open the seals, already sure who it would be from, and what it would say.

Marco, we need you—the time is at hand, read the scrawling, smudged hand. *There is none like you with a sword, with an inspiring speech. Where are you? Write as soon as you can. Domenico.*

Domenico de Lucca. Of course. Marco let the letter drop back to the desk. Domenico always thought the 'time was at hand', and that swords, not pens, were the answer.

There might come the day when he was proved right, when Marco would have to leave the scholarly life behind and become again the warrior. But he did not want Thalia to be near when that day came.

He would never put a woman he cared for in danger again.

Chapter Eight

Thalia fastened her pale blue spencer, turning before the mirror to judge its effect. Was the *à la militaire* cut stylish enough? Was it *too* stylish? Too—flirtatious? She did want to look pretty, but also serious. Scholarly. Trustworthy, so someone would want to entrust secrets to her.

She touched the braid trim along one of the well-cut lapels, wishing she had some garments that were not pastels. The blues, pinks, and sea-greens of her wardrobe were fashionable, and suited her fair colouring, but perhaps Marco would think her more intelligent if she wore black. Or brown. Or vivid Turkey red and jade green, as Clio favoured.

'Oh, blast it all!' she muttered, taking off the jacket and reaching for a plain pink pelisse. She did not care if Marco preferred Clio or Lady Riverton, or any woman, to herself. She had only agreed to this meeting out of courtesy and curiosity. She did not need his admiration or respect.

She did not!

Thalia scooped up her bonnet and gloves, and marched downstairs. Calliope was still asleep, exhausted by the assembly, and Thalia had breakfasted alone in the pretty little dining room. She was glad of that; no one to ask questions, to query her about her plans for the day. Now the house was quiet, except for Psyche's thin, high wail from the nursery.

Her niece obviously wanted attention and she wanted it *now*, Thalia thought as she paused before the looking glass in the entrance hall. The baby was not really well named, for she could not have foresworn looking directly at Cupid. She would have berated him soundly for even suggesting such a harebrained thing! Much like the rest of the Chases.

And maybe that was why Thalia herself was so nervous about meeting Marco. They would be in a public place, of course, but what if that burning curiosity, that cursed impulsiveness, overcame her? What if she knocked him down—if she could, which was doubtful, since he was quite tall—and demanded to know what he was doing in Bath?

It was all too likely, and the last thing Calliope needed right now was to deal with a scandalous sister.

'You must be calm and collected,' she muttered to her reflection, plopping her bonnet on her head. 'It is a quiet morning walk, nothing more.'

'Where are you off to this morning, Thalia?'

Cameron said. Thalia spun around to find him coming down the stairs, so quiet she had not even heard him.

Surely she could learn a lot about stealth from her brother-in-law. She had a feeling she was going to need it.

'I thought you were with Calliope,' she said, taking a deep breath as she tied the bonnet ribbons.

'I persuaded her to sleep a bit longer, then I will take her to the baths.' He paused at the foot of the stairs, leaning lazily against the balustrade. But Thalia was not fooled by the indolent posture. 'I would invite you to come with us, but it appears you already have plans of your own.'

'I doubt I could face yet more water,' she answered. 'Not just yet! I am going for a walk, then will do a bit of writing. I've been neglecting my work lately.'

'I'm glad to hear it. Calliope has been fretting that you will be bored.'

'How could I be bored in Bath? There are so many diversions.'

'So many admirers?' He grinned at her. 'You were surrounded by quite the horde last night.'

'They are diverting enough, I suppose, in their various ways.'

'And is one of them accompanying you on this walk?'

'They are not *that* diverting, Cam. Much like the water, I cannot face their prattle so early in the morning. I need to hear myself think.'

'And you cannot do that here?' Psyche let out a

great shout from above, and Cameron smiled ruefully. 'I suppose not.'

Thalia laughed, smoothing on her gloves. 'I won't be gone long.'

'Thalia,' Cameron said, reaching out to take her arm as she turned away. She paused, caught by the sudden seriousness of his voice. 'You aren't going to encounter Count di Fabrizzi on this walk, perchance?'

Calm and collected, Thalia reminded herself. She gave him a careless smile. Or at least she hoped it looked careless, not brittle and strained as it felt. But she wasn't the actress of the family for nothing. Cameron visibly relaxed at that smile, his hand falling from her arm.

'I have no idea who I might encounter,' she said lightly. 'But the Count does not strike me as being a morning sort of person.'

'You knew him in Italy, I think.'

'I'm not sure "knew" is the right word. He was in Sicily at the same time we were, and we encountered him at a few gatherings. Those of us who are interested in antiquities do seem to inhabit a very cosy world.' Thalia remembered the Pump Room, the crackling tension between Calliope and Cameron, and Marco. 'Perhaps you met him once or twice on your own travels.'

Cameron was half-Greek, and had spent much of his life travelling the Continent, pursuing his own studies. He and Calliope had made an extensive tour of Greece and Italy for their honeymoon. Surely he knew something of Marco's Italian life? But the caution in Cameron's eyes showed her that she should ease away, at least for now.

'I just don't think that he is a proper acquaintance for you, Thalia,' he said.

She laughed. 'Oh, Cam! Are you practising at playing the stuffy papa now? I think you have a few years before Psyche brings home any unsuitable admirers.'

He laughed, too, but it was rueful. 'I must begin some time, I suppose. But you are my sister now, and I want you to be happy.'

'And the Count is not likely to make me so? Oh, Cam, I do appreciate your concern. I always wanted a brother! You needn't worry, though. He is not at all my sort of gentleman.'

'Ah, yes. I have heard that ladies always scorn damnably handsome, titled Italian men,' Cameron scoffed.

'He is handsome, that is quite undeniable. But I am not all ladies, I am a Chase. My sisters have set quite high standards in their choice of mates.' Thalia gave him a quick kiss on the cheek. 'Tell Calliope I will go with her to tea at Lady Billingsfield's this afternoon. And if I see Count di Fabrizzi on my walk, I shall give him the cut direct.'

'I'm sure a brusque "good morning" will do the trick,' Cameron answered. 'And take an umbrella, for it looks like rain.'

'Yes, Papa,' Thalia teased. She caught up an

umbrella from the stand and hurried out of the door. The Crescent was quiet, with just a few maids out scrubbing the front steps and one carriage clattering past. The sky was indeed grey, but no rain yet fell.

Now, really! Thalia fumed, stabbing at a hapless rail with her umbrella. Why did everyone have to hide things from her? Have to protect her? Cameron and Calliope knew something about Marco, something surely unpleasant, and if they would not tell her she just had to imagine. To guess.

But she had a vivid imagination, and letting it run wild was never a good idea.

She hurried on her way, moving through the relative peace of the morning-time city. Everyone who was sensible was surely still at their breakfast table, thinking about an outing to the Pump Room, but Thalia had never claimed to be sensible. She rather wished that she was, though, as she stepped into the entrance of Sydney Gardens—and into she knew not what.

Marco was nowhere to be seen, and to distract herself Thalia took out the copy of Walks Through Bath she had tucked into her reticule. She sat down on a stone bench, opening it to read, 'Sydney Gardens is one of the most prominent, pleasing, and elegant features attached to the City of Bath. The hand of taste is visible in every direction of it; the plants and trees exhibit the most beautiful luxuriance. Upon gala-nights…'

A shadow fell across the page. 'Are you playing tourist, Thalia?'

She glanced up to find Marco standing before her.

Most of his features were shadowed by his hat, except for his white, teasing smile. She shut the book, holding it tightly in her gloved hands as she struggled not to grin at him in turn. What a ridiculous sight they would present, smiling away at each other like a pair of lunatics!

Sadly, that was how she often felt around him. Like a dizzy, giddy bedlamite, forgetful of everything else around her.

'It has been a long time since I was last in Bath,' she said. 'I don't want to miss any sites of interest.'

'Then there is not a moment to lose!' he declared, holding out his hand to her. 'Come, let me be your tour guide.'

Thalia laughed, slipping her fingers into his grasp as he helped her rise. Even through the leather of their gloves, she felt the elegant strength of his touch, the warmth of his skin. He quickly and properly let go, only to offer his arm.

Thalia had to lean close to take it, and the cool morning breeze carried his clean, exotic scent to her. That smell of lemon and ginger, of fine wool and starched linen. She glimpsed the curls of black hair that lay along his bronzed neck, the antique stickpin in his cravat. A helmeted Athena in profile.

'So, you are an expert on Bath now, are you?' she said.

'Oh, yes. I have been here nearly a fortnight now, and have seen many sites. The Abbey and the Hungerford Castle…'

'Those do not sound terribly exciting, especially for someone accustomed to all the glories of Italy.'

'Perhaps you are right. Most of the ancient sites here are hidden beneath the streets and buildings, or so I hear. But I have not yet seen everything Bath has to offer.'

'Oh? What have you missed?'

Marco's steps slowed, forcing her to slow with him, and he gestured to a wide pathway leading up to the top of the gardens. There resided a large stone pavilion, ringed around with pillars.

'I have heard that there are grand evening parties to be seen there,' he said. 'Music, fireworks—it sounds most, how do you say, convivial.'

'Ah, yes. I do remember how you liked the music and fireworks in Santa Lucia,' Thalia said. She gazed up at those false classical columns, remembering the real ones.

'As did you, *signorina*. You were the toast of Santa Lucia, just as you are here.' He gave her arm a gentle tug and they went on their way, their footsteps crackling on the gravel walkway. 'Bath is not Sicily, but we must take our merriment where we can find it.'

With Lady Riverton? Thalia thought. But she did not say it aloud; she was slowly learning caution. 'Bath has no shortage of diversions of its own. I seriously doubt I am considered any sort of "toast", but people seem glad to encounter new faces. We've had invitations to card parties, dances, theatre outings...'

Marco laughed. 'I am surprised, then, that you say you have not been to Bath in a long time.'

Thalia shook her head. 'When we were last here it was with my mother, when I was just a young girl. She had a very difficult birth with my youngest sister, and our father hoped the waters would restore her. Sadly, they did not. But I am certain of a more positive outcome now with my sister.'

'Thalia, I am so sorry,' Marco said quietly. His other hand reached up to cover hers, pressing her touch closer to his arm. Linking them closer together. 'I never meant to open a sad memory.'

'You did not.' Thalia smiled at him, easing away from his too-alluring touch. She could not give in to softer feelings for him, not when she was so intent on being angry at him! 'That was a long time ago. I intend to make new, happy memories in Bath now.'

He watched her closely for a moment, with those velvety dark eyes that seemed to see so much and gave so little away. At last he nodded, and they continued their promenade past benches and alcoves, past trees and hedges that were indeed the 'most beautiful luxuriance'.

'So, you are here for your sister's health,' Marco said.

'Yes. I am sure Calliope would prefer Clio as a nurse, but she is still on her honeymoon with the Duke.' Thalia studied Marco from the corner of her eyes, watching for a reaction to Clio's name.

He just gave a little half-smile, that damnably

attractive dimple flashing in his cheek. That dimple always filled her with a longing to kiss him just there, to feel his skin beneath her lips and discover exactly how he tasted. Like lemons and ginger?

'And how fares the new Duchess?' he asked, so polite. So neutral.

'Very well. We hope she will join us in London next year.' Though perhaps they would see her before then, now that Thalia had sent her the news of Lady Riverton's reappearance in Bath. 'But what of you? What are you doing in Bath, Count? I confess this is the last place I would expect to encounter you.'

'Why is that?' He gave her another teasing grin. 'Because I am so very sophisticated? Or such a picture of perfect strength?'

'Because Bath is so very far from your home.'

'Perhaps I am here for the same reason you and your sister are—for the sake of health.'

Thalia shook her head. 'There are spas in Italy, are there not? And you *do* look like the picture of strength to me.'

'Why, Signorina Chase! Is that a compliment? Are you remarking on my bright eyes and rosy cheeks? I am flattered. But surely Bath can also cater to wounds of the spirit, to ailments that cannot be seen.'

Thalia drew in a deep breath. Suddenly, she had heard enough. Enough of this dancing around each other, the constant dissembling. Enough of acting, of shadows. She wanted to stamp her feet on the ground, to yank out fistfuls of Marco's beautiful black hair until he was honest with her.

Until she was sure she could be honest with him. For she was sure of nothing any longer.

Just up ahead, she saw the entrance to the Labyrinth. Other walkers were appearing on the paths, but the Labyrinth's high hedge walls would surely shield any tantrum she might feel inclined to have. She tightened her clasp on Marco's arm, pulling him with her as she hurried toward the entrance.

Marco looked quite wary, but he paid their entrance fee readily enough, following her into the shadows. She let go of his arm and hurried ahead, turning right and left with no thought, no sense of where she might be going.

She could hear other voices in the Labyrinth, but they were muted and echoing, the words distorted as if they came from another world. She and Marco seemed all alone together, hemmed in close by leafy green walls.

She turned left again, only to be abruptly halted by a dead end. She spun around, the hedge at her back.

'What game do you play, Marco?' she demanded.

'Game? It is you, Thalia, who insisted we come in here and become hopelessly lost…'

Thalia suddenly lunged toward him, grabbing him by his impeccably tailored lapels and shaking him. She felt faintly ridiculous, for he was a good deal taller and a great deal more muscular than her. He could easily just flick her away.

But he just stared down at her with those impenetrable black eyes.

'You were our ally in Santa Lucia,' she said fiercely, shaking him again. He hardly moved at all, as solid as those stone statues in the garden. 'But now you are here alone, without a word to Clio and me. Here with Lady Riverton! The woman who stole that silver in the first place, who double-crossed her own partner in crime to spirit it away. Do you hope to charm the treasure out of her, to keep it all to yourself? Or…'

Thalia's hands dropped away and she stepped back, shivering. 'Or were you her accomplice all along?' she whispered.

At last there was a flash of real emotion across his face, a spasm of pain quickly erased. 'How little you think of me, *signorina*.'

'I hardly know what to think. To see you so cosy with Lady Riverton, after everything that happened in Santa Lucia…' Thalia swallowed, seemingly unable to finish her sentences.

'You surely know better than anyone that appearances can deceive. Are you not a most gifted actress yourself? The star of amateur theatricals. If you were not a baronet's daughter you would rival the career of Signora Siddons.'

'But I am a baronet's daughter, and not just any baronet—Sir Walter Chase. I've been schooled from the cradle on the importance of antiquities, of history and art. Lady Riverton is nothing but a petty thief of that history, the history of *your* land. I don't see how you can be her friend, let alone her…'

Lover. The word, even though unspoken, hung between them like a black cloud. Marco's jaw tightened, his back stiffened, and she glimpsed that heritage of his—Roman centurions, Renaissance grandees, men of iron wills and fierce warrior instincts.

'As I said—appearances can be deceiving,' he said, his Florentine accent thicker than usual. 'It is better that you know nothing more, Thalia. Pay no more attention to me, to Lady Riverton. Just enjoy your sojourn in Bath, your dances and partners.'

Fury wiped away that chill in a flash of flame. With a growl, Thalia flew at him again, pounding her fists on his chest. 'Don't you dare condescend to me, Marco! I will not be patted on the head and sent off to buy a bonnet, like a child. Don't you *dare*…'

Suddenly, his lips swooped down on hers, a hard, desperate, open-mouthed kiss that erased her fury as quickly as it had appeared. Replaced it with a fire of an entirely different sort.

Thalia closed her eyes, holding on to him tightly as the ground under her feet shifted, sending her tumbling down into that abyss where there was only Marco. Only the way he made her feel, all hot and dizzy and blurry. She touched the tip of her tongue to his, revelling in his deep groan that said he felt the same.

Through the warm, liquid haze of emotion, she felt his hand slide from her shoulder along her ribs, just skimming the sensitive curve of her breast. Startled by the force of her pleasure, by that burning touch, she arched into his body. The two of them fit together as if they had always been so, clinging to each other against the storm.

In Santa Lucia, she had often imagined what his touch, his caress, would feel like. As they had talked, she would watch his lips, the way their sensual lines curved up at the corners. That enticing dimple. She had wondered how he would taste and smell, how those lips would move over hers.

Now she knew, and it was far beyond any imagining. All the rest of the world, all the past, Clio, Lady Riverton—it all utterly vanished. She twined her fingers in his black hair, tugging him even closer, so close she could feel the very essence of him.

A burst of laughter from the other side of the hedge cut through that rosy cloud of sexual desire, sharp as a dagger. Shocked, cold, Thalia tore her lips from his, tilting back her head as she struggled to breathe. To think.

But in opening her eyes she saw Marco, and that just made everything worse. He stared down at her, his dark eyes wide with shock, as if he had never seen her before and had no idea how he came to be holding her. He had lost his hat, and his hair was tousled from her touch. His cravat was askew. And Thalia herself was just as much a rumpled, confused mess.

She stumbled away from him, his touch slowly sliding from her body, lingering heatedly on her waist.

'Thalia,' he said, his breath ragged and rough. His

accent so heavy she could hardly understand her own name. 'I do not…'

Another burst of conversation broke out from the other side of that hedge wall, moving ever closer. 'Shh!' she whispered frantically. She smoothed her pelisse, brushed back the curls that had escaped from beneath the brim of her bonnet. 'Not now, we can't talk now.'

'Thalia, *scusa*,' he muttered. He knelt to gather his hat and her reticule, both of which had tumbled to the ground. His hair fell over his brow, hiding his eyes, his expression, from her.

All she knew was his rueful tone, his words.

He was sorry. Of course. She was not the right Chase Muse, the one he wanted to be kissing.

Thalia didn't want to hear it, not yet. The kiss, the unexpected force of her emotions, left her feeling so fragile. As if she were made of glass, so delicate and transparent. So easily shattered.

'It doesn't matter,' she said hastily, snatching her reticule from him. Their hands brushed, and she pulled away. 'A grey day in Bath, after thinking about beautiful, sunny Italy, a quiet maze—a kiss was practically required. Just like in a novel. We need not speak of it again. I know that you want…'

'No, Thalia, I must say this…'

But whatever it was had to remain unsaid, for the chattering group came around the corner of the hedge and they were no longer alone. One of them was Lord Grimsby, her father's friend.

'Ah, Miss Chase! And Count di Fabrizzi,' he

declared heartily. 'I see you are quite as lost in this Labyrinth as we are.'

'I fear so, Lord Grimsby,' Thalia answered, laughing with a fine show of gaiety. 'My guidebook says to go right and left and left, yet it does not say what to do when one completely loses all sense of direction.'

'Well, then, let us be lost together,' Lord Grimsby said, leading her out of the clearing. The ladies of the party soon surrounded Marco, and they had no further chance for conversation. For apologies and explanations that would surely only make things worse. More confusing. Like this dead-end labyrinth.

But Thalia knew this was only a temporary reprieve. Sooner or later, she would have to confront Marco about what he was really doing in Bath. And confront herself about her feelings for him.

Then she would know the truth, whether she wanted it or not.

Marco stared at the entrance to Sydney Gardens, watching Thalia as she walked away with Lord Grimsby and his friends. They had offered to see her home so they could call on Lady Westwood, and Marco could devise no plausible excuse to keep her with him. To make her look him in the eyes and *listen* to him.

To kiss her again.

'Cazzarola,' he cursed. He tore off his hat, running his hand through his hair, as if pulling out the strands could pull out his burning desire for Thalia Chase.

Drive away the vision he had conjured of her in his bed, her pale skin naked against the sheets, her hair spread around her as she held out her arms to him.

He had felt that need, that pull between them, from the moment they had met in Santa Lucia. She was beautiful, true, an English rose with an irresistible vivacious charm. Yet he had known many beautiful women in his life. It was something far beyond that with Thalia, something that captured and held him. A hint of sadness in her eyes, a buried melancholy under all those smiles.

That wondrous imagination, and a fierce will he had never encountered before.

He longed to unearth those secrets of hers, to find out everything about her. Unfortunately—or fortunately, he had not yet decided—their lives seemed to be always drawing them in different directions. He had his work, the obligations to his family and country that had been his ever since he was born. It was not always a duty he welcomed, yet it was one he would never forsake.

It was also a burden he could never put on a lady like Thalia. No matter how her pretty pink lips tempted him to kiss her, to lose himself in her for ever.

She had turned the corner out of his sight, though he could swear he still smelled her perfume. The faint, lingering scent of springtime white lilacs that so suited her sunny beauty. He could still taste her on his lips.

He swung away from the crowded street, back

into the quiet of the park. He had much work to do today; he could not be distracted by Thalia, by anything. His time in Bath grew short; the letter from Domenico de Lucca proved that.

As he strode away, his glance fell on the bench where Thalia had awaited his arrival. Her umbrella lay there, forgotten.

Marco scooped it up, the bundle of black silk. The ivory handle, inlaid with a D for de Vere, was cold. But he gave in to a momentary romantic folly, raising it to his nose to see if it smelled of lilacs. Of the imprint of Thalia's touch.

It did not, of course, not really, and he laughed at himself as he tossed the umbrella in the air and caught it again, swinging it like a sword. He had long scorned the idea of his countrymen as hot-blooded romantics, and here he was behaving just so.

Thalia would surely laugh at him if she could see it. Her sister Clio, his old partner in mischief, certainly would mock him greatly!

Remembering Clio also reminded him of the promise he made her, the vow not to lead her sister into danger. Thalia was fully capable of throwing herself headlong into danger all on her own. And dragging him right behind her!

A promise was a promise. But he had never said he would refrain from returning lost umbrellas.

Chapter Nine

It is better that you know nothing more, Thalia. Pay no more attention to me…

Marco's words echoed in Thalia's mind, over and over as she paced the length of her bedchamber. Telling her she should not try to decipher what was happening was rather like telling the sun not to shine in the morning. It was impossible.

She wrapped the folds of her dressing gown closer around her, stopping at the window to peer down at the street below. It grew dark outside, evening crowding close. Only a few carriages passed by, hurrying homewards to prepare for parties and meetings.

Which was exactly what she should be doing. They were meant to be at the Grimsbys' card party soon, and she had not even chosen a gown. But how could she possibly concentrate on muslins and slippers, when all she thought about, all she saw, was Marco?

Thalia rubbed lightly at her lower lip, remembering the feel of his mouth on hers, the taste of him, so sweet and intoxicating. She had been kissed before, and she thought she knew what it meant. She had even imagined what it would be like with Marco. The reality was *nothing* like her imaginings. It was like nothing she had ever known before at all. It was—was an explosion of fireworks, dazzling, burning bright. Blinding.

And she wanted more. So very much more.

She bit her lip, tucking her hands into her sleeves. So, she knew Marco's kiss now, knew his touch, all too well. But she knew almost nothing else.

It was startling to realise just what an enigma he was to her. She knew he came from Florence, from an old aristocratic family there, but only because of his title. Because of that bearing of his that brought to mind a Renaissance warlord. Yet she knew nothing else, nothing of his parents, his education. Had he ever been married? Was he—horrors!—married now? How had he come to know Clio?

Thalia groaned aloud, leaning her forehead against the window. The cool touch of the glass did nothing to calm the fevered tangle of her thoughts.

No, she did not know Marco well at all. Yet somehow, deep down inside, she felt she knew him so well. She looked into his eyes and thought she saw recognition there.

Perhaps she was wrong. Perhaps their Sicilian playacting had gone to her head, made her imagine a connection that was not there.

But perhaps, just perhaps, she was right.

Thalia longed for someone to confide in, someone who could help her. But Calliope didn't need the worry, and Thalia could tell her sister held some secrets of her own. Secrets that made her not like or trust Marco. Clio was far away, and her other sister too young. Thalia had seldom felt quite so alone, so set adrift from all certainty.

She missed her mother. Celeste Chase would have known how she felt, what she should do. Calliope and Clio were their father's daughters, through and through; Thalia had been their mother's. They shared a certain wild impulsiveness, a romanticism her classical sisters lacked. Yes, her mother would have known what to tell her.

But Celeste was long gone, and Thalia just had to act on her own.

'Do I make the leap?' she muttered. Did she follow her impulse, or did she listen to Marco and forget about him?

A knock sounded at the door, and Mary, her maid, entered with two freshly pressed gowns over her arm, a pink tulle and silk and a pale green muslin. 'I'm sorry, Miss Thalia, did you say something?'

Thalia gave her a smile. 'Just talking to myself, I'm afraid, Mary. I cannot quite decide what to wear this evening.'

The Grimsbys' gathering was not quite the 'small family card party' they had promised, but neither was it a terrible crush where trains and slippers were in danger of being trod upon. Card tables were set up in their drawing room, along with various couches and chairs set close enough for comfortable chats. A supper was promised for later, but for the moment everyone seemed most content with their games of *vingt-et-un* and piquet, with a bit of diverting gossip.

Calliope and Cameron played *vingt-et-un*, but Thalia had never been much for cards. To be proficient required a patience, a stealth, she did not possess. So she played at the pianoforte instead, entertaining the company with some old Italian airs.

The songs would have to suffice, as there was no Italian *person* amid the gathering. Thalia remembered Lady Grimsby had mentioned including Marco in the invitation, but he had not appeared. And neither had Lady Riverton.

Thalia's fingertips danced lightly over the keys, weaving a tune of sunny, pastoral meadows and amorous shepherds, yet her thoughts were more like a thundercloud. Perhaps Marco and his be-turbaned escort had found a more amiable venue this evening. Some place darker, more solitary.

She crashed on a discordant note.

'Shall I turn the pages for you, Miss Chase?' asked Lady Anne, one of the Grimsbys' daughters.

'Thank you,' Thalia answered gratefully, sliding over a bit so the girl could sit beside her on the bench. Being alone with her thoughts and Italian music was not necessarily a good thing.

With the page turned, Thalia went on with the song, much more smoothly this time. She caught Calliope giving her a strangely thoughtful glance, and Thalia smiled at her.

'Have you been in Bath long, Lady Anne?' she asked.

The girl sighed. 'Oh, for ever and ever, it feels like! It was quite pleasant when we first arrived, but now it is dull.'

Thalia laughed. 'Dull? We have received a whole avalanche of invitations since we arrived here. There must be *some* sort of amusement out there.'

'Oh, yes! But I am not yet out, so cannot dance at the assemblies. I'm only allowed to watch until next year.'

Thalia smiled at her pout, at the disconsolate droop of her pretty red curls. How well Thalia remembered that feeling! That sense that time was moving so slowly, that all fun and merriment was just passing by.

But then she found that being a grown-up lady just meant *more* restrictions. More frustration.

'Observation can have its charms, as well,' Thalia said. 'There must be some interesting people in Bath. Some particularly handsome young man, perhaps?'

Lady Anne giggled as she turned the page. 'A few, yes. But surely they will all soon be in love with *you*, Miss Chase. My mother says you have turned down so many proposals, more than any other young lady she knows, and that if your father had any sense he would make you choose…' Suddenly, her eyes went wide. 'Oh, I am sorry! My mother also says I prattle on far too much.'

Thalia laughed. 'Not at all. It is true I have had one or two offers of marriage, but I have not yet met the right man for me. I shan't marry until he comes along, and neither should you.' She gave Lady Anne a conspiratorial nudge with her elbow. 'Do you have any favourites among the handsome men in Bath?'

Lady Anne peeked to make sure her mother wasn't watching. 'The Count di Fabrizzi! He is just like a hero in a novel. So dark and dashing! He *never* talks about shooting or cricket, like all the English gentlemen do. All my friends are quite in raptures over him, Miss Chase.'

Thalia smiled wryly. Of course all the ladies sighed over Marco, just as she did. 'So, the Count is your fancy, Lady Anne?'

The girl blushed and giggled. 'Of course! But he never looks at me, or any of my friends. He dances attendance on Viscountess Riverton, who is so very *old*. I cannot account for it.'

Nor could Thalia. Not yet, anyway. 'Do you hear much talk of the Count around Bath?'

'Ever so much. Yet no one seems to really know anything about him. Isn't that strange?'

'And the mystery only makes him more intriguing, yes?'

More giggles. *Lud*, thought Thalia, had she ever been that silly as a girl? If so, no wonder Cal and Clio had not wanted her always trailing around behind them back then. At least her own fifteen-year-old sister Cory was too preoccupied with art to be so giddy.

'But you can see for yourself, Miss Chase,' Lady Anne whispered as the drawing-room door opened. 'For there he is at last. Mama will be so happy that he came after all.'

'Rather late, I must say,' Thalia murmured. 'Is it an Italian custom, do you think?'

'Oh, Miss Chase! How can you be so calm? I feel so very flustered just looking at him,' Anne whispered. 'I should faint dead away if he spoke to me.'

Thalia feared she, too, might 'faint dead away' as she stared over the top of the sheet music at Marco. Lady Grimsby rose from her table, hurrying forwards in a cloud of amber-coloured silk to greet her new guest. Marco bowed over her hand, smiling that gorgeous smile of his.

Lady Anne quite forgot to turn the page, so Thalia just moved smoothly into a Mozart divertimento she knew by rote. Her hands slid over the keys automatically, leaving her gaze free to follow Marco around the room. Just like every other lady there.

Her thoughts had been so full of him all day that it seemed they had never parted at all. As he laughed with their hostess, so handsome, so sunny and charming, she could almost feel foolish for imagining such dark things about him. Suspecting him of unknown plots, ulterior motives.

But then his gaze met hers across the room, and

an intense solemnity passed over his face, like a storm cloud. It was gone just as quickly, and she wondered if she had imagined it. He gave her a small nod, an almost imperceptible quirk of his brow. Then he turned away.

Thalia's breath escaped in a great 'whoosh', her chest tight from holding it in. She stared down blindly at the keys, at her hands.

After a moment, when she was sure she could smile blandly, pleasantly, again, she glanced up. Marco was seated between Lady Grimsby and Mrs Smythe-Moreland on a sofa by the windows. And there was no sign of Lady Riverton. Was he, could he be, alone tonight?

She saw Calliope give her a long look over the cards in her hand, and Thalia just went on smiling and smiling, hoping she looked like a normal person and not an escapee from Bedlam. But inside her mind raced. Would she be cautious, forget Marco as he told her to? Or would she be bold?

She came to the end of the Mozart, resting her wrists at the edge of the keyboard to the sound of applause.

'That was lovely, Miss Chase,' Lord Grimsby said. 'Will you grace us with another?'

'I fear I grow weary, Lord Grimsby,' she answered. 'But I should so love to hear your daughter play. I hear she is quite accomplished.'

Thalia smoothly relinquished her seat to the blushing Lady Anne, surreptitiously tearing off a corner of the sheet music as she went. She used one of the little pencils from a card table to scrawl a message, and strolled past the sofa where Marco was enjoying his coze with the two ladies.

As she walked by, just for an instant her pink tulle skirts hid Marco from view. She dropped the tiny paper square onto his hand, and kept moving.

At the tea table, she peeked back over her shoulder to find him watching her again. She gave him a quick nod.

Yes. She would follow her own nature, and be bold. Bold!

No. She was not bold, not really. She was more like a scared little mouse.

Or at least she felt like one, as she stood alone in the dark little ante-chamber off the Grimsbys' foyer. The only light shone from an arched window overhead, falling in shifting patterns over a clutter of dainty chairs and tables. She could hear nothing beyond the closed door, no reassuring party patter.

This had seemed as good a place as any, this little room she had glimpsed as they had come in. But now, all alone in the stuffy darkness, she was not so sure.

Thalia pressed her back against the wall, her heart pounding so loudly she was sure everyone could hear it. Had all those classical heroines, Antigone, Persephone, Eurydice, felt afraid when they went down to the underworld?

But somehow it was not fear she felt in that heart-pounding, cold-tingling moment. It was sheer excitement. Sheer—aliveness. Such as she had not felt in many months, not since Santa Lucia.

At last, she heard something besides her own erratic heartbeat. A footstep, just outside the door. The door handle turned, opening slightly to let in a bar of candlelight. It fell across the toe of Thalia's slipper, and she held her breath.

'Are you there?' Marco whispered.

Thalia reached out and grabbed his hand, pulling him into the room and slamming the door shut again with her foot. They were all alone in that heated darkness.

She spun around, pushing him back against the wall, their bodies pressed together. In the absence of light, all her other senses were heightened. The sound of his breath, the feel of his lean body against hers, so lithe and powerful. So alive and vital against hers. The way he smelled, of that gingery cologne overlaid with the saltiness of his skin.

She couldn't help herself. Her palms flattened on his shoulders, sliding up over his starched cravat, the arc of his throat. She traced the sharp line of his jaw, the roughness of whiskers over his smooth, warm skin. Her fingers tangled in his hair, the silken tendrils curling around her bare hands. She went up on tiptoe, pressing even closer against him.

His breath hissed, and she felt tension in every line of his body. Yet he did not move away. He watched her intently, the two of them wrapped around in that shadowed spell.

'What are you doing, Thalia?' he said tightly.

She hardly knew. She hadn't planned so far ahead when she lured him here with her note. But now she wanted nothing more than to stay just as they were. 'I could ask you the same thing,' she whispered. 'What are *you* doing, Marco, here in Bath? What game are you playing, really?'

'*Cara*, I warned you once—forget about me,' he said, his accent heavy as fine satin. Suddenly, quick as a lightning strike, he seized her by the waist, lifting her off her feet as he twirled her around. Before she could even draw breath, their positions were reversed, and he held her captive.

She tightened her grasp on his hair, holding on as the whole world tilted around her.

'But you would not listen,' he murmured in her ear, his warm breath stirring her hair. She shivered, her thoughts turning hazy and unreal. 'I will not warn you twice.'

And he kissed her, but not just any kiss. His mouth crashed down on hers, hungry and hot. Thalia's lips parted, his tongue darting out to seek hers, to taste her deeply.

His body arched into hers, pushing her back against the wall until there was nothing between them, not even a particle of light. His hand roughly skimmed down her ribs to her hip, grasping at the tulle foam of her skirts as he drew them up and up.

Thalia cried out into his mouth as she felt his callused palm on her bare thigh, just above the edge of her stocking. His strong, lean fingers curled around her bare skin, lifting her higher against him.

If he sought to frighten her, to make her run away, she thought, he failed miserably. The way his touch, his rough kiss, made her feel just made her more determined to stay.

She wrapped her legs around his waist, revelling in the feel of his iron erection against her, the proof that he wanted her, too. *This*, then, was what she had read about in all those novels! This was what she saw on Greek vases and Pompeian murals. It was sex—it was life. And she wanted more and more of it.

Marco's mouth tore away from hers, but her cry of protest turned to a moan as she felt his wet lips trail over her cheek, along her neck. He licked at the sensitive spot just where her shoulder curved, and her head fell back against the wall. Behind her closed eyes she saw the explosion of stars, green and red and silver.

One of her slippers fell off, clattering to the floor, and she slid her stocking foot along the tight, hard curve of his backside. It clenched under her touch, but she couldn't pull away. She might never get a chance to satisfy this curiosity again.

'*Maledetto*,' Marco muttered against her bare shoulder. She felt the light, delicate touch of his lips on the swell of her breast, and she gasped. Was this *always* how it was, this spiralling ache of burning, raw need? No wonder Calliope and Cameron couldn't keep their hands off each other, despite the baby screaming…

At the thought of babies, her eyes flew open. That was where this led, all this delicious lust, sweat, naked skin, panting need. She felt as if she were dangling off a precipice by her fingernails, rocks clattering around her as she nearly fell into oblivion.

Yet even then she could not quite let go of him. Could not quite untangle her legs from around his waist.

But Marco seemed to sense her realisation—or perhaps he had one of his own. He leaned his forehead on the wall just beside her, their ragged breath mingling in the humid silence. Slowly, ever so slowly, his hand slid away from her thigh. He unwrapped her from around him and lowered her to the floor.

As he stepped back, Thalia pressed her hands hard back against the wall, holding herself upright. As she concentrated on not collapsing, she heard the rustle of his clothing straightening, the silken sound of his fingers raking through his hair.

'Remember, Thalia,' he said, that accent now so thick she could hardly understand. Or maybe it was the blood rushing in her ears. 'I will not warn you again.'

Then he was gone, slipping out of the door as swiftly as he had appeared. For an instant, he was silhouetted against the light from the foyer. And Thalia was alone again.

She finally allowed herself to slide down in a boneless, shivering puddle on the floor.

'Ouch,' she muttered as something jabbed at her hip. She reached under her skirt and came up with the lost slipper. Cinderella in reverse.

'Bloody hell,' she whispered. She stuffed her foot into the shoe, staring out into the darkness. She had the distinct sense that the rules of the game had just changed irrevocably. Yet she still had no idea what they were.

Marco paused in the foyer, bracing his palms on a small carved table. Every fibre of his being cried out for him to smash the ridiculous furniture to bits, to throw it across the room and howl like a barbarian. Maybe then his boiling lust, the heated rage in his blood would cease. Then he could think straight again.

But he doubted it. Nothing could cool that fever except going back into that dark room and grabbing Thalia into his arms again.

'Cazzarola,' he growled, pounding his fist on the table. He could still feel her body wrapped around his, taste the sweetness of her lips, her skin. Hear her breathy cries in his ear.

Never, not even when he was a callow boy, had he been so carried away by desire for a woman. And the fact that she wanted him, too, only stoked the bonfire higher. Thank the gods for that one tiny, piercing ray of sanity that had stopped him from having her right there against the wall.

Marco shook his head hard, trying to clear it of that sensual haze. Thalia Chase was a lady, his friend's sister, not some common doxy! He had to be strong, stay away from her, and concentrate on what he had to do. But truly, stealing back that silver would be simple and easy, compared to forgetting about that one soft spot where Thalia's neck met her white shoulder.

'Blast it all,' he muttered. He stood up straight, adjusting his cravat and waistcoat, smoothing back his rumpled hair. He thought he could still smell the faint, intoxicating fragrance of white lilacs on his coat, but that was surely only his heated imagination. His memory of the way her soft golden hair smelled.

From along the corridor, he heard the click of the drawing-room door opening, the swish of a muslin skirt. Quickly, he pasted a polite smile on his lips, preparing to face whoever he encountered and make a hasty exit.

But it was Calliope Chase—no, Lady Westwood now—who emerged. She was adjusting a shawl over her shoulders, a concerned frown on her face as she glanced around. Every time Marco saw her, he remembered that dungeon in Yorkshire, the eerie space cluttered with ancient treasures hidden away by the Duke of Averton. And Calliope coming upon him and Clio in the act of stealing the Alabaster Goddess.

That escapade had not gone so well, and as she spotted him there in the foyer he feared this would not go well, either.

'Lady Westwood, lovely as ever,' he said, giving her a bow.

Her frown deepened. 'I am looking for my sister,' she said shortly. 'Have you seen her?'

'I fear not. The last time I saw the lovely Miss

Chase, she was playing at the pianoforte. A most exquisite performance.'

Calliope stepped closer to him, her sherry-brown eyes smouldering in her ivory face. 'I do not know what game you play, Count di Fabrizzi,' she said. 'But I will not let you involve Thalia. She is young and romantic, and far too impulsive. I won't see her hurt, not for any of your schemes.'

'Lady Westwood, I think perhaps you underestimate your sister,' Marco answered. 'Impulsive she might be, but she is no fool.'

'I think I know my sister better than you! I vowed I would take care of her while we are here, and I won't see any repeats of what happened in Yorkshire. The Lily Thief is finished.'

'I am not sure what you speak of, Lady Westwood. But I have no ill intentions toward Miss Thalia—or any of the Chases.'

Calliope studied him carefully for a moment, those eyes practically burning holes in his flesh. Finally, she turned away to stalk back toward the drawing room. 'I will be watching you, Count,' she called over her shoulder. 'And so will my husband.'

Magnifico, he thought wryly. That should make his work ever so much easier in Bath. It was just one more incentive to stay away from Thalia Chase.

And yet, yet—that lilac scent was so haunting.

Chapter Ten

Thalia sorted through the pages of her play *The Dark Castle of Count Orlando*, studying the blotted, crossed-out, rewritten words of that half-formed story. She had conceived of it in Sicily, and the tale made perfect sense there, amid the ruins and windswept plains, the dark schemes that seemed part of everyday life. But the story of the Robin Hood-esque prince and his unwilling young bride in that crumbling castle all seemed silly here in England, its Gothic twists and turns beyond her writing skills.

After last night, though, secret passions and heady, irresistible cravings for the forbidden seemed all too close. All too real.

Thalia reached for her pen and ink, staring down at the half-finished scene before her. It was the wedding night of the robber-prince Orlando and his reluctant bride, the hot-tempered Isabella. She had been sold into marriage by her wicked stepfather to this mysterious man. A man she had heard many terrible stories about, but she could not deny the fascination he held for her. That maddening, drugging desire that drew her inexorably to him.

Oh, yes, indeed. Thalia knew what poor Isabella was feeling.

She envisioned the stage setting, a chamber in one of the ancient castle's towers. A vast, red-curtained bed looming in the background. The locked chest holding unimaginable horrors. The full, amber-coloured moon beyond the barred windows. Isabella's white nightrail stood out as a bright beacon in the shadows. And the prince held out his gloved hand to her, beckoning, enticing…

But as Thalia pictured it, the scene shifted. It transformed from a tower chamber to a little dark ante-room, warm and close in the night. Echoing with her own gasps and moans of desire.

Thalia pounded her hand down on the desk, scattering droplets of ink over the manuscript. 'Enough!' she muttered. She had stayed up all night going over and over that kiss in her mind. Remembering the way his hand felt on her bare skin, his taut backside against her foot.

Going over and over it all solved nothing. It didn't make the events, or her feelings, disappear. It just made her want to do it all again.

Isabella: Oh, the wickedness of it all! Why must you torment me so? Have you no mercy?

Prince Orlando: You are my wife now. There can be no torment in the joys of the marriage bed…

The sudden flow of words was just as abruptly ended by a knock at the door. Thalia glanced up, startled. Calliope and Cameron had gone off to the Pump Room, leaving her alone in the little library. The house should be quiet enough, at least until Psyche rose from her morning nap.

'Come in,' Thalia called, sliding the play under more respectable-looking letters.

It was the butler, bearing a single card on his silver tray. 'There is a caller, Miss Chase.'

'A caller? At this hour?'

The butler gave a disapproving sniff. 'That is what I said to him, but the gentleman was most insistent.'

Thalia rose, hurrying around the desk to take the card. *Count di Fabrizzi*, it said, bold black letters on fine cream-coloured vellum. Just as she feared. Or hoped.

Yet she stared down at it, frowning, as if the words might somehow change. Become something, someone, else. 'You told him Lord and Lady Westwood are not at home?'

'Of course, Miss Chase. He says it is you he wants to see. I put him in the drawing room, but I could send him away.'

Thalia shook her head. She had to get this encounter over with sooner or later. It might as well be 'sooner'.

Surely, here in her own house, in the light of day, she could be in no danger of losing her senses? It had just been the night, the smell of his cologne, her own frustrations at being shut out—again. That was all past now.

Right?

'Right,' she said aloud, slapping the card down on the desk. 'I will see the Count. If you will be so good as to send in some tea?'

'Of course, Miss Chase,' he said, sounding rather disapproving.

Disapproval had never had much impact on Thalia, not from butlers *or* older sisters. She hurried out of the library and down the quiet corridor before she could stop to think.

The drawing-room door was half-open, and she paused to peek inside. Marco stood by the window, gazing down at the street as the grey morning light outlined his profile. His glossy black hair was brushed back behind his ears, and he was clean shaven, leaving just the sharp, elegant lines of his face. He looked like an ancient coin, solemn and timeless. A Roman emperor. Count Orlando in his black tower.

Had this man really held her in his arms in the darkness, gasped her name as he caressed her shoulder, her breast? As he kissed her so passionately?

Thalia stepped slowly into the drawing room, leaving the door open behind her. At the soft rustle of her skirts, Marco looked up, giving her a half-smile.

'You have a good view from here,' he said.

She moved to his side, peering out at the Crescent Fields beyond. The street was crowded with walkers at that time of day, people scurrying on their way to the baths or the shops. On the walkway just below was a small child with his hoop, helped along surprisingly not by his nurse but by his well-dressed father.

'I do like it here,' she said. 'We see everyone in Bath going by. It is better than the Pump Room, and not as noisy!'

She remembered how she had seen Marco walking past once or twice, with Lady Riverton. But there was no sign of her today, just as there had not been last night.

'My father would never have time to do such things with me,' Marco said lightly, gesturing to the child with the hoop. 'As a child, I was scarcely allowed out of our palazzo! My mother was sure gypsies were just waiting to snatch me away.'

Fascinated by this fleeting glimpse behind Marco's façade, Thalia smiled up at him. 'Were there so many gypsies in Florence?'

His own smile widened. 'A few, here and there. I was most interested in them, but they had far better things to think of than stealing one spoiled little boy. At least I usually found it so, when I sneaked out.'

Thalia laughed. 'Somehow I am not surprised to hear you were a disobedient child, Marco! You are fortunate you never came to any harm.'

'As you did not?'

'Me?'

'Come, Thalia *bella*. I would wager you were something of a little mischief-maker yourself as a child.'

She thought of swimming in the pond at Chase Lodge when told not to, of stealing a nip of brandy or a glimpse of one of her father's hidden erotic etchings from Pompeii. 'Perhaps I made a bit of mischief, once or twice.'

'Ah, yes. Some things never change.'

Thalia swallowed hard, remembering their 'mischief' of last night. 'Marco, about the party last night—'

But she was interrupted by the servants bringing in the tea. Once they had finished laying out the silver and china and departed, leaving her alone again with Marco, she found she did not know what to say.

'Would you care for a cup of tea?' she asked weakly, leading him to the coral satin couch.

'Grazie,' he said, sitting down beside her. He was unseemly close, and she could feel the heat of him, smell his scent, reaching out to her. Reminding her.

And always he watched her with those inscrutable dark eyes, as if he knew her every thought. Her every need.

She busied herself pouring the tea. 'Tell me about your father,' she said. 'Is he still living?'

'Alas, no. I have sadly lost both my parents, to a fever in Florence many years ago.'

'And you have no siblings?' she asked. His fingers brushed hers as she passed him the cup, their slightly rough caress against the smooth china yet another reminder. The way they slid over the swell of her breast last night…

Thalia drew quickly away, causing a single amber drop to fall on his hand. She dabbed at it with a napkin.

'I was the only one of their children to live past infancy,' he said smoothly, as if ignoring her ridiculous agitation. He slid the napkin out of her tight grasp. 'Perhaps that was why my mother worried so.'

Or perhaps the poor woman realised the havoc that would ensue once Marco was released on the unsuspecting female population.

'That is sad,' she murmured, taking a careful sip of her own tea. 'My sisters can sometimes be infuriating, but I don't know what I would do without them.'

'I would have liked a sibling to have adventures with.'

Thalia laughed ruefully. 'Oh, we did have adventures! My mother often had fits, as yours did. But Calliope kept us in check, she was always the sensible one.'

'And your father—he must have been busy, like mine.'

'Yes. As a scholar, he was often preoccupied with his studies. He always read to us in the evenings, though, and made certain we were well versed in the works of the ancient world.' She offered the plate of cakes and bread and butter. 'Was your father also a scholar? There must be so much scope for such work in Florence.'

'My father was a writer, but his focus was on the Renaissance, the ideals of the Republic,' Marco answered, taking a little sandwich. He munched on it thoughtfully, as if considering how much to say, before he continued, 'When Napoleon first took over Tuscany, my father had hopes of him, of the new rule. He hoped it would sweep away the old feudalism, bring in a new day of law and order, of expanded education and greater justice. He and his friends wrote pamphlets of such things, held endless meetings.'

'And did he see his hopes realised?' Thalia asked quietly.

Marco shook his head. 'Not surprisingly, Napoleon let down their liberal ideals, just as everyone else had. My father grew to bitterly resent the lack of any real power for old families like the Fabrizzis; the lack of any real change for anyone at all. He and his friends were beginning to call for a constitutional government, but he died before any real work was accomplished. Now, with the Austrians entrenched, such a thing seems further away than ever.'

Thalia was fascinated by this peek into his past, into a life she could scarcely imagine. A life of politics and high ideals, of real, important work. 'And do you write, too, Marco? Do you follow in your father's footsteps?'

But the veil dropped back into place. He gave her a careless grin, holding out his empty cup. 'Now, *cara*, what would I write about? I could compose an ode to your sky-coloured eyes, your beautiful, firm—'

'Please do not.' She snatched the cup from his hand, unaccountably disappointed. As she refilled it, she said, 'I would rather see a monograph on Florentine history.'

'Then you must write one yourself. As I recall from Santa Lucia, you are a most gifted author.'

'I just scribble little vignettes. I fear I had no such inspiration as the Duomo right outside my door.'

'No, you had something far better.'

'What is that?'

He held on to her hand as she passed back the cup, folding her fingers into his warm, strong clasp. 'A close and loving family.'

Thalia slowly drew her hand away, watching as he placed the cup on the table. 'Marco—why are you here today?'

'To bring you this.' He reached down to the floor beside the couch, bringing up the umbrella she had lost in Sydney Gardens. 'I thought you might need it, in such a rainy place as Bath.'

'That is kind of you,' she said slowly. 'But surely you could have sent a servant?'

'I could not entrust a servant with the rest of my errand.'

'The rest of your errand?'

'This.' Marco reached out to gently cup her cheek in his palm, cradling it softly like the most delicate porcelain. Slowly, as if to give her time to draw away, he lowered his lips to her.

But Thalia had absolutely no desire to turn away. Indeed, she could think of nothing at all, nothing but the feel of his mouth on hers, the slide of his caress along her cheek. She parted her lips, meeting his tongue with hers. Just like last night, she felt herself sliding down the steep slope of heady desire.

She clutched at his shoulders, her empty teacup falling to the carpet. He was her only anchor in the whirling world, even as he was the only cause of that dizziness. The sole source of that burning need.

She wound her arms around his neck, the silk of his hair falling over her hands, binding her to him. He groaned against her mouth, his own arms drawing her even closer into the hard length of his body.

'Thalia *cara*,' he muttered, pulling away to press soft little kisses on her cheek, her closed eyelids, her temple. She felt his chin rest atop her head, yet still she could not open her eyes. Could not quite face reality.

'There are so many reasons why I must stay away from you,' he said roughly. 'But you must know that is the hardest thing I have ever done.'

'Then don't stay away,' she whispered. 'Be here with me now, completely. Tell me your reasons.'

'I can't. *Scusa, cara.*' He kissed her brow once more, and she felt his hands ease away from her body, felt the space beside her grow cold in his absence.

Still, she did not open her eyes. Not until she heard the drawing-room door click shut. Then she leaped up, running to the window to watch in dazed dismay as he walked away down the street. The brim of his hat hid his expression from her.

Thalia's hands curled into fists against the glass of the window. Perhaps he thought to scare her off with his kisses, his warnings. But that just showed how little he really knew her. She was a contrary Chase Muse, and telling her she should *not* do something only made her more determined on it!

She had always wanted to be a part of her family's doings, to impress her sisters at last! Now she wanted to impress Marco, too. To make him see who she really was.

Especially after that kiss. She knew now that he had feelings for her, despite whatever was going on with Lady Riverton or Clio. She couldn't let that go, not yet. No matter what.

Chapter Eleven

After their very memorable encounter in the drawing room, days went by without Thalia seeing Marco again. She went to the assembly rooms, ate ices at Mollands with Calliope and Psyche, played cards at Mrs Smythe-Moreland's, and listened to a concert of Italian music—and Marco did not appear at any of them. Not even the concert, which she felt sure would draw him out.

She knew he wasn't there, for she always looked. She also checked the book at the Pump Room for his name, and it wasn't there. Yet neither had she heard tell of his departure, and in the small world of Bath everyone seemed to know everything about everyone else. Except for Marco. No one knew about him at all, least of all Thalia.

Lady Riverton was still in town. Thalia saw her at the assembly, a new young escort in tow. Had Marco broken with her, then? Was that why he was no place to be seen?

Or was it something she, Thalia, had done? Those kisses changed so much for her, changed—well, everything. Perhaps he did not feel the same. Perhaps her ardour had driven him away! But that did not seem likely. Marco seemed all about passion; he was surely not easily driven away.

Thoughts like these, ever twisting and changing, plagued her. Yet one good thing came of those days—she put that confusion, that frustrated desire, into her writing. New scenes for the play flew from under her pen, scenes where poor Isabella was plagued into melancholic bad health by her dark, mysterious husband. By the evils that lurked around the towers of the castle. By the force of passionate, undeniable love.

Thalia was hardly going to swoon away, like Isabella. Yet she did wonder, and watch.

'Will you go to the Pump Room with me today, Thalia?' Calliope asked over the breakfast table, on the latest of those 'wondering' mornings. 'Cam has to answer some letters of estate business, and I simply cannot face more of that water on my own! But if you are writing…'

Thalia smiled at her over the chocolate pot. 'Of course I can go with you, Cal. I am rather stuck on my play's next plot point, actually. Some fresh air will help me work it out in my mind.'

'I am not sure how much fresh air can be had at the Pump Room! It is always such a crush. But there are sights to be seen. Lady Wallington, for instance, has taken to wearing a blonde wig.'

'A blonde wig! Whatever for?'

'I think she fancies herself a Norse goddess. She should save such things for our Venetian masquerade.'

'Speaking of which, I have nearly finished writing out the invitations,' Thalia said, reaching for the pile of cards. 'If there is no one else you would like to add to the guest list, they will be ready to be delivered tomorrow.'

'We must be certain to invite Lady Billingsfield and her nephew,' Calliope said, with a teasing, sidelong glance. 'Young Mr Dashwood sent flowers again this morning, I see.'

'They already have a card—despite Arthur Dashwood being a bit of a nuisance.'

'I think he is rather sweet, and so attentive. He is definitely one of the most handsome men in Bath, especially since Count di Fabrizzi is no longer to be seen.'

'Is he not?' Thalia said, shuffling through the invitations. 'I fear I have not noticed, as I have been so busy of late.'

'Hmm,' Calliope said doubtfully. But she let the subject go. 'Thank heavens Cam let us engage rooms at the Queen's Head Inn for the masquerade ball! We could never fit everyone into this house. We need to hire the musicians, too. Tell me, Thalia dear, have you chosen your costume yet?'

'Who is *that*?'

Thalia heard the two ladies chattering behind her in the Pump Room. For several minutes it had just been an indistinct blur of fashion tittle-tattle, a little silly eavesdropping to divert her while she waited for her sister. But with those awestruck words, the tone of the conversation changed.

'I have no idea, Matilda,' the second lady said. 'But if I had ever met him before, I am certain I would remember.'

Thalia peered toward the door to see what they were talking about, going up on tiptoe to see around the crowd. It had seemed a most dull morning at the Pump Room without Marco to distract her; any new diversion would be quite welcome!

Then she saw the focus of the ladies' attention—and had to struggle to keep her own jaw from dropping in astonishment.

Indeed, it was not just their attention that focused so suddenly on the entrance, but that of every lady in the room. Even dowagers bundled up in their Bath chairs raised their quizzing glasses; young girls giggled into their gloved hands.

Thalia had never seen a man so beautiful before. He was a veritable Apollo, tall, slim, with golden, curling hair to match his almost-shimmering golden skin. Even across the room, she could see how vivid his violet-blue eyes were. He surveyed the elegant room like a god, too, as if everything and everyone in it belonged to him.

As it very well might, Thalia thought wryly, as she watched the ladies flocking toward him. He swept a dazzling smile over them all, drawing them into his sparkling net.

Yet Thalia found she was not drawn in. No matter how lovely this newcomer was, he could not compare with Marco's dark mystery. She had always preferred the tales of Hades to those of Apollo.

'Good heavens,' she heard Calliope say. 'Has the sun landed in our midst?'

Thalia turned to her sister, laughing. 'So, you see Apollo, too?'

'One could scarcely help it,' Calliope said. 'It's a good thing I am so in love with my husband, or I might be tempted to simper and swoon like everyone else.'

'When have the Chases ever simpered?'

'Never, of course. Mother would never have allowed it, and we have never had the time! But surely one can admire from afar.'

'Oh, yes. Like an Archaic statue or a red-figure krater,' said Thalia.

'Exactly so, sister.'

Thalia took a sip of the water Calliope brought her, watching the golden man bow over a myriad of gloved hands. 'Do you know who he is?'

Calliope shook her head. 'Come, let's check the book.'

They hurried to the open arrivals book, scanning the list of fresh names. 'This one!' Calliope declared, pointing. 'This must be him.'

'Signor Domenico de Lucca,' Thalia said. 'Has there even been a more suitable name?'

'Dom-en-ico de Luc-ca,' Calliope drawled, and they laughed. 'It doesn't say where he's from.'

'Rome, or Milan, surely, with a fine name like that.'

'So many Italians in Bath suddenly. Are we being invaded again?' Calliope tapped her finger to her chin. 'Maybe he's from Venice.'

'Naples, actually,' a rich, melting voice said from behind them. Thalia and Calliope exchanged an incredulous glance over the book, before turning as one to face this Domenico de Lucca.

He stood there with Lady Grimsby and her daughter Anne, smiling at them. His eyes *were* violet, Thalia saw, like the Sicilian sky just before dusk. But he had no dimples, like Marco did.

'Do you know Naples?' he asked.

'Of course they do,' Lady Grimsby said. 'These are two of the daughters of the famous scholar, Sir Walter Chase. They have traveled everywhere in Italy and Greece!'

'Infatti?' Signor de Lucca said, his tone eager and enthusiastic. 'How truly wondrous, to meet two such lovely ladies who know my home.'

Lady Grimsby laid her hand on his arm, as if to remind him of English proprieties—or perhaps just to touch him. 'Lady Westwood, Miss Chase, may I present Signor de Lucca? He has come to Bath to study some of the Roman sites. Signor de Lucca, this is the Countess of Westwood and her sister, Miss Thalia Chase.'

'Of course,' he said happily. 'The Chase Muses! Your scholarship is known even in Naples.'

'Indeed, *signor*?' Calliope answered. 'We do love

the art and history of the ancient world, but I am certain our knowledge is nothing to that of the people who live in Italy. Surrounded on all sides by such glories.'

A small, sad frown creased that golden brow. 'Alas, Lady Westwood, so many there do not appreciate their own culture. Their own heritage.'

'Are you a scholar yourself, Signor de Lucca?' Thalia asked.

'Of an amateur sort only, I fear. My duties in the army take so much time! But I study when I can. I have recently read a series of writings from the third century on the settling of Bath—do you know them?'

'My sister is reading them even now!' Calliope said. 'Is that not so, Thalia?'

'Oh, yes,' said Thalia. 'I enjoy reading of the building of this city, the founding of the cult of Sulis Minerva.'

He gave her a delighted grin, which made him appear even more the sun god than before. 'Exactly so, Signorina Chase! In fact, I hope to see the sites of which those ancients write while I am here in Bath, so I can make some sketches and notes. The sites that can still be seen, that is. Along with the Abbey and the pastries at Mollands, of course. I am told those cannot be missed.'

Lady Grimsby gave him a speculative glance. Thalia feared she had seen that sort of look many times before—the dawning of a fit of matchmaking. And indeed she was proved right, as Lady Grimsby gave him a tiny push in Thalia's direction.

'Miss Chase is a great expert on ruins,' Lady Grimsby said. 'She has just returned from a long tour of the Continent, and I am sure she knows all about the ancient sites of Bath already.'

'Oh, no, not at all...' Thalia began, but her protests were overridden.

Calliope said, 'My sister is so eager to explore all the Roman ruins, but alas my health has not allowed me to go with her. She would be an excellent guide for any newcomer to the city.'

'I would be most interested to hear any advice Signorina Chase has to give on the best sites,' Signor de Lucca said, still smiling at her. Really, he should stop it, it was most disconcerting! 'Will you take a turn about the room with me, Signorina Chase?'

Thalia glanced at Calliope, who gave her an encouraging nod. 'Do go, Thalia. I must speak with Lady Grimsby about the arrangements for the masquerade.'

'Very well. Thank you, *signor*, I would enjoy a bit of walk.' Thalia took Signor de Lucca's outstretched arm. As she turned with him toward the windows, she gave her sister a long look over her shoulder. A look that promised retribution later. Calliope just tossed her a happy little wave before chatting with Lady Grimsby, as Lady Anne stared after her wistfully.

They walked on, pausing next to one of the tall windows, gazing down at the covered baths, the glimpse of columns and red-stained stone. 'I'm afraid it's not much,' Thalia said. 'Especially to someone accustomed to Naples!'

Signor de Lucca laughed, and she was struck again by how very bright and handsome he was. Yet, strangely, she was not moved by standing so near to him. There was none of the giddy shivers she felt with Marco, the tingling *awareness*. She could admire Domenico de Lucca, definitely, but there was a distance to it, as if she admired a particularly fine painting.

She could never mistake Marco, with all his dark, simmering heat, as a painting.

'What are we looking at, Signorina Chase?' he asked. 'I fear I am not much use at interpreting ruins.'

'Are you not? And here I thought a knowledge of antiquities came to every Italian through their nurse's milk.'

He laughed. 'Perhaps we are given an appreciation of such things as a birthright, *signorina*, but knowledge—that requires dedicated study. I have recently begun such a course, but before I did not have much time to properly apply myself. I am an army man, you see.'

Thalia nodded, though honestly she could not envision Apollo marching through the mud. 'And what do you study, now that you have the time?'

'My special interest is in temples,' he said. 'Their architecture and contents, the nature of their rituals. They speak so much to the glorious heritage of my country.'

'Perhaps you came to the right place, then. Ancient Bath was centred on the temple of Sulis Minerva, of course. There is little of it left, I fear.

They say the Saxons dismantled it and used the stones for their own monastery—even the altar!'

'Barbarians,' he scoffed. 'Where is the site now?'

Thalia shrugged. 'Under the cathedral, perhaps. But I am told there is a small museum, the Bath Society of Antiquities, showcasing some of the votive offerings thrown into the sacred spring. I have not yet had time to visit it.'

'Perhaps then you and your sister would accompany me there some afternoon? For I can see that you are an excellent tour guide.'

Thalia laughed. 'You mean I am an excellent talker! I fear I do tend to prattle on so about antiquities.'

'Not in the least.' Signor de Lucca leaned closer to her, his violet eyes luminous in the light. 'Such intelligence and beauty in one lady—it is rare indeed. And precious.'

Thalia opened her mouth to reply, then closed it again, hardly knowing what to say. She wanted to laugh, yet she had to admit her vanity was flattered by his comment.

'I can see that Italians also learn one other thing in infanthood, along with history,' she murmured.

'Oh, yes, *signorina*? What is that?'

'Flirtation, of course. You are far more adept at it than Englishmen!'

He gave a startled laugh. 'Indeed, Signorina Chase? Do you know many Italian men, then?'

There was a small, distracting flurry of commotion near the door. Thalia glanced over Signor de

Lucca's shoulder to see Marco making his entrance to the Pump Room, as if her thoughts of flirtatious Italians had summoned him. Lady Riverton was again at his side, smiling happily up at him from under her fruit-laden bonnet. Though he smiled back, Thalia thought she saw a shadow over his face, a wisp of some taut tension.

'I know a few,' she said.

Signor de Lucca glanced back, following her stare. He was turned away from her, but she noticed his hand tighten on the ivory head of his fancy walking stick.

'Are you acquainted with the Count di Fabrizzi?' she asked, then felt silly. As if all Italians, whether Venetian, Florentine, or Neapolitan, knew each other!

But he nodded. 'I do know him. We are old friends.'

'You are?' Thalia said, amazed. 'What a coincidence, to find each other here in Bath.'

He faced her again, still smiling. But there was a new crease on his brow, just between those beautiful eyes. 'Perhaps not, Signorina Chase. For was not ancient Bath a place for exiles from Rome? A place where they tried to make a new home in the image of the old.'

Puzzled, Thalia glanced at Marco to find him watching her. Lady Riverton still chatted brightly up at him, yet he looked quite solemn. She gave him a tentative smile, suddenly quite conscious of how close to her Signor de Lucca was standing. Of the burning power of Marco's dark stare.

'Shall we go and say hello to the Count, then?' she said, uncharacteristically hesitant. 'I am sure he will be happy to see a friend from home.'

Signor de Lucca laughed. 'Perhaps. But he appears to be occupied at the moment. Shall we take a turn about the room instead?'

Thalia nodded, taking his proffered arm and letting him lead her into the milling crowd. Yet she could swear she felt the heat of Marco's stare on her back, even across the room.

Maledetto! What was Domenico de Lucca doing in Bath? And with Thalia?

Marco stared, incredulous and angry, as Domenico laughed with her, the two of them standing together by the windows. The milky-grey light fell over them, a pair of perfect golden creatures cast down from the heights of Olympus to the dull reality of the Pump Room.

Domenico was not a *bad* person; he had been Marco's friend for a long time, since they were youths in the army, cast into a situation they could not yet understand. He was a good drinking companion, as well as a fine friend for discussing deeper issues. As far as Marco knew, Domenico had never mistreated a lady.

But Marco also knew that, beneath Domenico's affability, there lurked a soul devoted to his own cause, his own ideals. If he thought Thalia could help him in those aims, he would not hesitate to use her. If she could not…

Marco watched as Thalia pointed at something outside the window, and Domenico edged even closer to her. No, he could not let Domenico involve Thalia in any way with whatever scheme he was planning. Marco had worked too hard to protect her. Had tried to stay away from her, to ignore the lure of her kisses even as his heart urged him not to let her go.

She had no place in his life, and he certainly had none in hers. But he would never let Domenico, or anyone else, hurt her. Not after what had happened to Maria, just because she loved him, and had followed him to battle. Because he loved her, and yet had caused her downfall.

As if she sensed his stare, Thalia turned. For one unguarded instant, she looked happy to see him. Her eyes widened, and a smile touched the corners of her lips.

Then something seemed to fall over her, some concealment, and she merely looked—polite. Domenico turned, too, and she said something to him.

'Excuse me, *signora*,' Marco muttered to the still-chattering Lady Riverton. 'I will return in a mere moment.' He hastily kissed her hand, and headed across the room toward Thalia and Domenico, who now strolled arm in arm. Domenico was speaking quiet words to her now, close to her ear, and Marco could not help imagining what those words might be.

Surely Domenico could tell her a great deal Marco would prefer she not know, if he chose.

'Ah,' Domenico said with a welcoming smile. 'It is my old friend, the Count di Fabrizzi!'

'Such a surprise to see you here, Domenico,' Marco said, carefully maintaining his polite affability. 'So very far from home.'

'I feel I have never left Italy at all,' Thalia commented, glancing between them. 'Who would have known that all of Naples and Florence could be found right here in the Pump Room! The town's hostesses will be most delighted.'

'Oh, I am sure Signor de Lucca will not be here long enough to partake of Bath's splendid social offerings,' Marco said. 'He is very busy.'

'Not so busy as all that,' Domenico protested. 'If all of Bath is as amusing as the portion I have already met, I must stay longer. I have never encountered so much charm and beauty in one place.'

Thalia laughed delightedly. 'Now you *are* bamming us, Signor de Lucca! I have travelled in Italy myself, you know, and Bath's ruins are just a patch on the ones there.'

Domenico gave her a soft smile. 'I certainly was not referring to the ruins, *signorina*.'

Thalia laughed again, as Marco itched to strangle his 'friend' with his bare hands.

'My sister is hosting a Venetian masked ball,' Thalia said. 'You must at least stay for that.'

'If Lady Westwood wishes to include me on the guest list, I would be most happy to attend,' Domenico answered.

'Excellent! Now, I am sure you two, er, friends have much to discuss, and I must rejoin my sister. Good day, Signor de Lucca. Count di Fabrizzi.'

Thalia turned and strolled away, her pale pink-clad figure quickly swallowed by the milling crowd. As soon as he was sure she was gone, Marco turned on Domenico, who watched him with an air half-amused, half-wary.

'What are you doing here in Bath?' Marco muttered.

'You would not answer my letters,' Domenico answered. 'I grew concerned, and thought I should find out what was happening for myself.'

'I am near my goal. But things are precariously balanced. Your presence could tip that balance beyond recovery.'

Domenico shook his head. 'The silver is not so important now. The time is very near, Marco! We need you in Naples, with or without the altar set.' His voice dropped to a harsh whisper. 'We need your warrior skills now. Your sword.'

'I have told you…' A passing couple gave them an interested glance, and Marco reined in his temper. He raked his hand through his hair, forcing himself to smile.

It felt as if his face would crack with the effort. Just as all they had worked so hard and sacrificed so much for would crack and vanish, if foolish hotheads like Domenico had their way.

'We cannot talk here,' Marco said. 'Meet me at Brown's Coffee House on Horse Street this afternoon.'

Domenico nodded, though he looked as if he longed to argue right there in the crowded Pump Room. As he turned away, Marco growled, 'Domenico—stay away from Miss Chase. She has nothing to do with any of this.'

Domenico glanced back, one brow arched. 'The oh-so-pretty Miss Chase? Of course she has nothing to do with it. She is a just a woman. Most gallant of you to protect her, *amico*. Most gallant indeed.'

He departed, yet that burning urge to hit something did not leave Marco. It only burned brighter at the slur on Thalia's intelligence!

Just a woman? Ha! If only Domenico knew the force of nature that was the Chase sisters, he would not be so dismissive then.

And Marco could not afford to underestimate her, either. No matter how far ahead he stayed, how he worked to protect her, she was always just a step behind. Closer and closer.

'Who was that?' Lady Riverton asked, slipping her hand onto his arm. 'A friend of yours?'

'An old acquaintance from home.'

'Indeed? He looked most intriguing, Marco dear. Why did you not introduce us?'

'He had an errand,' Marco answered shortly.

'Oh.' Lady Riverton pouted. 'Well, I'm sure I will meet him soon enough. Shall we depart, then? I have an appointment with the milliner I simply must keep. And then I must find a modiste to make my costume for Lady Westwood's party. I was thinking Anne Boleyn, but I fear you would make a most unconvincing Henry VIII! Perhaps we could be Paolo and Francesca?'

'Whatever you like, Lady Riverton,' Marco answered amiably. But his thoughts were very far away—with Domenico. And Thalia. He had the brooding sense that matters had just become even more complicated.

Chapter Twelve

'The post has just arrived, Miss Chase,' the butler announced, presenting a stack of missives on his silver tray.

'Thank you,' Thalia answered, glancing up from her writing. Now that she was inspired, the play was moving along quite satisfactorily. She was about to add a new character—a handsome, sunny-natured gentleman, who might be the one to save Isabella from her mysterious husband.

Or he might cause her even more trouble. Handsome gentlemen usually did, whether in theatre or in life.

But her hand was beginning to ache, and she was glad of the distraction of letters and invitations.

'Is Lady Westwood still out?' she asked, sifting through the stacks.

'Yes, Miss Chase. I believe she said she would have luncheon with Lady Grimsby after she took the waters.'

'Oh, very good.' So, she still had a few hours of quiet before she had to face Calliope's questioning looks again!

Not that Calliope had said anything about Marco or the very flattering Signor de Lucca after they had returned from the Pump Room yesterday. They had spent a quiet evening dining at home and playing some new songs at the pianoforte, and never once had the subject of Italian men arisen. But Thalia could tell that Calliope had been thinking about it. Wondering what she and de Lucca had talked about.

Thalia wondered herself. On the surface, it had all been polite, as everything was in Bath, if a bit flirtatious. But when Marco had joined them, she sensed a new tension in his manner. And she was growing mightily tired of deciphering coded behaviour! It was such a vast waste of time.

She glanced down at her play, at the smudged lines of ink. *Ah, the plot thickened.*

But she did not have long to ponder the puzzle of the two Italians. At the bottom of the pile of letters was a thick bundle addressed in Clio's distinctive bold hand.

'At last,' Thalia whispered, eagerly slicing through the red wax imprinted with the Averton ducal seal.

My dearest sister Thalia, she read. *I cannot say how happy I was to receive your letter! It was a wonder it reached me, as Edward and I have stopped in Naples, which is full of disquiet, following yet another false lead about the silver. You can imagine my astonish-*

ment that Viscountess Riverton has arrived in Bath*! And without the silver. Ever curiouser.*

We will depart at once for England, of course, and I look forward to seeing all of you again. In the meantime, dearest Thalia, as you have guessed the biggest part of the tale, let me enlighten you as to the whole.

Thalia read on in delighted astonishment as Clio filled in the outlines of their Santa Lucia adventure. Thalia had known, of course, that Lady Riverton had stolen the ancient silver altar set, with the help of her companion Ronald Frobisher and a team of dangerous *tombaroli*. Clio and her now-husband discovered that theft, and asked Thalia for her help in devising a theatrical trap. It seemed to work—until Lady Riverton slipped away, and showed up in Bath. With Marco.

What Thalia did not know was that Clio had once been the infamous Lily Thief. Two years ago, this thief had plagued unscrupulous antiquities collectors, snatching their treasures out from under their noses and leaving a fresh lily in their place. The Chase sisters' own Ladies Artistic Society had tried to solve the mystery, to no avail.

Of course, I have quite given up such things. It would hardly befit a duchess! Clio went on. *Now I must follow more, shall we say, legitimate methods. I am not too sure about the Lily Thief's former partner in crime, though. I understand he is also in Bath? The Count di Fabrizzi. He is just as passion-*

ate as the Chases about ancient history, and twice as tenacious. I am not surprised he found Lady Riverton before Edward and I could. He was a good thief, and a good friend.

But, my dear, I beg you to be careful. I have heard things here in Naples. Marco plays at games you and I have no part in, and he follows his own path. Stay close to Cal, until I can be with you both. Kiss baby Psyche for me, and all my love to you all—Clio.

Thalia slowly lowered the letter to the desk, staring out sightlessly at the little library. She laughed aloud, suddenly overcome by a strange sense of lightness. Of floating free.

Marco and Clio had been partners in crime only, not love. That was the only secret they had between them. The reason for their whispered conversations and secret glances. It all made a bizarre sense! Except…

Thalia remembered Clio's wedding, Marco's solemn mien as he watched Clio become the Duchess of Averton. It was friendship on Clio's side, of course, but Marco?

Well, regardless, Clio was married now, and Marco was on some sort of mission.

I have heard things here in Naples.

And strange things were afoot in Bath, too. She was sure of it.

Thalia refolded the letter, tucking it between the pages of her play. Real life was suddenly much more interesting than any fiction. She was not terribly surprised Clio would engage in something like being the

Lily Thief. She had always been the boldest, the wiliest of the Chases. Thalia wished her sister was with her now, to tell her everything! To help her decipher everything.

But Clio was not there, and Calliope should not be distracted while she recovered her health. Thalia was on her own. It was her chance, her one chance, to prove herself to Marco.

And she was suddenly quite restless. The walls of the house seemed too close. She had to get out, move about.

Above her head, she heard a loud wail. Someone else seemed to feel the same.

Half an hour later, she set off along the Crescent, pushing Psyche in her pram. Thalia had waved away the nurse's protests, saying she was surely capable of taking care of her niece for an afternoon. So far, she seemed correct. Psyche waved her tiny hands, cooing happily amid her ruffles and ribbons as sunlight warmed her little limbs.

She was as happy to be out and about as her auntie.

'What do *you* think of all this business, Psyche darling?' Thalia said. 'Stolen antiquities, intrigue…'

Psyche laughed, waving her hands more energetically.

'Quite right,' Thalia answered. 'It's a great deal of fun. Come, I know where we can go.'

She turned the pram down the gravel walk that led to Queen's Square, heading for the little museum called the Bath Society of Antiquities. It was surely never too early for Psyche to begin her education.

When a portion of the old temple of Sulis Minerva was uncovered, a dried-up sacred spring had been discovered. For many years in ancient Bath, the faithful had tossed their offerings down into the waters, such as coins and thin, rolled-up pewter sheets. Curses, spells and requests were etched onto those sheets, all in the desperate hope of an answer from the gods.

Now, whatever had not been pocketed by curious workmen was housed in the Bath Society. And the Society was little visited, Thalia saw, as she wheeled Psyche through the doors. It was a dim, dusty place, lined with cases of objects and three or four larger statues. Just a few people browsed the galleries, half-hidden in the gloomy light, which was just as Thalia liked. No one to watch her, no one to make inane chatter with, just the wondrous silence of ancient beauty. The power of old wishes and hopes.

Psyche seemed to feel it, too, for she grew quite uncharacteristically quiet as they strolled past displays of coins and those pewter sheets. She popped one tiny finger into her mouth, staring about with her wide brown eyes.

Thalia paused before a stone head of the goddess Sulis Minerva, and lifted the baby from the pram so she could observe it. 'You see, Psyche,' Thalia said quietly, as Minerva's empty stone eyes regarded them dispassionately, 'this is Sulis Minerva, the patron goddess of the hot baths here. Since it was believed that those springs came directly from the underworld, she guarded a connection between this bright world and the dark mysteries below. By throwing all these offerings into the springs, her acolytes believed they could communicate with the underworld itself. That they could appeal to her wisdom.'

Psyche cooed, stretching out a tiny hand to the statue. 'That's right, Psyche love,' Thalia murmured, cradling the child close against her shoulder, savouring her sweet baby smell. 'We should ask her to help in healing your mama, so that she will feel entirely herself again.'

Putting her back into the pram, Thalia pushed Psyche into the next gallery, which housed a miniature model of the old temple. 'The great altar was here, you see, with its concave top for…'

Her words trailed away as she saw they were not alone in the room. Marco di Fabrizzi stood on the other side of the temple watching her with quickly concealed surprise.

'Oh,' she gasped, startled. Her face felt suddenly warm, her stomach full of butterflies as she was faced with him unexpectedly, with no time to prepare herself. 'I—I did not think to see anyone here.'

And immediately she felt like an idiot. 'Did not think to see anyone'—in a public museum?

But Marco just smiled at her, moving closer around the temple. 'Neither did I. Everyone seems too occupied with gossip and drinking vile-tasting water to pay attention to the history under their feet. I should have known *you* would be here, though, Thalia.'

'And I you.' Psyche suddenly gave a coo, kicking her tiny feet.

Marco smiled down at her. 'This must be the newest Chase Muse.'

'Indeed,' Thalia said with a laugh. 'This is Lady Psyche de Vere, and she does not care to be ignored.'

'I doubt she will have to fear. No one could ignore such a beauty.'

'Such a noisy beauty.' Thalia tucked the blanket around her niece, fussing about with it to avoid looking Marco in the eye just yet. With her new knowledge from Clio's letter, she wasn't entirely sure what to say to him.

'I see you have begun her classical education,' he said. 'As befits a proper Chase.'

'Yes, poor baby. She will have gods and goddesses for her bedtime stories from now on! At least she seems interested in it all.'

'Will she be a writer, like her *zia*?'

'If she is, I hope she will be a much better one.' Thalia curled her hands tightly around the pram handle, facing Marco squarely. He watched her with a half-smile on his lips. 'And I am sure she will be far more observant than I am. She will not be always leaping to conclusions.'

Marco tilted his head. 'What do you mean?'

'I mean, I received a letter from Clio this morning.'

'Ah. And how is the lovely *Duchessina*?'

'She is well, and on her way back to England. She had a most intriguing tale to tell. One of masquerades, disguises—thieves.'

Marco nodded, a dull red flush spreading across his bronzed face. 'So, you know, *cara*.'

'I am sure I do not know *everything*. I only know more than I did before. That you were in league with my sister as the Lily Thief.'

'So I was, but that was long ago, I assure you. My methods are entirely legitimate now.'

Thalia laughed. 'Forgive me, Marco, but I cannot believe you could be *entirely* legitimate!'

'True,' he answered, giving that warm, secret smile that always made her toes tingle. Just like in a horrid novel. 'But I promise, I am trying to be good.'

'Not *too* good, I hope,' Thalia murmured.

'For you, *cara*—never.' He laid his hand lightly over hers on the handle, hot and alluring even through the leather of their gloves.

She remembered all too well their passionate kiss in the Grimsbys' ante-room. And in her drawing room. And in Sydney Gardens. She peeked up at him through her lashes, avidly studying the curve of his lips, the sharp line of his jaw. The way his black hair curled over the nape of his neck, beckoning her to touch it. She yearned to press a kiss to that hollow just below his ear, and taste the sweet saltiness of his skin.

She tore her stare away, her breath tight in her chest. 'Why did you not tell me about the Lily Thief?' she whispered.

He still watched her. She could feel the burn of his eyes, of that all-seeing dark gaze. 'It was not my secret to tell, it was Clio's.'

'And the part of it I don't know? Is that Clio's, too?'

'What makes you think there is something you still don't know?'

'Because there is *always* something I do not know. My family thinks I am too stupid to know the truth about anything, and that I must be sheltered.'

'If anyone thinks you stupid, Thalia, then they are a fool indeed,' Marco said. He reached up and softly touched one curl escaping from the edge of her bonnet. 'Yet I can see why the great urge to, as you say, shelter you.'

'Because I am just a silly female?'

'Because you have a light in you,' he said, his caress still so gentle against her hair. Thalia fought the urge to lean into his touch, to close her eyes and revel in that sense of *him*. That sense that the two of them were folded into their own secret world that always came over her when they were together.

'A light that burns with the pure joy of life itself,' he said. 'You are more alive than anyone I have ever known. To see that vitality dim, that light flicker under the weight of ugliness—that would be a tragedy.'

She covered his hand with hers, holding it tightly. 'But it is that very life—*real* life!—that stokes that fire. Without it, surely existence is just a pale echo? The life of books and dreams. I need more. Don't you?'

He laughed harshly, raising her hand to his lips for

a lingering kiss. 'Life as we found it in Santa Lucia? With thieves and danger around every corner?'

'Exactly like Santa Lucia. I had a purpose there, my work mattered.'

He stared at her over their entwined hands, his black eyes burning like winter coals. 'What of life as we found it in that dark little closet, hmm?'

Thalia swallowed, feeling again her legs tight around his waist, the touch of his tongue on her skin, on the pulse that beat with her life's blood.

'That, too,' she said hoarsely. 'Perhaps especially that.'

Marco groaned, pressing her palm to his cheek. Her fingers curled around the sculpted contours of his face, caressing. 'Thalia, *mia*, what you do to me!'

'Tell me, Marco. Tell me what I do to you. Because if it is even half what *you* do to *me*…'

'I did not come here to seduce you,' he said, dropping her hand. 'You—a respectable young English lady! My friend's sister.'

Thalia stepped back, trying to take in a deep, cleansing breath. 'Why did you come here? To resurrect the Lily Thief? To find the silver? To what end?'

'That is also not my secret alone.'

She shook her head. 'Just know this, Marco. I want to help. I know I *can* help you! You can't protect me, no one can. I just have to be myself, be a Chase Muse. If, when, you want to tell me something, I am always ready to listen. To do anything I can for you, for I know we care about the same things.'

That speech took every bit of Thalia's courage. She turned away before he could break her heart by dismissing her again, pushing the pram as fast as she could out of the gallery. Psyche seemed enthralled by the little scene, staring up at Thalia in wide-eyed silence.

'We need not mention meeting the Count to your mother,' she said as they emerged into the daylight. 'It would only upset her unnecessarily.'

Psyche sucked on her fingers, as if contemplating the new joys of secret-keeping. Thalia felt terrible about corrupting her, but it could not be helped.

She was not quite ready to go home yet, not until she had fully composed herself. She went to Bond Street, hoping that a bit of window-shopping would do the trick. As she neared the end of the street, she caught a glimpse of Lady Riverton emerging from a shop, the scarlet plumes of her elaborate hat quite unmistakable. Thalia kept to the edge of the pavement, watching her as she strolled off, followed by package-laden attendants.

Thalia peered closer at the shop window, and saw that it was the modiste where she herself intended to commission a costume for their Venetian masquerade.

'Modistes always have the best gossip,' she told Psyche, resolutely pushing the pram toward the door. 'Shall we just stop here for a moment and look at some ribbons, my dear?'

If Marco wouldn't tell her what was going on with Lady Riverton, she would just have to find out for herself.

Chapter Thirteen

The Theatre Royal was crowded, every gold-and-crimson box in the three tiers filled with fine gowns and sparkling jewels, every seat below in the stalls overflowing with rowdiness. As Thalia slid into her velvet chair, she gazed around at the way the chandelier light glinted off the gilding.

And she studied every face in the surrounding boxes through her opera glass. But the one she sought was not there. Either Marco had no taste for Shakespeare, or he was one for fashionably late arrivals, as at the Grimsbys' card party.

Lady Riverton was obviously not. She was most prompt, sitting across the u-shape of the theatre in her own box, comfortably ensconced with—Domenico de Lucca.

As Thalia stared through the glass, Lady Riverton leaned close to her golden-haired escort, the green plumes in her turban nodding. Signor de Lucca smiled, seemingly enraptured by whatever she was saying.

Well, well, Thalia thought, lowering her glass. Another little wrinkle in the plot.

She recalled her little chat with the gossipy modiste. Thalia had delicately dug for nuggets of information about Lady Riverton as she chose fabric for her costume. When Thalia mused that she was not sure what she wanted to portray, but that she did not want to look like anyone else at the party, Madame Sevigny had tsked.

'Just as long as you are not Cleopatra, *mademoiselle*,' she had said. 'My client who just departed, that is her choice. I told her that might be a soupçon too youthful, but *alors*! She will not listen. Now you, *mademoiselle*—you would have made a *magnifique* Cleopatra.'

Yes, Thalia had thought wryly—if the Queen of the Nile decided to masquerade as a fluffy blonde shepherdess. So, that was what they decided on, a shepherdess. And now she knew of Lady Riverton's disguise, *and* the fact that she hoped to lure an admirer with her fine, er, asp.

Which admirer was it, though? Marco, or Signor de Lucca? Or maybe the young man she had arrived with at the Pump Room? And where, by Jove, *where* had she hidden the silver?

'Isn't this lovely, Thalia?' Calliope asked, taking her seat next to Thalia. 'Just as up to the mark as London.'

'And just as crowded,' Cameron said. 'We'll be lucky if we can hear a word the actors say.'

His wife playfully tapped his arm with her fan. 'You will just be looking at the pretty actresses anyway!'

'Not at all,' he protested. 'I will be far too busy looking at *you*, Cal. You outshine every other lady here.'

He kissed Calliope's blushing cheek, and the two of them exchanged such a sweet, intimate smile that Thalia had to turn away. Their love glowed so brightly, like a corona of sunlight that enclosed only them in its blessed light. Just like Clio and her Duke.

'One would think you two were newlyweds, instead of old married parents,' she murmured teasingly, staring down at her programme. 'Shall I leave you alone?'

Calliope laughed, blushing an even deeper rosy pink. She *was* looking better, Thalia thought happily, not as pale and tired. 'Speaking of parenthood, Thalia dear, I hear you committed an act of great courage today.'

Thalia started guiltily. Had Calliope heard of her conversation with Marco at the Bath Society, then? Or the way she had grilled the modiste for gossip? 'Whatever do you mean?'

'The nurse told me you took Psyche out in her pram. Quite alone.'

'Oh, yes,' Thalia said, laughing. 'We went to the Bath Society of Antiquities to look at the offerings to Sulis Minerva. She seemed to enjoy it.'

'She was sleeping like an angel when we left for the theatre,' Cameron said. 'A most silent angel. You, sister dear, are a miracle worker.'

Thalia shook her head. 'Just read her some ancient myths. I'm sure it will do the trick when you want her to be quiet.'

'Yes. She is a Chase, after all,' said Calliope. 'Did you meet anyone else on your outing?'

Thalia thought of Marco holding her hand. Staring deep into her eyes, as if he could see all her most secret thoughts and dreams written there. 'Not really. I went to Madame Sevigny's shop to discuss costumes. She had the loveliest white silk, Cal, which I'm sure would do well for you.'

Calliope peered at her suspiciously for a moment, but she just said, 'I must get there myself, then. Perhaps I will feel up to it tomorrow, if you will go with me.'

'Of course. I can buy some new ribbons for my bonnet.'

Cameron said something to his wife, distracting her, and Thalia went back to perusing the audience. It was only as the curtain was rising that her patience was rewarded.

Marco appeared in a box, just a few down from hers, strangely alone. He slipped into his seat, his attention on the stage as the Montagues and Capulets appeared in a burst of Renaissance bellicosity.

'"What, drawn and talk of peace! I hate the word, as I hate hell, all Montagues, and thee…"'

Thalia studied Marco through her glass for several long moments, sure that he must feel the weight of her regard. Yet he never glanced toward her, never turned from the stage.

Puzzled, Thalia focused her own attention on the actors. She was quickly absorbed into the action, into the lush, romantic, dangerous world of Verona. *Romeo and Juliet* was one of her favourite plays; she watched it whenever she had the chance, and knew all the lines by heart. Yet it never failed to engage her. And she never failed to hope, deep down inside, for a happier ending.

To love like that, so freely and openly, so passionately that not even decades of hatred could stop it—how glorious. How full of life.

She watched through her glass as the Capulets' masked ball burst into music and colour. As Juliet, so wide-eyed with wonder—despite the fact that the actress was obviously no longer close to fourteen herself!—danced with one partner, then another, until she met a man she did not know. A stranger—yet she felt, so very strongly, that she knew him well. Knew him intimately. And nothing would ever be the same.

'"Thus from my lips, by yours, my sin is purged."'

'"Then have my lips the sin that they have took."'

'"Sin from my lips? Oh, trespass sweetly urged! Give me my sin again."'

Suddenly, Marco rose and left his box. Thalia slumped back in her chair, as if released from a tight, binding cord. But she knew very well that the invisible ties between her and Marco were only briefly loosened. They could not be undone, not yet.

The scene on the stage shifted, from the noisy

party to Juliet's ivy-covered balcony. She appeared there in her white nightrail, sighing with all the wistful frustration Thalia felt in her own heart.

"'...if thou wilt, be but sworn my love and I'll no longer be a Capulet.'"

Thalia could not bear it any longer. The helpless desire, the longing that led only to disaster yet could not be stopped. She felt as if she couldn't breathe, as if she was being drawn inexorably into that Verona world and leaving her own behind.

She whispered a quick excuse to Calliope and left the box, hurrying into the dimly lit corridor. Even there she could hear the muffled, distant words from the stage.

"'My bounty is as boundless as the sea, my love as deep; the more I give to thee the more I have, for both are infinite!'"

Thalia pressed her hands to her ears, shaking her head. *No!* She did not want to feel that way, not for Marco. Not for someone she didn't completely understand. Someone who refused to trust her. She couldn't be like Juliet, dashing heedlessly toward love.

'Are you ill, Thalia?' she heard Marco say, that musical, caressing voice so concerned. So gentle, and alluring.

She opened her eyes to see him emerging from the shadows. He was so much a part of them, with his black hair and black velvet coat, his fathomless dark eyes, she had not seen him. He was always a part of the shadows.

'I just needed some fresh air,' she managed to say.

'Yes,' he answered. 'The play—it affects me, as well.'

Thalia leaned back against the wall, grateful for its support. 'Were you like Romeo when you were a youth?'

Marco laughed, leaning beside her. The soft fabric of his sleeve brushed her bare arm, just above the edge of her glove. She shivered, but did not move away.

'Was I always fighting, you mean?' he said. 'Or mooning over heartless Rosalines? I have to confess, yes to both.'

'I can't imagine that even Rosaline would ever spurn *you*, Marco.'

'She did not. But her protector rather took exception, and he challenged me to a duel.'

Engrossed in the story, in the sound of his voice, Thalia slid her fingers across the wall between them, just barely touching his hand. 'What happened then? Did you kill him?'

'I never had the chance. My father heard of it, and decided he had had enough of my youthful foolishness. He packed me off to the army.' Marco paused, entwining his fingers with hers. 'I did my killing there, and learned my lesson very well.'

'And your Rosaline? What happened to her? Did you ever see her again?'

He shook his head. 'A gentleman never tells.'

'Are you a gentleman now, Marco?' she teased. 'Despite your fine title, I am not sure…'

'I try to be, *cara*. But some people do not make it easy.'

She swung around to face him, bracing her arms against the wall to either side of him. He could easily brush her aside like a piece of tulle, but she liked the illusion of holding him prisoner. Of being in control for once in her life.

'I am sure you cannot mean *me*,' she said softly, going up on tiptoe so their bodies brushed together.

'Not only you,' he answered roughly. His eyes were completely black in the shadows, his shoulders tense. 'There are also your sisters. You are misnamed the Muses. You are surely as stubborn and dangerous as the Furies.'

'Did you say such things to your Rosaline? If so, Marco, no wonder you had such trouble with her!' Thalia pressed closer to him, revelling in his body's reaction to hers. If she was going to fall heedlessly, she didn't want to go entirely alone.

'Tell me what happened,' she whispered. 'Did she come to you the night before the duel? Throw herself into your arms? Like this?' She pressed a soft kiss to his jaw, just above the folds of his cravat, inhaling deeply of his scent.

'Thalia.' He seized her shoulders, setting her away from him. 'We can't do this here.'

She glanced along the corridor, suddenly coldly aware of how right he was. Anyone could have walked past and seen them, just like at the museum. It was probably yet another sign that she was headed straight to Bedlam. Yet she could not quite make herself care. Not yet.

She took his hand, drawing him with her down the hall until they found a quiet, contained niche, storage for chairs. 'What about here?' she whispered.

'Thalia, *bella*,' he groaned, taking her into his arms at last. 'I was wrong in naming you a Fury.'

'Then what am I?'

'Aphrodite herself, surely.'

Thalia chuckled, and at last pressed her lips to his, their breath mingling. Whenever they were alone like this, enclosed in the sweet darkness, wrapped up in each other, the rest of the world just melted away. There was only Marco, the essence of him and how he made her feel. As if she could soar free. As if he was the other half of herself, and in his arm all illusions dropped away. There was only their bodies, their spirits—together.

But that in itself was surely the greatest illusion of all. Marco's whole life was made of smoke and mirrors, a black curtain she could only part an inch and glimpse the whole, shining truth for an instant.

She eased away from the lure of his kiss, resting her head against his chest. Through layers of linen and velvet, she heard the pounding of his heart, echoing her own.

She closed her eyes, holding on to him tightly. 'Are you going to vanish now,' she whispered, 'and leave only a white lily in your place?'

He went very still. 'I told you, *bella*. I have changed my ways. Surely your sister also told you *that*.'

'She told me many things.'

'Ah, yes, I am sure she did.'

'Is that all you have to say about keeping such a secret?'

'I told you, it was not only my secret to keep, it was your sister's. And I am glad you know now.' Marco gently framed her face in his hands, turning her gaze up to him. He was pale in the shadows, all stark black and white angles. 'I hate keeping secrets from you, Thalia.'

'Then don't!' She pressed her hands over his, holding him to her. Holding on to that connection between them. 'I will hold all your secrets safe.'

'What do you want me to tell you? What do you want from me?'

Thalia laughed, but it was a humourless sound. 'I hardly know where to start. Just tell me the truth about Lady Riverton. You have come to find the silver altar set she stole from Santa Lucia, yes?'

He nodded shortly.

'And have you found it?' she said.

'If I had, I would no longer be here. I would be taking it back to its home. And if she does still have it, she keeps it very well hidden.'

'Perhaps she has already sold it?'

'My connections in the antiquities trade have heard about no such object coming onto the market. And anyone who bought it would not hesitate to brag of it!'

'Very true. So, Lady Riverton has it still—and you are after it. But why?' Thalia frowned up at him in the dark. 'Why come all this way? To get it for yourself?'

'Thalia…' he began. There was a sudden burst of conversation from the corridor outside their niche. Startled, Thalia jumped back from him, his touch falling away from her.

'We cannot talk now,' he muttered as the noise increased, intruding on their little world.

Thalia glanced back over her shoulder. Time grew short for them, as it always did. Yet she could not quite let him go. 'But you *will* tell me?' she said hastily.

He nodded, a crooked half-smile on his lips. 'If I do not, you will certainly hound me until death.'

'Of course I will! I can never resist a puzzle.'

'Then go now. We will talk later.' Marco kissed her once more, quick and deep, and spun her around, nudging her towards the corridor.

Thalia quickly smoothed her hair, the bodice of her gown. She glanced back, but he had already melted into the shadows. Taking a deep breath, she dived into the crowds of people emerging from their boxes for the interval.

She did not see Calliope and Cameron, so they were surely still in their box waiting for visitors—and for Thalia to return. Yet Thalia could still feel the heated blush in her cheeks, and she did not feel quite up to facing her sister's too-observant eyes. Instead, she turned toward the stairs, thinking to seek out some refreshments.

On the landing, she caught a glimpse just up ahead of Lady Riverton's plumed turban, the tall feathers nodding above everyone's heads. They were moving towards the foyer.

Without thinking, Thalia followed those feathers as quickly as she could, dodging elbows and hem-treading shoes. At last she emerged into a quieter space, just in time to see Lady Riverton pause next to a tall, burly man clad in footman's livery. In a flash, she handed him a folded slip of paper and continued on her way. The note disappeared up the man's sleeve.

It happened so very fast that Thalia wondered if she was imagining things. But she knew she was not. After all, she herself had recent experience with surreptitious message-delivering!

The man glanced back over his shoulder, and Thalia saw that he had a square, dark face, and a thick ridge of a scar down one cheek and over his jaw.

Then he vanished out of the theatre doors, and Thalia plunged on after Lady Riverton. That woman joined Domenico de Lucca, who handed her a glass of punch, and the two of them laughed as if they hadn't a care in the world.

Thalia spun around, determined to find Marco, to tell him what she had just seen. To ask him what it meant. But she was brought up short by her brother-in-law.

'There you are, Thalia,' he said, smiling. 'Calliope was getting worried about you.'

'I just needed some air,' Thalia answered, forcing

herself to breathe slowly, normally. To calm down, and smile. 'I didn't mean to worry Cal.'

'Not to worry, I left her chatting with Lady Billingsfield,' Cameron said. 'Shall we fetch some lemonade for her?'

Thalia nodded, taking his offered arm. She would just have to tell Marco about Lady Riverton and the scarred footman later.

But was it not strange, she mused, how quickly she moved from suspecting Marco, to seeing him as an ally? And how long could *that* possibly last before the tables turned yet again?

Marco stayed in the dark niche for several long moments after Thalia departed, taking deep breaths as he fought to bring his rebellious body under control. It would never do to cause a Bath scandal by displaying an iron erection in those damnably fashionable tight breeches!

Whenever he was near her, whenever he looked into her eyes or so much as touched her hand, all his hard-won control crumbled. Even now, surrounded by the scent of her perfume in the darkness, he could think only of *her*. Only of the taste of her, the feel of her skin. Of having more of her, ever more.

Blast it all! He did not need such a distraction now. He was set to meet with one of his contacts in the hills outside the city later that night. Things were moving forwards at last, and he needed all his wits about him to bring everything to a satisfactory conclusion. Then he would be done with England, and on his way back to Florence and his work.

But he *was* distracted, and Thalia made matters so much more complicated. He should have known she would work things out, with or without Clio's help. Thalia was too intelligent, too willing to throw herself into any scheme, with no thought of her own safety.

He loved that about her, loved her shining spirit, her passion. She would be an asset to any plan, undoubtedly.

But Marco's soul would die if anything happened to her, as it had to poor Maria. He would just have to put Thalia off—if that was even humanly possible! But first, he had to meet his contact.

He peered cautiously into the corridor, now filled with people chattering during the interval. Soon they would all find their way back to their boxes. Hopefully, Thalia was already ensconced in hers, under the watchful eye of her sister, the cautious Lady Westwood.

If only she could stay there until he left Bath. But he knew that Thalia would never stand for such confinement. His best hope was to finish his work here fast—and leave her to her safe, secure life.

Yet he knew very well that when he *did* go, he would leave a part of himself behind, held in Thalia's soft, white hands.

He resolutely pushed away such foolishly romantic thoughts, concentrating only on that upcoming meeting. He made his way into the crowd, smiling and bowing at acquaintances as if he had only pleasurable diversion in his mind.

As he turned the corner, he saw Lady Riverton just ahead—holding on to the arm of Domenico de Lucca.

Cazzarola! he thought. His two greatest obstacles, together. Had they joined forces, then? Or perhaps Domenico played his own game with the Viscountess. Well, there was only one way to find out.

'Ah, Lady Riverton, *bella*!' Marco said happily, striding forwards to catch up her hand and press a gallant kiss to her wrist. 'How I have missed you. But I see my friend has supplanted me already, alas.'

Lady Riverton laughed, tapping his arm with her closed fan. 'You were very naughty, Count di Fabrizzi, to go running off without a word to your friends! I needed an escort, of course, and Signor de Lucca has been so charming.'

Marco peered at Domenico over the lady's plumed turban. Domenico gave an innocent shrug, but Marco was not fooled.

'I cannot bear to see such a lovely lady lonely, even for a moment,' Domenico said.

'I hope you two shall not fight a duel!' Lady Riverton trilled. 'I assure you there is no need. There is room for both of you to sit in my box.'

'Alas, my lady, I must decline for this evening,' Marco said, pressing his hand to his heart. 'But I hope to see you again very soon. Both of you.'

'Come to tea tomorrow, then,' she said. 'I am having a sort of salon, with visitors I'm sure you would enjoy.'

Marco bowed once more over her hand, and she turned away with Domenico. *Buono*, Marco thought with a soupçon of satisfaction. Lady Riverton would surely keep him distracted for the rest of the evening.

And Marco could take care of his own business, unseen.

Chapter Fourteen

Thalia raised her mask to her eyes, peering at herself in the mirror. Through the narrow perspective of the gilded leather eyeholes, the world appeared quite different. Rather than the vast myriad of colours and sensations she had always thrived on, the dizzying surfeit of possibilities, there was only one.

Help Marco find out where Lady Riverton had hidden the silver altar set. Who the scarred man in the livery was.

She lowered the mask, studying her costume. She didn't look like a Fate or a Fury at all tonight, not like someone to be wary of in the least. Her shepherdess costume was of pale pink brocade and silver tissue, the puffed sleeves tied with silver satin ribbons. More ribbon caught up the hem in bunches, revealing glimpses of her silver shoes and pink stockings.

Her hair was concealed under a powdered wig and a large straw hat, trimmed with yet more ribbon.

With the mask, and a quantity of rouge and pearl powder, she was hardly recognisable.

Yes—she looked like a completely unthreatening bonbon. All the better to trail Lady Riverton and find out if she had a secret rendezvous with the alleged footman.

'Thalia, dear, are you ready?' Calliope called from the corridor. 'The carriage is waiting.'

'Just a moment!' Thalia answered, tying the satin strings of her mask. She reached for her crook with its fluttering ribbons, and the little sheep toy on wheels borrowed from Psyche's nursery. She was armed and ready.

Under Calliope's direction, the ballroom at the Queen's Head Inn had been transformed from a large, rectangular, rather bare space into an evening in Venice. Hangings of gold and midnight blue draped from the beamed ceiling, shimmering like twilight. Musicians played on a dais at one end of the room, a long swath of parquet floor cleared before them for dancing. On either side were small card tables draped in more blue and gold, and chairs set in groups for a quiet coze.

At the other end of the room was a large painting of the Rialto Bridge at night, making the whole space feel removed from the rest of Bath. Lifted out of England altogether, and set down whole in the magic of Italy.

'Oh, Cal,' Thalia whispered, staring around her. 'It is perfect.'

Calliope, dressed as Athena in white silk draperies and a gilded helmet and shield, shook her head. 'I do wish I could have procured some orange and lemon trees! Or perhaps an olive or two.'

'I told you, my love, we are meant to be in the *city*,' Cameron said, taking her hand. He, too, wore a white chiton and gold sandals, a wreath of gold wheat sheaves on his dark head. Together, they looked perfectly god-like, as if they had just descended from Olympus to grace the world with their beauty and wisdom. 'No one expects an orchard in St Mark's Square. Your decorations are perfect.'

Calliope didn't seem convinced. Her gaze lingered critically on the draperies. 'Perhaps not. But I must make sure the refreshments are correct. Oh, if only we had the room in our own house for this party!'

The two of them hurried away, leaving Thalia near the door. It was very early in the evening; no guests had yet arrived, and the musicians were just tuning up for the dancing. A few servants scurried about, setting up glasses of wine and trays of those refreshments Calliope was worried about.

Thalia always liked this part of any evening. There was so very much to look forward to—so many possibilities.

Pulling her little sheep behind her, she strolled around the edge of the room, adjusting the draperies, arranging some glasses, examining the painting of the Rialto at night. The deep violet sky shimmered above the white stone, casting a Venetian spell of mystery and decadence over the evening. She remembered Italy, the vast beauty of it, the way the ancient buildings seemed to call out to her, tempting her to be a part of it all. To lose herself in its beauty for ever.

Much like an Italian *person* she knew.

'Thalia!' she heard Calliope call. 'Come, my dear, the guests are arriving.' And there was no more time for musing on the mysteries of Italy.

After nearly an hour of greeting people, directing them to the refreshments and to likely dance partners and of calming Calliope, Thalia was at last able to excuse herself from receiving the trailing end of the guests and to make her way into the crowd. It hardly seemed possible this was the same quiet, empty space as when they had arrived! A lively set wove its way around the dance floor, a strange mix of Greek gods, medieval queens, robed sorcerers, and bright-coloured gypsies joining hands and skipping along the line.

The card tables, too, were crowded, several Henry VIIIs and Catherine de Medicis placing their wagers. And Calliope surely had no need to worry about the refreshments, for everyone seemed to be snabbling them up with alacrity!

But she saw no Cleopatra. And no one who could possibly be Marco, either. Surely no matter what disguise he chose, she would know him.

She tucked her sheep under her arm, smiling at

greetings and compliments, waving at the dancers. She glimpsed Calliope at the other end of the room, consulting with two of the footmen. Cal would surely be distracted for the rest of the evening—she loved nothing more than to co-ordinate events! Be the general of her own social army.

It was a pity Cameron showed no inclination for politics, Thalia mused, for Cal would see him Prime Minister in no time. But, like all of them, Cameron and Calliope were only interested in history.

'Speaking of ancient history…' Thalia murmured, watching the doors as Cleopatra made her entrance. Lady Riverton wore a turquoise-and-gold gauze gown, held in place by a wide jewelled collar and a gold sash, gold snake bracelets around her bare arms and turquoise sandals on her feet. It was a good thing Thalia had got the inside story from the modiste, for the Viscountess was quite concealed by a black wig and gold mask.

She held on to the arm of a tall, muscular pharaoh, his impressive chest and arms barely concealed by folds of white gauze. He, too, wore a black wig, along with an elaborate gold headdress and mask. But Thalia saw the edge of a thick scar on his unsmiling face.

All that was missing was a barge.

She made her way toward the door, cursing her decision to wear such a puffy costume as her ribbons got caught on a knight's pasteboard sword. What had she been thinking? A shepherdess could not be surreptitious! She saw Cleopatra and her pharaoh take glasses of wine from a footman's tray, but they did not seem to be conversing. Indeed, they were each staring off in different directions, as if completely distracted.

So occupied was Thalia in studying Lady Riverton's curious behaviour that she didn't notice a hand reaching out to clasp her wrist. Before she could even cry out, she was reeled behind a midnight-blue drapery and into a pair of strong, velvet-clad arms.

'Wh…?' she gasped, her words broken off by lips pressed enticingly to hers.

Lips she knew well now. Their taste, their feel—the way they fit together so very, very well.

'Marco,' she whispered, tilting back her head to smile up at him. He was a Renaissance prince, her own Romeo in a black-and-white velvet doublet, his face half-concealed by a black leather mask. His hair fell over his brow in inky waves. His smile in the shadows was very white. 'You're here!'

'Of course I am here. Along with everyone else in Bath.'

Thalia laughed. 'Calliope does enjoy playing hostess. But how did you come in without me seeing you?'

'Ah, so you were watching for me?' he teased. 'You could not wait to see me, yes?'

'I was merely helping my sister by observing *all* the guests.'

'I slipped up the back staircase,' he said.

'Of course,' Thalia whispered. 'You have secret observations of your own to make.'

'I wanted to observe one thing in particular.'

'And what might that be?'

'A beautiful pink shepherdess.' And he kissed her again, pulling her even closer to the arc of his body.

Her sheep and crook fell to the floor, and she twined her arms around his neck. As always, when she was near him, when she was in his arms, she didn't hear the rest of the world. Didn't *want* to hear the world. Despite everything, despite all the puzzles swirling around them, around *him*, she felt safe in his embrace.

She felt entirely like herself, in a way she couldn't be anywhere else.

But a burst of raucous laughter on the other side of the curtain reminded her that, for good or ill, they were always in the world.

Thalia drew away, pressing her finger to his lips as he moved to follow. 'I should go and see if my sister needs my help,' she murmured.

'*I* need help, *cara*,' he whispered roughly. He pressed a kiss to her earlobe. 'Stay with me, just for a moment.'

Thalia laughed. 'I can't!'

'Then dance with me. Remember Santa Lucia? The masked ball in the piazza? How we danced all night.'

'Of course I remember. I think about it all the time,' she said. 'I wish…'

'Wish what, Thalia?'

'I wish I could go back there,' she said, all in a rush. 'Back to Italy. I miss the sun, I miss…' She kissed him quickly. 'Yes, I will dance the next set with you.'

Before he could reach for her again, tempt her into staying, she ducked out from behind the curtain. She scooped up her crook and hurried away, in her dazed state completely forgetting to tell him about the scarred footman.

After pausing before a mirror to straighten her wig and mask, she found Calliope. Her sister seemed content for the moment, playing a hand of cards with Cameron and the Grimsbys, and the ball was well underway.

As Thalia left Calliope's table, she caught a glimpse of turquoise gauze at the back of the room. Lady Riverton—it had to be, no one else wore such a colour tonight. Thalia hurried after her, finding herself in a dimly lit stairwell.

She heard footsteps clicking away just below, and she rushed to follow, holding her skirts close to muffle their rustle. At the foot of the stairs, a doorway opened to a dark courtyard, piled high with coal and barrels of kitchen supplies. The odour of fish and rotting produce was strong through the half-closed door, but Thalia ignored it, hiding behind one of the barrels just inside the entrance.

She heard the fierce exchange of voices outside. One of them was assuredly Lady Riverton; Thalia had heard her use such a tone in Santa Lucia, when she was unhappy with poor Mr Frobisher. The other voice was low and gravelly, masculine, with a heavy Northern accent.

Thalia could only hear words here and there, and she cautiously edged closer.

'…meet your friends yet?' Lady Riverton said. 'We haven't much time!'

'Patience will…' the man said, his tone full of mocking laughter. 'Folk like this can't be rushed.'

'They were quick enough to take my money! When will it be delivered?'

'I told you…'

'No, *I* told *you*! I have waited long enough. The cave is in readiness for the transfer. I will wait another week and that is all. If you and your so-called friends want the rest of your coin, you will do as I say.'

'Here, now.' The mockery fell away, replaced by the unmistakable tang of threat. 'You wouldn't be thinking of cheating us, eh? Because that wouldn't be very clever.'

'Only if you cheat me first. This shipment is very important, and I will do anything to protect it.' Lady Riverton's voice lowered, and Thalia leaned forwards to hear. 'Anything.'

'Aye, you've proved that well enough, I'd say.'

There was a rustle of gauzy cloth, and the unmistakable sound of breathy kisses. Thalia wrinkled her nose, drawing back into her hiding place. She definitely did not need to see such details of Cleopatra and her burly pharaoh!

But the shipment and the caves—now that was the

sort of information she needed. The 'shipment' was surely the silver, or some equally rare piece of ancient art that was soon destined to be lost for ever. The cave—well, that could be anywhere, of course. Bath was ringed with hills filled with such hidey-holes.

She had to tell Marco. He would know what to do next.

A cry of pleasure from outside the door made Thalia look up sharply. Yes, she had to tell Marco, but not here. Not at a public ball. Every time she tried to speak to him quietly at a party, they always seemed to end up much like Lady Riverton and the pharaoh. It was only a matter of time until they were caught.

Holding on to her skirts, she backed away until she was out of hearing distance. The she turned and ran up the stairs, back to Venice.

She caught up a glass of wine from a passing tray, taking a deep swallow of the bracing liquid. Her heart was pounding, her stomach all full of flutters. Now she could see why Clio and Marco had created the Lily Thief. Subterfuge was most exhilarating.

'Have you perhaps lost your sheep, *signorina*?' she heard Marco say. She glanced back to find him standing behind her, holding out Psyche's toy with a grin.

'I am a poor shepherdess, I fear,' she answered, trading her empty glass for the sheep.

'But, as I remember, a very fine dancer.'

'I do enjoy a lively dance.' She studied him carefully from behind her mask. 'Especially with a skilled partner.'

'Ah, *signorina*! As I think we have discussed before, my dancing skills are of the highest calibre.' He deposited her empty glass with a footman, and held out his hand. 'Shall we?'

Thalia nodded, reaching out for him. Reaching out to let him lead her into the dance, and whatever adventure waited.

Chapter Fifteen

'So, Thalia *mia*, what was it you wanted to talk to me about?' Marco asked as they strolled the pathways of Sydney Gardens again.

It was the morning after the masquerade, and the skies were that same lowering pearl-grey they always were in Bath. But Thalia scarcely noticed the clouds; she still felt the tingling excitement of the night before. The incandescent joys of surreptitious spying, of having some real purpose again. Of possibly impressing Marco at last.

She gave Marco a smile, holding on to his arm as they strolled along, for all appearances like any other stylish couple out to take the air. But she had not asked him last night to meet her this morning for a spot of gossip and light flirtation. She had to tell him what she had overheard at the ball.

Lady Riverton's words had kept Thalia awake all night, thinking of stolen 'shipments' and hidden caves. Surely, Marco would know what to do about it. For was he not a thief himself?

But surely not of the same brand as Lady Riverton and her scarred cohort? She did not know Marco's full story yet, of course, but she could not quite picture him so consumed by greed.

Was he?

There were too many people on their path, smiling and nodding as they passed by. Eager to speculate with their friends on what Miss Chase was doing so cosy with Count di Fabrizzi. Eager to listen to other people's conversations.

Thalia steered Marco around a corner, along a quieter path. The few people there were obviously far too intent on each other to pay attention to anyone else.

'Have you discovered yet where Lady Riverton might be hiding the silver?' she said quietly.

Marco arched his brow in inquiry. 'Not entirely. Someone told me—'

'Someone?'

'One of my contacts in London. He saw one of Lady Riverton's servants at the docks, speaking to a rather, how do you say, questionable ship's captain. He deduced that she must be expecting an important delivery very soon.'

'I think that delivery may have already arrived,' Thalia said. She clutched tightly to his arm, unable to contain her excitement. 'I heard her last night…'

'You *heard* her?' Marco caught her by the shoulders,

his stare very black and burning as he studied her intently. 'What do you mean? Were you following her?'

'Not following exactly,' she said. 'I just happened to see her slip away from the party last night, and I may have caught a word or two. She was conversing with that man in the ridiculous pharaoh costume.' Conversing, and other things, of course. But Thalia didn't find it necessary to mention that. Especially with Marco glowering down at her.

'Thalia, you should not have done that,' he said darkly. 'What if you had been caught?'

'Give me some credit, Marco! I was most quiet and careful. There was no time to find you—I had to decide what to do in only an instant.'

'You do not know these people, *cara*. They will do anything to protect themselves and their illegal trade. If you had been hurt…'

'But I was not! Besides, don't you want to know what I heard?'

Marco shook his head ruefully. 'Have I a choice?'

'No!'

'Then tell me, Thalia, what did you hear? A romantic rendezvous?'

'Well, yes. But more than that, I heard that the shipment is to be delivered to one of the limestone caves outside town.' She frowned at the memory of her frustratingly truncated eavesdropping. 'I did not hear which cave precisely, or when. But I am sure I can find out!'

'No!' His clasp tightened on her shoulders. 'I will

find out. I do not want to hear of you breaking into the Viscountess's house, or holding up her carriage on the road.'

Thalia grinned up at him. 'Very well. No playing highwayman, though I must say that is an excellent thought. I did a good thing, didn't I? A helpful thing?'

Marco laughed, some of that black anger dissipating like the grey clouds overhead. He drew her closer, pressing a quick kiss to her brow. 'You did indeed. A very good thing.'

'So, I am not so very useless after all,' she murmured.

'Thalia, *useless* is the very last word I would use for you,' he answered. 'But sadly, *cautious* is also not one that springs to mind. I want you to be careful from now on, you must promise me.'

'Oh, yes! I will never jeopardise your mission, Marco, I vow.'

'That is not what worries me.'

'Then what is it? If Clio can help you, I know I can, too.'

'Thalia.' He held her hands tightly between his, staring down at her. 'I told you. If you were hurt, I could not bear it.'

She swallowed hard against the sudden dry knot in her throat. The sudden fluttery rush of emotion at the thought that he possibly cared about her. 'I will not be hurt. And neither will you! Please, Marco. Let me help you. Tell me why the silver is so important.'

He glanced over her head, at the pathway behind them. 'Not here.'

'Then where? We are never alone.'

'Later, *cara*, I promise.' His voice lowered, his accent heavy. 'I owe you that much at least.'

Thalia shook her head in frustration. Why did she always feel that one step forwards took her three back? The day seemed overcast again, the world merely ordinary. 'You do not owe me anything, Marco.'

'On the contrary. Come, let me buy you an ice at Mollands. Then perhaps I can give you some information in exchange for yours.'

He stepped back, offering his arm for her to take again. Thalia accepted it, letting him guide her back through the Gardens. Perhaps it was not much really, but he *had* admitted that she was useful. And that was all she could hope for.

For the moment, anyway.

Bath was silent in the late-night darkness, blanketed in a damp mist. Only a few windows shone through, amber-gold and blurry.

The assembly rooms were long closed, and even the gaming clubs were darkened. Everyone was tucked up in sleep, except for insane Italians, Marco thought. He was the only one abroad on such an inhospitable night.

He tugged his cap lower over his brow, keeping to the edges of the walls as he made his way through town. The meeting with his contact had gone very well. Thalia was right about Lady Riverton and her companion at the masquerade. The man, known in his criminal circles by the unoriginal moniker of 'Scarred Jack', was trying to arrange for the Viscountess's newest treasure to be stored in one of the small limestone caves in the hills and be picked up there.

Where it would go after that remained to be seen. It would probably vanish, like so many of his country's ancient treasures. Pieces of its glorious history, broken up and scattered.

But not this one. Marco was most determined on that.

And, so it seemed, was Thalia Chase.

He made his way along a narrow gravel walk between the Circus and the Royal Crescent, the soles of his boots crunching the rock underfoot. It was the only sound he heard, even when he turned to face the sweep of fine houses along the Crescent.

Thalia's home was near the end of the curve—he had walked past it many times now, and he paused there. He had to be absolutely sure all was quiet and peaceful with her, before he returned to the inn. That she was safe.

And he saw that he was not quite the only person awake in Bath. One window of the house was lit, a single square of warm candlelight. A burning beacon in a cold night.

Marco stared up at it like a ridiculous Romeo, even though he could not be entirely sure it was *her* window. He could see only a faint silhouette against the filmy draperies, a lady with long hair writing at a desk.

And yet he was sure it was her; he could sense her very presence. Just the sight of her safe in her own home reassured him. Even if the fact that she was up late working on who-knew-what did not.

He remembered the shimmering excitement in her sky-blue eyes as she told him her information about Lady Riverton and the caves. The passionate enthusiasm inside of her that resonated with his own, that called out to him to share it with her. Share everything with her, his bright Muse.

But even as she wound her way irresistibly around his soul, he knew he had to pull her back from the precipice she dashed towards all unheeding. He remembered very well what had happened to Maria. He would be damned if he watched it happen to Thalia, too.

Marco laughed ruefully as he stared up at the window. Oh, but he was damned anyway! Ever since the moment he had seen her in Santa Lucia he had been lost.

There was a sudden flurry of movement as the curtains were brushed aside, and Thalia appeared behind the wavery glass. She wore a white dressing gown, her blonde hair loose over her shoulders in wild curls and waves. With the candlelight behind her she seemed all covered in gold, an ancient goddess.

She leaned on the windowsill, staring down at the street. She did not seem to see him there in the fog, and so was unguarded in her solitude. Unguarded—and strangely sad.

He wanted to know what she was thinking,

feeling. Wanted to know everything about her. She pressed her fingertips to the glass, as if she would push that barrier aside and fly free into the night.

Marco forced himself to turn away, to leave her behind. Even as he wanted only to climb up to her chamber and take her into his arms. The two of them alone against all enemies.

He walked out of the Crescent, not looking back.

Thalia stared out over the misty Crescent Fields, all grey and silver in the muffled moonlight. It did not look like Bath at all. It was a fairyland, where the everyday was transformed and nothing was as it seemed.

She gazed up at the sky, dotted with only a few faint stars, and wondered what it would be like to leave the house behind. To leave her whole life behind, and float free into the clouds. To be able to look down and see everything clearly at last.

She glanced back at her desk, at the pages of her manuscript scattered across its smooth surface. Right now she felt a bit like poor Isabella, trapped in a dank castle where things could only be half-seen, glimpsed from high, high windows.

But both she and Isabella were learning more every day. About the men in their lives—about themselves. Soon, she would see the whole.

A high wail went up from above, Psyche waking and wanting attention. Wanting to be heard, acknowledged.

'Believe me, Psyche darling,' Thalia murmured, 'I do understand.'

She turned back to draw the curtains closed, and glimpsed a movement on the street below. A mere shadow, a ripple in the fabric of the night. She peered closer, and saw a tall, black-clad figure walking away.

At the edge of the walkway, he turned, and she saw that it was Marco. No one else could possibly have such a beautiful Florentine profile, limned in the moonlight.

Surprised, she half-lifted her hand, opened her mouth to call to him. Yet he was already gone.

Had she only imagined him? Imagined him watching her house, wanting to be with her, because she longed so much to be with *him*? Whether he was a dream or not, he was quite gone now, and she was alone again.

But not for long. She was determined on that, and when a Chase Muse was determined—well, the world had best prepare itself.

Chapter Sixteen

Thalia crouched low behind a wrought-iron railing, gazing down at the servants' entrance of the White Hart Inn. Yawning maidservants had deposited the night's refuse several minutes ago, but a light still burned behind the high, small windows.

Her stomach lurched with trepidation and impatience, and she had to force herself to remain perfectly still. To stay in the shadows, where her black wool breeches, coat and knit cap could not be seen, and not go running about shrieking like an escaped Bedlamite.

She had broken into places where she should not be before, of course. On that one memorable occasion in Santa Lucia, she had even broken into Marco's own house, when she thought he might have eloped with Clio. But she had never attempted a place like an inn, where there were so many people, so much coming and going. What if her information was incorrect, and she went bursting into the wrong room?

She glanced over her shoulder, suddenly tempted to turn around and go home. To forget this fool's errand. But even as she studied the quiet street, she knew she had come too far to go back now. Marco would never tell her the whole story of what was happening, would never really let her help him. He was too protective, too *Italian*, for that.

She simply had to take matters into her own hands, and it had to be now. Before he vanished from her life again.

A cat suddenly leaped on to the railing, making Thalia cry out. She pressed her hand to her mouth, her heart pounding. Yes, it certainly did have to be now, or she would lose her nerve!

The light went out at last, and all was silent. She took a deep breath, and ran down the stairs. Her thin wire lock pick, a useful trick learned from Clio, made short work of the flimsy door lock. She was soon in the darkened kitchen, where the fire was banked for the night and all the servants were tucked away in their own rooms.

She hurried around crates and tables, the soft soles of her boots whispering on the flagstone floor. She had studied the layout of the inn, planned how to reach Marco's room from the warren of back stairs. But studying and planning were very different from actually doing.

She went up the steps, listening carefully at the door before she opened it and slid out into the narrow corridor. A few lamps were still lit along the way, guiding her to the next set of stairs, the next servants' corridor, until she came at last to the right one.

Behind a few of the chamber doors, she heard voices laughing, arguing—crying out in raw pleasure. But there was no one on the landing, and she soon found the one room she sought.

Holding her breath, she leaned close to the polished wood, her ears straining for any hint of movement. At first, all seemed quiet, so when a voice burst out in a flurry of Italian, she fell back a step in startlement.

'…will never convince anyone of the rightness of what we seek,' Marco said, as Thalia swiftly translated in her head. His words were muffled, but the forceful anger of them was impossible to miss. 'Our cause is just, and violence will only damage our credibility with those whose support we seek. Surely you see that!'

'I see only that you have abandoned us!' another man said, also in rapid Italian. Thalia could scarcely keep up, even with her ear pressed directly to the door. 'You, our strongest comrade.'

'I have not abandoned anyone,' Marco said, low and tense. 'I work for our cause every day. Why else am I here in Bath, so far from my home? The silver—'

'The silver cannot free us! It cannot take up arms and fight for us. The time for such symbols is past.'

'I cannot leave my work here. Not for such rash actions that are doomed to failure.'

'You cannot leave the pretty Signorina Chase, you mean.'

There was a sudden crash, like a fist coming down on a table, rattling pottery. Thalia sucked in a breath at the mention of her name.

'You will leave her out of this,' Marco growled. 'She has nothing to do with it.'

'I think she does. We know about her family, about how they were messing about in things that are none of their business in Santa Lucia.'

'That is not true. They were interested in antiquities, like everyone else. They are scholars.'

'They were interested in *stealing* antiquities, like everyone else. And now you are panting after the *puttana* like—'

A great thud, like a body hitting the door, reverberated right in Thalia's ear, and she toppled back onto the corridor carpet.

'Never speak of her again!' Marco insisted. 'I tell you, she has nothing to do with this. I will work in my way; you do what you must. But if you dare harm her…'

The door abruptly swung open. Thalia gasped, scrambling into the shadows just an instant before Domenico de Lucca emerged from the room. His golden hair was rumpled, a large bruise forming on his cheek as if he had just been hit.

'I will not leave this godforsaken place until you see sense, Marco,' he said over his shoulder, tugging his coat into place. 'Our plan is the only one that will work. If you are not with us in this, you must be our enemy.'

Marco appeared in the doorway. The lamplight behind him outlined him in flickering red-gold, like a dark Hades emerging from the underworld, burning with fury.

'I am not your enemy,' he said fiercely. 'But I will be if you come near the Chases, if you involve them in this in any way.'

Domenico just dashed away, disappearing down the stairs as Marco slammed the door behind him.

Thalia crouched there in the sudden silence, hardly daring to breathe. Had she just imagined that whole strange scene? Why was de Lucca arguing with Marco? What was their 'situation'? And where did Lady Riverton and her pharaoh fit in?

She shook her head. Truly, real life was far better than anything on offer at the Theatre Royal! It was enough to make her even angrier that Clio had shut her out of all the excitement for so long.

She would *not* be shut out any longer.

Thalia pulled herself to her feet, and marched over to pound on the door. Marco swung it open, growling, 'Domenico, I will not—'

She launched herself past him before he could realise who it was and lock her out. 'You will not—what?' she said, taking off her cap to let her hair fall free.

Marco laughed wryly, crossing his shirtsleeve-clad arms over his chest. 'Thalia,' he said. 'I should have known you would make an appearance. You have such a theatrical sense of timing.'

She leaned back against the closed door, crossing

her own arms. 'So I am told. Was that Domenico de Lucca I saw departing in such a hurry?'

'It was.'

'And what did he want here?'

'I think a better question would be—what do *you* want here? Surely this is not the way a well-bred English lady should behave?' he said, tsking at her teasingly.

Thalia tilted back her head, studying his closely. 'And surely you know by now, Marco di Fabrizzi, that I am not a typical English lady.'

'I may have gleaned that about you, Thalia, given the *unusual* nature of most of our meetings. What I cannot decide is what made you so. You are a puzzle.'

'Not nearly the puzzle that you are,' she said. He stood there in his thin linen shirt and loosened cravat, his glossy black hair rumpled over his brow, smiling at her as if he hadn't a care in the world. As if it was every day he had a fight with a countryman and then discovered a lady lurking outside his door clad in breeches.

No, she did not understand him one whit. But she wanted him, wildly and beyond all reason. Even now, when his overheard quarrel with de Lucca told her for certain he played at some dangerous game, she could think of little but kissing him. Of feeling his arms around her, his body against hers, and knowing that they were meant to be together.

If only he felt that, too.

'I have to be this way—it is my nature,' she said. 'If I sat at home sewing all day, I would miss out on too many interesting events. No one ever tells me anything, so I had to learn how to discover things on my own.'

He arched one of his dark brows. 'And what have you discovered tonight, *mia*?'

'Not a thing,' she said blithely. 'Yet.'

She took a step closer to him, then another and another, slowly reaching out to clasp his hands. She held them tightly in hers, unfolding his arms. The flickering candlelight behind him illuminated the lean outline of his body in that thin shirt, the soft fabric rippling against his muscles. He did not move away, just watched her intently, waiting to see what she would do.

Thalia wasn't at all sure herself what she would do. She was acting only on pure instinct, emotion. She went up on tiptoe, pressing her lips to the edge of his jaw.

A muscle flexed under her kiss, and she heard the sharp intake of his breath. She tightened her grip on his hands, but he did not draw away. Emboldened, she traced the tip of her tongue to the dimple low on his bronzed cheek, delicately licking at that enticing spot, tasting the salty sweetness of his skin.

'Maledetto,' Marco groaned. His arms swept around her tightly, lifting her off her feet as he kissed her lips. Their mouths met, open and hungry, full of all the passionate longing that had carried them to this one inevitable moment.

No, she had *not* known what she sought when she

came here tonight. Yet now she knew. It was this. It was him. She loved Marco, and in that love she would give herself to him. Nothing that felt like this kiss could be a mistake.

She wrapped her legs around his hips, her arms about his neck, holding him so close there could be nothing between them. No past, no future, no regrets. Only Marco and Thalia. Together.

She tugged his cravat loose, dropping it to the floor as she slid her lips to his throat, to the bare vee of his chest, exposed at the parting of his shirt. He tasted so delicious, of sunshine, salt, the dark essence of *him*. She wanted more and more, wanted everything.

She drew in a deep, unsteady breath, trying to inhale him into her very soul, to memorise him so she would never forget.

'Thalia,' he muttered, kissing her hair, the pulse beating so frantically at her temple. 'You are killing me, *bella*. We shouldn't do this.'

'No,' she gasped, tightening her legs around his hips, pressing herself close against his erection. 'We shouldn't. But…'

'But we have no choice,' he said flatly.

She shook her head, her hair swirling around them in a pale golden web. 'Our moment for turning back passed long ago.'

He laughed roughly. 'Thalia, we never had such a moment at all. I tried to fight it, deny it. I cannot.'

Their lips met again. The kiss held no art, no

thought—just raw feeling, desperate need, wild emotion. The rest of the world, the rest of their lives, did not exist. Only the two of them in that moment.

She felt him move against her, but their kiss did not part. Not even when he lowered her to the bed, coming down atop her as she slid her legs higher, cradling him in the curve of her body. His fingers entwined in her hair, holding her as if he feared she might fly away. But she could not have left if she wanted to. She could never tear herself away from him.

She moaned, turning her head to the side as his lips traced the line of her cheekbone, her closed eyelids. He nipped lightly at her earlobe, and she shivered with the hot wave of longing that swept through her. She caressed the hollow of his spine with her fingertips down to the waistband of his breeches, feeling the heat of his body through the linen. In one quick, desperate move she yanked his shirt loose and over his head, tossing it away.

She arched her head back, studying him in the candlelight. He was more beautiful than she could have even imagined, his skin taut and glistening with the light sheen of sweat over his rippled muscles. A fine line of black hair traced down his chest, disappearing into those horribly concealing breeches.

She pressed her open mouth against his heartbeat, feeling the frantic drumbeat of it echoing her own. His breath hissed, and he drew back from her touch.

'No…' she began, but her disappointment faded as he slid down her body to stand by the bed. He drew off her boots and stockings, kissing the sensitive arch of her foot, the curve of her ankle. As he moved up, kissing and caressing every inch of her, he took her clothes away, throwing them down to join his shirt on the floor. Soon, she lay naked before him, stretched out on his bed with only her hair to shield her.

Suddenly shy, she tried to draw the blonde strands over her bare breast, but he would not let her. Gently, he took her hands in his, holding them to the mattress as he leaned over her. He trailed soft kisses along her neck, the line of her shoulder, easing away any concealment until she was completely bare to him. Until she was writhing with longing for more and more.

But his hands held her still for his mouth, his tongue. For the alluring torment of his caresses. His open mouth slid over the swell of her breasts, licking between them lightly, teasingly. Closer and closer he would come to her aching, pouting nipple, then he would ease away, leaving her panting.

'Marco, please,' she groaned, arching her back, pressing closer to him.

He chuckled deeply, the sound of it echoing against her skin. At last he gave her what she wanted, taking her nipple into his mouth. He rolled it against his tongue, letting go of her hands to slide his touch over the arc of her ribs. He weighed her other breast lightly on his palm, pinching and rolling the nipple, caressing, until she moaned.

His kiss trailed wetly away from her breast over her hip, the curve of her thigh. Gently, slowly, he eased her legs further apart, kneeling between them.

She felt so heavy and damp down there, aching with a dark, primitive longing she only half-understood. He traced the intimate opening with his fingertip, and she shuddered. The flash of sensation was overwhelming, frightening—delicious.

And she wanted more of it. Much, much more.

When she sensed his touch leaving her, she seized his wrist, holding him to her.

'Are you quite sure, *cara*?' he said tightly. His eyes were completely black and fathomless as he stared down at her, burning. His accent was rough. 'If we go any further, I don't think I can turn back.'

'I don't want you to turn back,' she whispered. 'I only want you, Marco. Please.'

He kissed her again, their mouths and tongues desperate as his finger plunged inside her. She moaned at the rough, wondrous friction of it, the startling sensation. He pressed hard against one spot, and bright stars exploded behind her closed eyes.

'Do you like that?' he muttered. 'Do you like it when I touch you there?'

'Yes!' she gasped.

'And what about—here?'

Those stars caught fire. 'Yesss…'

As he kissed her, she faintly sensed his movements as he loosened his breeches, as he spread her legs even wider.

'I'm so sorry, *angelina*,' he whispered against her lips. 'I promise it will not hurt long.'

'Hurt...' she said, still dizzy with the pleasure of his most intimate caress.

'Hold on to me tightly,' he said.

She wrapped her arms around his shoulders, and he eased himself inside her, inch by careful inch.

Thalia knew what was happening; she could hardly help it, growing up surrounded by ancient statues and vases, and with two married sisters. But she gasped at the sudden ache, the burning sense of fullness. He pressed deeper into her than she would have thought possible. Then there was the strangest sensation, a flash of pain, of tearing.

'Oh!' she cried, digging her nails into his shoulder.

'Scusa, scusa,' he said again, over and over, his body resting heavy and still against her, his penis buried deep within her.

Was this *it*, then? she thought, puzzled. Was this what made her sisters so crazy for their husbands? It was not terrible—indeed, the burning ache was already fading away, leaving a nice warm sensation. But neither was it so very grand.

Marco drew back and thrust deep again, kissing her neck, her cheek, murmuring soothing, sexy little Italian words. Back and forwards, that friction building again, growing inside her. Their bodies found their rhythm together, their profound connection, and she moved with him.

And then she knew. This *was* grand! It was—sublime.

She tightened her legs around him, learning his movements, responding to them. They were as one, wrapped around by a spell of passion and need too long denied.

Deep, deep inside, she felt a new pressure building. She couldn't breathe, couldn't think. There was only feeling. Only Marco. At last, that pressure burst, and those wondrous white-hot stars showered down on her again. Red, blue, green, burning away everything but the wonderful, glorious pleasure.

'Thalia!' Marco cried out, his body taut over hers, his head thrown back like an ancient god. Then he collapsed to the bed beside her.

Exhausted, exhilarated, Thalia stroked his glistening shoulder, his hair. He shivered, his eyes tightly closed. Without opening them, he took her hand in his, kissing her fingers.

'Grazie, cara mia,' he whispered.

'Oh, no,' she said. 'Thank *you*.'

And she curled up beside him, the curve of her body against his chest as she gave in to the lure of weak, blissful sleep.

Marco studied Thalia's face as she slumbered. The dying candlelight cast a shadowed amber glow over her, making her look like an ancient Venetian mosaic of an angel. Serene and peaceful—deceptively so, for he knew well that she was anything but serene! She was a force of nature, throwing herself passionately into what she believed in.

There was no artifice to Thalia Chase, and he loved that about her. He felt as if most of his life had been spent in illusions, hiding behind masks, behind cool calculation. Thalia's theatrics, though, were so full of vibrant, irresistible life.

He smoothed her tousled golden hair back from her brow, letting it flow over the white pillows. She sighed in her sleep, rolling toward him until they were nestled together. The two of them against all the world outside.

Marco softly kissed her cheek, holding her close. Her body was soft and warm against his, so trusting in sleep, so very, very beautiful.

He knew that he had made a great mistake tonight. After all his plans to protect Thalia, to stay away from her and end whatever this was between them, he had instead made love to her. Made everything far more complicated. More dangerous. For he knew Thalia was involved too deeply in his work to ever be easily shut out.

From the moment he had seen her outside his room—no, far earlier, from the moment they had met in Sicily—their coming together had taken on a forceful inevitability of its own. He had held it at bay for as long as possible, but now the floodgates had broken free. Their lives were inextricably linked.

Marco remembered half-forgotten tales his mother used to tell him when he was a child. The Contessa di Fabrizzi had shared her husband's love of the Renaissance, of that time that was so gloriously colourful, passionate, and dangerous. She had told him of Medicis, of Romeo and Juliet, of Dante and his Beatrice. The golden beauty he could only worship from afar.

Thalia reminded him so much of those tales. Of life that burned free and hot and true. Of all he never really knew until he found her.

She murmured in her sleep, stretching against him. As he watched, fascinated, her eyes fluttered open. For an instant, her brow creased, as if she could not remember where she was. Then she smiled, and reached up to gently touch his cheek with her fingertips.

'So it was *not* a dream,' she murmured.

He caught her hand in his, kissing her fingers, her rosy-pink palm. She smelled of white lilacs, of the cool night. He slid the tip of her littlest finger into his mouth, sucking at it until she shivered.

'Not unless you want it to be,' he answered, holding her hand to his cheek. Perhaps she would rather this night vanish—until they could marry, and a more proper wedding night take its place.

'Never!' she declared, arching up to kiss him. 'I never want to forget tonight, for as long as I live.'

'Nor do I. Though I fear there is not much of it left.'

Thalia glanced toward the clock on the mantel, as it ticked away the moments until dawn. Until he would have to take her home, and they would have to resume their old lives, their old selves, again.

She sat up, gathering the folds of the sheet around her bare shoulders. She shook her hair back, and gave him a sweet, beguiling smile he had learned could not always be trusted.

'Then you must tell me something quickly,' she said.

'Oh, yes?' Marco said warily. He sat up against the carved headboard, watching her.

'What were you and Signor de Lucca arguing about? What is he doing here in Bath? It seems that this pokey old town is attracting the most interesting of characters this season!'

'Including the Chase sisters? You are surely the most interesting of all, *cara mia*.'

'My reasons for coming here are very simple—my sister's health. But I must say I am very glad we came. Bath is proving to be far more amusing than London could ever be.'

'Amusing until someone gets hurt,' Marco warned sternly. 'Thalia, you do not know the kind of people you are dealing with. They are devoted to their own ends, and they will be ruthless in seeing them through.'

'I have seen ample demonstrations of that, both here and in Santa Lucia. I am impulsive, perhaps, but I hope I am not stupid! I won't get hurt—and I won't let anyone hurt Calliope and Psyche, either. Now tell me, how do you know Signor de Lucca really? Or perhaps I should ask him. He does seem rather charming, when he isn't raging about…'

Marco laughed. 'Very well, *bella*, I surrender! You don't have to ask Domenico anything. It is all very simple. I knew him as a boy, when my father sent me away to school after my mother died. And then we were in the army together. We were friends.'

'*Were* friends?'

'Our opinions have taken diverging courses since then.'

'Your opinions on what?'

Marco reached out to touch one silken curl against her shoulder. 'Are you always this inquisitive?'

She smiled at him unrepentantly. 'Of course.'

'I should have known. You *are* a Chase, after all. And to answer your question—ever since we were young, Domenico and I have both seen the terrible course our country is following, dominated by foreign powers, losing its history and culture. The city-states all separated from each other, cut off from any real self-determination. We, and many of our friends, determined to do something about it. To make our homeland stand for something important again.'

Thalia leaned closer to him, her eyes wide and serious. 'But you no longer agree on how to do that, yes?'

He frowned, remembering all the long nights of impassioned discussion in taverns and coffee houses. All the hard work, the plans. 'I am not sure we ever did agree. I had the idea that recovering the lost heritage that had been stolen from us was of great importance.'

'And that is why you joined Clio as the Lily Thief?'

He nodded. 'I write pamphlets, you see, about art and history, about what they mean to my country. They are read by many English scholars, who then offer their help and support. Your sister was one of them, though her "support" went further than anyone else's.'

Thalia swallowed, shifting her gaze away from his. 'She became your great friend.'

'Indeed she did. She helped me recover many pieces of great symbolic importance. Pieces that helped others see how we can be great again. How our past is a part of us, and how it can be part of our future, too.'

'And that is what the silver is.'

'*Si.* The altar set was spirited away from Demeter's temple in the face of invasion by a brutal foreign force. It was buried by the goddess's loyal acolytes, hidden. And it is so extraordinarily beautiful, unlike anything else that has ever been found. Surely that makes it a vital symbol of our culture, our resistance. I must find it before it disappears.'

'But Domenico de Lucca does not agree on how important it is?' she asked quietly, hugging her knees against her as she listened to his story.

Marco shook his head, overcome by the emotion of his quest. Of sharing it with Thalia. 'He and his old army friends in Naples are planning an armed uprising. They feel that force of arms is the only thing that will be heard. They don't understand that bloodshed will turn our valuable allies, like your own family, against us. It should be only a final resort, and we are not yet at that point. If I could find the silver, show everyone what it means…'

She suddenly kissed him, holding on to him fiercely. 'Oh, Marco! Let me help you. Please.'

'Thalia…'

'No. I know I am not Clio. I'm not clever like her. But I'm a good actress, I can discover people's secrets before they even realise they have revealed them. Before they realise I am not really a fluffy bonbon. I can help you, I am sure of it! I *want* to help you.'

He took her hands tightly in his, bending his head to kiss them. To hold her close, his precious, passionate Muse. 'I know you can give invaluable help, *cara*. Woe betide anyone who ever thinks you a—what? Bonbon? But I could not let you be hurt.'

'I won't be. Not with you to protect me. If finding this silver will bring you new allies, will help to save lives and prevent violence—I want to do what I can.' She settled back against the headboard, a thoughtful frown on her face. 'Now. What about Lady Riverton and those caves?'

And Marco knew she was his new ally. Whether he wished her so or not.

Chapter Seventeen

Thalia was uncharacteristically beginning to have some doubts about this midnight venture.

She usually welcomed anything at all out of the ordinary way, and planning to meet Marco to explore the dark hills and search out Lady Riverton's hiding place was assuredly *not* ordinary. It was better than any play or opera for sheer drama and excitement! She had found a partner, a place, at last.

But now, holding tight to Marco's waist as he guided their horse along a twisting lane, she began to wonder if she was indeed entirely sane. Anything could happen out here, with who knew what lurking around every corner.

Then she tilted back her head, her gaze taking in the silvery swath of stars in the clear black sky. She hugged close to Marco, to his warm strength, and suddenly those fears vanished like a puff of smoke. Drifting away into that magical sky as if they had never been.

This was truly where she was meant to be. What she had been waiting for all her life.

'Va bene?' Marco asked, turning his head for an instant to smile at her.

'Oh, yes, quite well,' she said, resting her chin on his shoulder. 'Are we almost there?'

'We'll have to leave the horse just up ahead and walk the rest of the way,' he answered. 'The path gets narrow and rocky.'

'You've reconnoitered, then?'

'In my work, *cara*, it pays to be prepared. As prepared as one can be, anyway, where everything is so unpredictable.'

Thalia turned her cheek against his shoulder, the rough wool of his sleeve. 'I do like unpredictable.'

He laughed. 'So I have noticed.'

He drew up the horse near a ramshackle little cottage, nestled in a craggy valley below the limestone outcroppings. He leaped down from the horse, reaching up to help her alight. His hands lingered at her waist, his expression serious, half-shadowed in the moonlight.

'You can wait here for me, if you prefer,' he said.

Thalia gazed around at the darkened cottage, the smoky bits of clouds drifting across the sky. Listened to the distant howls of night creatures. 'I would be far more frightened alone here, wondering what was happening,' she said. 'Please, Marco. You did say you would let me help you.'

For an instant, he looked so very solemn she was

sure he would refuse, would break the fragile, shining bond of their new-found partnership. She braced herself to argue, but he just nodded brusquely.

'Stay close to me,' he said.

'Of course.'

Marco lit a lantern, its faint, golden circle their only light as the clouds grew thicker, hiding the moon and stars. He took her gloved hand in his tightly, leading her into the limestone hills.

As they hurried on, the path growing narrower, steeper, their boots grinding on the loose pebbles and dirt, Thalia remembered all she had read about this place. The steeps and valleys were littered with Iron Age barrows and old Roman mines. Full of ghosts and legends.

'I heard there was a witch living in one of these caves,' she whispered.

'A witch?'

'Yes. She used her wicked spells to lure unsuspecting mortals into her rocky lair.'

'Ah, yes?' Marco said softly. 'And then what did she do with them?'

'I'm not entirely sure. Ate them, perhaps. Until she was turned into a pillar of stone for her misdeeds. They say you can still see her there.'

He smiled back at her. 'If she is stone, *bella*, then we need not fear being eaten.'

'Oh, but I think there is some spell that can release her from her terrible state. Then she will be the servant of whoever frees her, bound to do as they command. Until she kills them and takes her final revenge.' Thalia realised she was probably babbling on, but thinking of witches and spells kept her mind away from the rocky shadows looming around them. 'Such a creature seems quite appropriate for wicked smugglers, doesn't she? Someone to guard their treasure, until they fall under her wicked spell.'

'Believe me, Thalia *mia*, witches and smugglers are never any match for a Muse.'

Thalia laughed. 'Have I just been complimented—or insulted?'

'Complimented, I assure you.' He squeezed her hand. 'I have never met a woman as formidable as you, Thalia Chase.'

Absurdly pleased, Thalia followed him into a narrow crevice between two tall stone walls. Their lantern light took on an eerie halo-glow, their footsteps echoing.

'Where did you hear such a tale, the one of the witch?' he asked quietly. 'Is it in your new play?'

'My new play is about an ancient haunted castle, and a man who is not what he seems,' Thalia said. 'But a witch in the story would not come amiss. I must add one.'

Her words trailed away as they emerged into a vast cavern-chamber. The walls, an undulating pale silvery colour, rippled up to a sharp peak.

'Oh,' she breathed, taking in the strange luminescent glow. From somewhere far away she could hear the steady, slow flow of water. 'Is this it?'

'I think so. Look.' Marco held the lantern higher, taking in wall sconces attached to the stone for torches, along with stacks of crates draped in oilcloth.

Excitement built in a warm bubble inside Thalia, and she pressed her hand to her stomach. 'The silver?'

'I'm not sure,' he said darkly. 'But whatever it is, I am certain it has no business being here.'

He dropped his knapsack on to the pitted stone floor, kneeling down to draw out a lock pick and a crowbar.

'Hold this,' he said, handing her the lantern. She held it aloft for him as he took one of the crates from atop the tall stacks and slid the bar under the edge of its nail-studded lid.

The wood splintered and broke as he pried it off, and Thalia peered eagerly over his shoulder.

But the light caught not the sheen of silver, but the dull glow of a black krater. Nestled in sawdust, the ancient vessel once used to mix water and wine at fine banquets looked lonely, the red figures caught at some Dionysian revel forlorn.

'It is so lovely,' Thalia murmured, reaching out to reverently touch one of the twisted handles. 'And remarkably intact. It looks as if it was made only days ago!'

'The Italian soil has preserved it,' Marco said fiercely. 'Until it was snatched away.'

She laid her hand on his shoulder, feeling the coiled tension of his muscles. 'What is in the next box?'

Together, they opened up several more crates, finding coins, sculptured marble heads and hands, and one half-broken funeral stele of a young girl. Thalia knelt down beside the flat stone, gazing solemnly at the beautiful, long-dead child with her downcast eyes and elaborate curls and draperies.

'I'm so sorry,' she whispered. Somehow, that stark beauty made her see, really see, what Marco meant when he spoke of the importance of these objects. What *tonight* meant, beyond any lark or adventure.

It meant what her parents had always tried to teach her, to teach all their daughters from the time they were in leading strings. The past *mattered*; it had power and value. It had irreplaceable lessons to teach, and those who would steal it for their own gain had to be stopped.

That was what it meant, really, to be a Chase Muse. And her whole life had led her to this one place. To Marco, and all they could do and be together.

She traced the raised pattern of the girl's profile, feeling a sudden deep kinship to her. They were connected, even over thousands of years, and Thalia had to help her.

'Thalia!' Marco suddenly said, his voice deep and urgent. 'Look.'

She turned away from the stele to see that he had opened a crate on the other side of the cavern. He stared down at it, perfectly still.

She rushed over to his side. There, packed in sawdust and crumpled newsprint, was what they sought. The silver altar set from the temple of Demeter in Santa Lucia. A welter of libation bowls, ladles, an elaborate incense burner carved with a relief of Demeter, an offering plate depicting sheaves of wheat. Even slightly tarnished from their long journey, they glowed with an unearthly light.

Thalia carefully lifted one of the small libation cups, turning it on her gloved palm. Reliefs of acorns and beechnuts entwined with a profile of Demeter. Scrawled on the bottom, in scratches of ancient Greek graffiti, were the words 'This Belongs to the Gods'.

'Marco,' she whispered, hardly daring to speak, or even to breathe. Not daring to break the enchantment of the silver. Marco was right—this was a potent symbol indeed. A symbol of sublime beauty, snatched from the terrors of war. 'We have found it!'

He gave an exultant laugh, reaching out to take her hand, pressing her fingers over the little bowl. 'Yes, *cara mia*, we have found it!'

He kissed her, a hard, swift, deep kiss that tasted of victory. Of the wondrous thing they had accomplished, together.

But their triumphant embrace was shattered by the sudden skitter of rocks outside the cave's entrance. The clank of steel and the mutter of low, rough voices.

In one swift motion, Marco kicked over their lantern, extinguishing the light. In the darkness, he slid the lid back over the silver's crate and pulled Thalia behind the stacks of boxes.

They crouched there, pressed tightly together. A bolt of ice seemed to slide down Thalia's spine, holding her immobilised. The quick spin from exultation to panic was terrifying. She clutched the bowl, holding it against her pounding heart as she sucked in her breath.

Marco slid his body in front of hers, pressing her back to the hard stone wall and shielding her from whatever was coming.

The voices grew louder as they approached the cave, the words more distinct until Thalia could hear that two men were speaking—and one of them had a pronounced northern accent.

'Why do we have to move them now?' the man said. Surely he had to be the lusty pharaoh from the party.

'You said next week,' the other man said sulkily. 'All the arrangements were made. Why tear me out of my cosy bed tonight?'

'Quit moaning like a pair of scullery maids,' a woman said. 'I told you there has been a change of plans. You're being well paid, so I don't want to hear another complaint from either of you. Understand?'

Lady Riverton. Thalia clutched the bowl even tighter. Of course. She *would* be here tonight. This was all her own plan, after all.

Thalia pressed her forehead to Marco's taut shoulder, listening for whatever would happen next.

Her chest ached with holding her breath, with the unbearable tension. In front of her, Marco was as still and steady as a rock. They sat there, listening as Lady Riverton and her two henchmen argued and shifted crates about.

Every scuff of wood on stone, every clank of precious marble and pottery, made Thalia long to scream. To fly out from her hiding place and beat them senseless for all their careless greed.

But even as her fingers curled into tight fists, she knew she had to stay put. To rely on Marco. If the villains killed her, what good would that do the artworks? What would her sisters say?

What have I done? she thought.

'Don't be so careless!' Lady Riverton snapped. 'Just look at the haphazard way your hirelings piled up these crates. Lax! You will not be paid if a single piece is broken, I can promise you that.'

'Listen here,' the pharaoh said, 'I've had about all I'm going to take from you!'

'A truer word was never spoken,' Lady Riverton answered. 'You'll get no more coin if—let go of me!'

There were the unmistakable sounds of a scuffle. Boot soles sliding on stone, cloth tearing, a ringing slap. Then another one, a crack of palm on skin, echoing off the walls. Thalia had the terrible urge to laugh hysterically at the whole melodramatic scene, and she bit down on the tip of her glove to stifle the guffaws.

But her elbow nudged the crate she was wedged against. The merest whisper of wool against wood, yet suddenly the cave went very, very still.

'Here, pipe down, you two,' the non-pharaoh man said. 'Did you hear that?'

Marco's back tensed, the air around them crackling.

'Probably a bat,' the pharaoh said, a quaver of—

was it *fear* in his voice? Who knew someone like that could fear bats? 'I hate bats!'

'Hush,' Lady Riverton commanded. There was the ring of footsteps, the hollow clatter of something tapping on a crate. First one, then another, edging ever closer to their hiding place.

In a flash, Marco spun around and caught Thalia in his arms, bearing her down to the floor. 'Close your eyes,' he whispered.

Unable to think, to breathe, Thalia did as he said, squeezing her eyes shut as she clutched at his shoulders. He wrenched open her coat and shirt, baring the top slopes of her breasts as he buried his face between them, wedging his body between her legs.

It hardly seemed the moment to be amorous, but she just had to go along. She slid the tiny bowl beneath her before driving her fingers into his hair, pushing him closer.

There was a sudden rush of cool air and torch light as Lady Riverton pushed aside the crates forming their impromptu hiding place.

If this was to be her last moment, Thalia thought wildly, at least it was a good one. With Marco's lips on her skin, his silken black hair falling over her hands, she could die satisfied.

Almost.

'Well, well, boys,' Lady Riverton said, her voice laced with an unmistakable strain of amusement. 'It looks as if our hiding spot has become a cosy little love nest. How charming.'

Marco leaped to his feet, dragging Thalia with him and swiftly covering her bare skin with the loose folds of her shirt. His quick movements also hid the glint of the knife that slid from his sleeve into his palm.

The two burly men crowded in behind Lady Riverton, their torchlit faces avid and very, very scary.

Thalia did not have to pretend ashamed bewilderment as she blinked at the sudden light, holding her coat tightly closed with one hand and sliding the bowl into her pocket with the other. It washed over her in cold, abundant waves.

'Laura, what are you doing here?' Marco said hoarsely, his accent heavy.

Lady Riverton arched her brow, tapping her riding crop against the skirt of her habit. Unlike Thalia, she looked cool and elegant despite being in a dirty limestone cave in the middle of the night. Skullduggery became her.

'I could ask you the same thing, Count di Fabrizzi,' she said. 'But I can clearly *see* what you are up to. Good evening, Miss Chase.'

Thalia stared at her in silence for a long moment before muttering, 'And good evening to you, Lady Riverton. Such a surprise to see you here.'

'That is most apparent,' Lady Riverton said.

'Here, you said no one knows about this place! That it was safe,' the non-pharaoh man said menacingly.

'And that is exactly what *I* was told,' Marco said, somehow managing to sound icily indignant. The offended aristocrat. 'This cave seemed the perfect place to celebrate my betrothal to Signorina Chase. Notwithstanding these dusty old crates of smuggled French brandy, it is quiet and isolated…'

'And ever so romantic,' Thalia cooed, latching onto Marco's sleeve and gazing up at him in what she hoped was a vacant, adoring manner. 'My sister watches me so closely, I hardly have a moment alone with my handsome fiancé. Convention is such a nuisance, don't you agree? Of course you do, or you would not be here with your own coterie. Would you, Lady Riverton?'

'Oh, yes, I agree. Convention is a nuisance, to be done away with whenever possible,' Lady Riverton said with a sly smile. 'I am just surprised to find you a devotee of rebellion, Miss Chase. Or perhaps not. You were rather—spirited in Santa Lucia. You and your sister. How is the Duchess, by the way?'

'So, are we going to kill them now?' the pharaoh said impatiently. Without his fancy headdress, his scarred face was even more frightening.

'I'd like to see you try, knave,' Marco growled. 'I will flatten you like Attila did Rome.'

'Oh, will you now, Italian pig?' The pharaoh lunged forward, drawing a wicked-looking dagger from the sheath at his waist. The non-pharaoh cackled with glee.

Before Thalia could scream, Lady Riverton stopped him with a hand to his chest. 'Now, Jack, none of that. Bloodshed would be so messy with all this—brandy about. We have a betrothal to celebrate!

I do love an engagement. Let me be the first to wish you both happy.'

She stepped close to Marco, running one gloved fingertip down his rumpled shirtfront. 'I must say, Marco darling, I am surprised. Flirting with me to disguise your feelings for Miss Chase. It is so—clever. So very unlike you.'

Marco gazed down at her, eyes narrowed. 'I must have hidden depths.'

'To say the least,' Lady Riverton said. 'Are you sure she is woman enough to plumb them?'

Thalia yanked on Marco's arm, turning him from Lady Riverton's touch. But the Viscountess just laughed, spinning around to stroll back to the cave's entrance.

'Ah, yes, I do love *love*!' she said merrily. 'Come, Jack darling, do as I say and put that knife away. We must see the lovebirds safely back to town before sunrise.' She glanced over her shoulder. 'I look forward to calling on you and your sister later, Miss Chase, to officially offer my best wishes. Perhaps you will have another masquerade ball to celebrate! Jack and I do love a masquerade, don't we, darling?'

As Lady Riverton and the two men left the cave, Thalia tightened her grip on Marco's sleeve. 'We can't leave without the silver!' she whispered urgently. 'What if they—?'

'Shh, *cara*,' Marco muttered. He took her hand firmly in his, but his gaze was still on the entrance. 'Do not worry. I will think what to do, now that we know where it's at. For now we must celebrate our engagement with our new friends.' He grinned at her, raising her hand to his lips. 'You will make such a lovely bride.'

Chapter Eighteen

'Thalia, dearest, are you quite certain this is what you want to do?' Calliope asked. 'I know he is handsome and rich and, well, Italian. But do you really know him well enough?'

Thalia stared out of the drawing-room window, not really seeing the carriages dashing past in the rain. She had been asking herself just that same question all morning—was this really what she wanted to do? Did she know Marco well enough? Just not quite in the same way Calliope meant.

She tightened her fingers over the crumpled note in her hand. The missive had arrived at breakfast, written in Marco's bold, dark hand. *Thalia, cara*, it said. *Please do not worry—you won't be trapped with me for the rest of your life, and neither will I with you. We must only playact a little while longer.*

Playact—just when she was taking everything so very seriously. She had seen last night in the cave how very important, and dangerous, Marco's work was. How much she wanted to be a part of it all.

But he seemed to be pulling away from her again. Even now, when he was in the library asking Cameron for permission for their 'betrothal'.

Their sham betrothal, which he obviously did not want. Yet perhaps a fake engagement was better than none. At least it bought her some time, gave her an excuse to be in Marco's company without exciting more gossip.

She turned to smile at her sister. Calliope sat on the couch, cradling Psyche in her arms. For once, the baby was quiet, gazing around with her wide, dark eyes, as if aware of the seriousness of the moment.

'I am sure this is what I want to do,' Thalia said, sitting down beside her. 'I know that you have all been worried I would never find a gentleman to suit me. Well, now I have.'

'Thalia, I have not been worried you would not marry! You have had far more offers than the rest of us put together. I worry that you will marry the *wrong* person. The Count is exciting, of course, but will he make you happy?'

'Is there something you want to tell me about Marco, Cal?' Thalia asked carefully. 'That day at the Pump Room was not the first time you had encountered him, of course.'

Calliope shifted Psyche to her shoulder, not quite meeting Thalia's gaze. 'You are right, Thalia. I did not tell you the entire tale. That time we visited

Emmeline Saunders and her family in Yorkshire, and we went to Averton's castle…'

'You saw him with Clio, trying to steal something from the Duke. Probably the Artemis statue.'

Calliope's eyes widened like her daughter's. 'You knew?'

'Of course. You told me, remember? And so did Clio, once she finally decided I could be trusted. But that is all over now. His work is entirely aboveboard, and so is Clio's.' Except for sneaking into caves in the middle of the night. But Thalia saw no need to mention *that*.

'Oh,' Calliope said weakly. 'Well, if you know about all that and still wish to marry him…'

'I do!' Thalia took her sister's hand. Somehow, it was so important that Calliope understand. That she, and all the Chases, accept Marco. Surely no one could help him more in his cause than her family. 'Oh, Cal, I thought I would never find someone who could understand me as Cameron does you. Someone who doesn't care that I am wild and impulsive.'

Calliope laughed, bouncing Psyche in her arms. 'I am quite sure the Count has no room to complain about anyone else's impulsiveness!'

Thalia smiled ruefully. 'No, because we are alike in so many ways. My life with him will never be dull. Never be without purpose.'

'We Chase Muses do like to have a purpose, don't we?'

'Of course. And we want others to see the rightness of that purpose.'

'And make them do as we say?' Calliope shook her head. 'I doubt the Count will ever follow your orders, sister dear. Or you his.'

Thalia laughed. 'Much like you and Cameron?'

'Well, a quarrel or two to clear the air in a marriage never comes amiss. If he makes you as happy as Cam makes me…'

'Then I will be abundantly blessed. So, you will agree to this engagement?'

'Yes. *If* you wait for Father and Clio to come home before you marry.'

'I could not have a wedding without them.'

'Then I hope you will ask the Count to dine with us tonight, before our guests arrive for cards. There is a great deal I would speak to him about, I think.'

'Oh, thank you, Cal!' Thalia exuberantly kissed her sister on the cheek, and then her startled niece. 'You will not be sorry. You'll see how wonderful Marco is.'

Psyche wailed, kicking her feet at all the excitement. 'I hope so, Thalia dear. And just think—soon you might have a Psyche of your own.'

Thalia stared down at the baby's red cheeks, biting her lip as she remembered that wild night in Marco's bedchamber. Her legs wrapped around his waist as their bodies moved and thrust together.

All the more reason to quickly turn this sham betrothal into a real one. If she could. She was determined, but was she determined enough?

'Not too soon, I hope,' she murmured.

* * *

'You are very quiet today, *cara mia*,' Marco said.

Thalia left off picking at her pastry at their table in Mollands window to smile at him. 'It makes a change, does it not?'

He laughed. Her dark knight of the caves was gone, and he was the light and charming escort again. 'But it means I hardly know if it is *Thalia* I am with, or her strangely silent twin.'

'I'm sorry. I was just thinking over everything that has happened.'

'It is a great deal to absorb.'

'Surely not for you. I'm sure your entire life must be full of such excitement! Caves, daggers, midnight meetings…'

'Not every night, I assure you. I am quite sure my nerves could not stand it.' He held out his empty teacup for her to pour. 'Most of my time is spent being a hermit in my library, writing letters and pamphlets, working on my monograph. Only since I met you has my life become like one of your English Minerva Press novels.'

'Tell me about your home in Florence, then,' she said, stirring her tea. Two people she had never met before strolled past the window, grinning when they saw her and Marco—just as so many people had done today. Lady Riverton's gossip about their betrothal had spread fast. She ignored them. 'Is it so very ancient?'

'Ancient enough,' Marco answered. 'It was built in the fourteenth century on the Via Larga, but an ancestor expanded it greatly a hundred years later. He was a great collector, of course, and he needed not one but three great courtyards to display his sculptures. My mother, she loved these courtyards, and she added new fountains and so many rosebushes. In the summer, the air is full of their perfume.'

Thalia closed her eyes, picturing it all in her mind, just as in the beautiful villas she saw on her travels. An arcaded *cortile* with marble pillars supporting arches overhead; marble cameo medallions gazing down on classical statues, columns, twining vines and flowers. She imagined sitting on a cool marble bench under the shade of the portal, listening to the whisper of the fountains, inhaling the musky-sweet scent of summer roses. In her dream, Marco sat down beside her, dropping one of the blossoms into her lap as they laughed together. 'It sounds perfect.'

'It is, very nearly. Sadly, the rest of the house needs a bit more care. I get caught up in my work, and since my mother died there is no one to see to it properly. It needs care and attention, someone to love it. I fear no one will want to take on such a burden.'

'I am certain there could be far more onerous tasks in life than taking on the restoration of a Renaissance work of art!' Thalia protested. 'Making it truly elegant once again, a showplace.'

'Ah, but whoever took on *that* would also have to take on me. And all my family relations, who are spread from the Veneto to Naples, and yet who are all certain they know how I should live my life.'

'It sounds like my own family. Surely no one

could be more opinionated than a Chase! We are all quite sure we know what is best for each other.'

Marco laughed. 'Are you sure you're not Italian, then?'

Thalia smiled at him. 'Sometimes I think we must be. But, speaking of my family, Marco, you needn't come tonight for dinner and cards if you are otherwise occupied. I don't want you to feel—obligated in any way.' She remembered his note, and her confusion only increased. He did not *want* this engagement; he had made that clear to her.

But he reached across the table and gently took her hand in his, in front of all the gossip-seekers. 'There is no place else I would rather be.'

'But what about…?' Thalia quickly lowered her voice. 'What about the silver?'

Marco glanced out of the window, his jaw tight. 'Did you know, *cara*, about the fireworks gala in Sydney Gardens tomorrow night?'

Thalia blinked at him, startled. What did fireworks have to do with the silver? Or with *anything*? 'Yes, of course. Cameron procured tickets for us. What can it—oh.' Of course! She felt suddenly foolish. The gala must be a cover for something.

'May I go with you?' she whispered.

That muscle in his jaw ticked. 'I was wrong to take you to the cave, Thalia. If something happened yet again…'

'It won't!' She tightened her clasp on his hand, unwilling to let him go now. 'If I hadn't been with you in the cave, you would not have had such a good excuse for being there. They might have—have hurt you.'

Her stomach lurched at the thought of Marco bleeding alone in the cold cave, with no one there to help him. He was so protective of her, yet now she found that she was every bit as protective of *him*. They needed each other, whether he wanted to admit it or not.

'I would have thought of something else,' he said roughly. 'And then you would not be in this position.'

'But could you have come up with something so fast?' She gave him a teasing smile. 'I am a fairly good actress, am I not?'

'Bella,' he said, with a reluctant smile of his own, 'you are far too good.'

'Then you can tell me what is happening during the gala. I won't get in your way, I promise.'

'We can't talk about it here.'

Thalia glanced around the crowded shop, all the curious people eating their pastries and ices. 'Let us walk, then. I need some fresh air.'

But there was no privacy in walking, either. So many people stopped them to proffer their good wishes and sly questions that there was no chance for a quiet word at all. Thalia began to wonder how her sisters and their husbands had ever managed to court each other, with everyone watching!

'Tonight, then,' she whispered, when they had a scant moment between conversations. 'We can meet in my chamber after the card party. No one will miss us then!'

* * *

The game of Speculation was in full fervour.

Marco glanced across the table, to where Thalia was examining her hand of three cards. In front of her was the upturned trump card. In her concentration, her brow was creased, her lips pursed in an alluring little pout. Slowly, she drew in her lower lip, worrying at it with her even white teeth before she suddenly smiled and laid down a card.

And Marco shifted uncomfortably in his chair, once again cursing the fashion for tight breeches. They were a blasted inconvenience whenever he was near Thalia.

His fiancée looked especially beautiful tonight, with the candlelight turning her upswept curls to molten gold, her cheeks a glowing pink as she laughed. She wore a gown of pale green silk trimmed with frills of fine white lace, which made her look like an Aphrodite emerging from the foam of the sea. *Si*, she was so very beautiful, so sensual and so innocent at the same time.

She peeked at him from beneath her lashes, giving him a secret little smile. 'Do you wish to sell your card, then, Count di Fabrizzi?' she murmured. In those simple words seemed a wealth of shared mischief.

In only a few days, she had surely become an inextricable part of his life. His lover, his partner. His friend? Somehow now he could hardly imagine going on in his work, in his life, without her.

And that knowledge was dangerously distracting. It turned him from his work, and worse put Thalia herself in danger. He had to be very vigilant, to make certain this false engagement never took on the appearance of a real one. No more than it already had, anyway.

He frowned, staring down at his cards again. 'Not at the moment, my dear Miss Chase,' he murmured. 'I think I see more advantage in holding on to what I have now.'

They played with Lord Grimsby and his daughter Lady Anne, with Lady Westwood and her husband at the next table. The arrival of the other guests had been a welcome distraction after a supper spent being pelted—politely, of course—with questions. What were his properties in Italy? In England? Where did he intend for Thalia to live? How often would he bring her to visit her family?

Thalia had brought the inquisition to an end by laughingly declaring they would surely be living in a cave in the Apennines, where they would raise goats and make wine. And perhaps write poetry all day. For was that not what counts and contessas did?

All of which sounded strangely charming to Marco. To be alone with Thalia, with only the goats to watch them and gossip about them. Where he could kiss her, touch her, whenever he wanted. It would be bliss indeed. And yet one more reason why he should stay away from her, and her intoxicating, amnesia-inducing smiles.

As if she read his thoughts now, Thalia gave him a puzzled glance before going back to chatting with Lady Anne.

Lady Westwood's whist partner at the next table was a new arrival in Bath, Lord Knowleton, head of the Antiquities Society, of which the Chases were such enthusiastic members. Marco was anxious to speak to him, as the Antiquities Society had been so active in the recovery and study of so many artefacts. He would be a most useful ally in Marco's work.

If, that is, he could cease being so distracted by the curve of Thalia's rose-pink lips…

'And when is the wedding to be?' Lady Anne asked eagerly. 'Will it be here in Bath?'

Thalia laughed. 'I confess I have not thought so far ahead! I will have to wait until we hear word from my father. Perhaps we will marry at Chase Lodge, where all my sisters can see.'

'Oh, no!' Lady Anne said with a pout. 'I was so hoping it would be here, and soon. You are sure to have the prettiest bridal clothes that ever were seen, Miss Chase.'

'Anne!' her father said, laughing fondly. 'Enough, my dear. You will have to forgive her, Miss Chase. She is a great devotee of weddings.'

'As am I,' Thalia said. 'There must be just the right amount of silk and lace, and the right sort of cake and wine. My sisters both had lovely nuptials, Lady Westwood at my father's London house and the Duchess of Averton at a little church in Sicily. I cannot be outdone by them.'

'Not when you are the most fashionable of us all,'

Lady Westwood said. 'No one will make a more beautiful bride than Thalia.'

'Perhaps you could find a Roman temple to marry in,' Lord Knowleton suggested. 'Surely no place could be more suited to two scholars of the ancient world!'

Marco had a sudden flashing vision of Thalia entering the shadowed hush of a pillared temple, a sheer veil draped over her golden hair. She was a part of that ancient world, of all the beauty of so many centuries. A part of *him*, of all he worked for and loved.

But then she laughed, and that ethereal vision shattered. She was only Thalia again, the woman he cared for so much he ached with it. He cared *too* much, and he feared he would never be cured of that, no matter how much he pretended. No matter how hard he worked to show Thalia theirs was not a betrothal in truth.

'Do not say that in my father's presence, Lord Knowleton,' she said. 'He would set to building a temple straight away.'

'And then your wedding would be delayed even further!' Lady Anne said sadly.

'And what do you think of such nuptial plans, Count?' Lady Knowleton, observing her husband's card game, asked.

Marco grinned. 'I think anything that makes Signorina Chase happy makes *me* happy.'

'Well put, Count,' Lord Westwood said. 'You are learning this marriage business quickly indeed.'

Marco suddenly felt the soft caress of dainty toes

against his ankle, brushing up his calf. A slow, alluring caress. Thalia had obviously slipped off her shoe beneath the drape of the tablecloth. She gave him an innocent little smile over the edge of her cards.

The false betrothal thing was not going well at all.

'He is indeed a very fast learner,' she murmured, her agile little foot sliding ever higher.

Marco carefully reached down and seized her ankle in his hand, running his fingers over the silk-covered arch. Thalia gasped and bit her lip. 'Not as fast as you, *signorina*.'

The drawing-room door opened, the butler slipping inside to announce, 'Lady Riverton and Mr de Lucca, my lady.'

'My dear Lady Westwood!' Lady Riverton trilled, sweeping in on a wave of blue feathers and musky jasmine scent, her hand on Domenico's arm. 'Do forgive us for being so late. We have come from the theatre.'

'Not at all,' Lady Westwood said, cool but polite. 'We were about to pause for some tea.'

'How lovely,' Lady Riverton said. 'I simply *had* to be here to wish the newly betrothed couple happy. They do seem absolutely made for each other, do they not?'

'I certainly think so,' Marco said, giving her a little bow and a polite smile. In turn she gave him a bland stare, giving away nothing of her knowledge of the cave. Of the dangerous game they had played all the way from Sicily.

'Then we must have a toast to the happy couple,' Lord Westwood said. 'We need champagne!'

'Oh, delightful!' said Lady Riverton, clapping her hands. 'I do adore champagne, and so does Signor de Lucca. Don't you?'

Domenico, too, smiled, but his glance was hard and tense as he stared at Marco and Thalia. '*Natura secondo*, but even more I love a true occasion for it—like a wedding. Though perhaps *prosecco* is more appropriate tonight, as the bridegroom is one of my own countrymen.'

'I fear I have no Italian wines to offer, *signor*,' Lord Westwood said affably. 'Perhaps once Thalia is the Contessa di Fabrizzi she can help me remedy that lack in my cellar.'

'Di Fabrizzi is an ancient name indeed,' Domenico said tightly, his words ever so slightly unfocused. Marco wondered warily if he had been drinking at the theatre. The only thing worse than a hothead was a drunken hothead. He rose smoothly from his chair, moving toward Domenico to stave off any possible outbursts.

Any revelations.

'It is very sad that now it will be so diluted by foreign blood, as so much of my country has been,' Domenico muttered. 'Reduced to sending wine to English cellars, playing at being a *scholar*. Where some of us must…'

Marco seized Domenico's arm in an iron grip. '*Basta,*' he hissed. 'If you have a problem with me, I will meet you on any duelling field you choose. But you will not insult Miss Chase or her family.'

Domenico tried to snatch his arm away, but Marco held fast. Just as he suspected, the unmistakable scent of brandy hung heavy around Domenico. His hair was rumpled, his fine velvet coat wrinkled.

Fool. What had he said to Lady Riverton while he was in his cups? A fine revolutionary he was.

'Oh, so *now* you will fight?' Domenico said sulkily. 'Now when your English *puttana* is insulted…'

Marco's fist came up in a flash, but his wrist was suddenly clasped by soft fingers. He glanced down to see Thalia beside him, drawing him gently but firmly away. At the same moment, Lady Riverton took Domenico's other arm.

'Do forgive him!' she trilled. 'He had a spot of punch at the theatre, and you know how these Neapolitans can be. Come, Signor de Lucca, I am sure Lord Westwood will show you some of his sketches from Greece.'

She drew Domenico away, helped by Lord Westwood. He went willingly enough, but the stare he tossed back at Marco fairly burned.

Thalia's hand tightened on his wrist. 'You would not really duel with him, would you?' she whispered.

He gave her a careless smile. 'Not tonight, *bella.* I will not ruin the celebration of our betrothal.'

She frowned, and he could tell by the flash of her eyes that she had much more to say. But she just shook her head.

'After the card games resume,' she murmured, 'meet me in the upstairs corridor.'

'*Cara*, how very scandalous. Are you trying to hurry along our nuptials?'

But she was not fooled by his banter. She shook his wrist. 'Just do it!'

Then she spun around and stalked away, hurrying to join her sister at the tea table. Lady Westwood whispered urgently in Thalia's ear, glancing toward him.

The Chase soirées were always endlessly entertaining, Marco thought wryly, rubbing at his wrist as if to hold Thalia's touch to his skin. One never knew what might happen. An evening began with a family supper and some innocent card games, and ended with belligerent Neapolitans and trysts in upstairs corridors.

It was almost too tempting, to stay here for ever and see what happened next. Forget what waited for him in Florence, the danger. Even as he well knew he could never turn back now.

Chapter Nineteen

Thalia paced the dark patch of corridor between her chamber door and a pier table, back and forth as she stared toward the top of the stairs. A single lamp at the end of the hallway burned steadily, but its light didn't reach her.

Her mind felt just as shadowed. Why had Lady Riverton shown up here, with Domenico de Lucca of all people? Was he her new pet Italian, since she had lost Marco? Or was there more to it than that—as there must be with Lady Riverton? And why did she seem determined to stay close to them, when by all appearances she had them cornered? She had forced a public betrothal on them, and she still had the silver.

At last Thalia heard the soft sound of footsteps on the stairs. She spun around to see Marco there on the top step, the lamp behind him outlining him in impenetrable darkness.

Thalia ran to him, grabbing his hand and drawing

him with her into her chamber. She closed the door behind them, and they were alone at last in the shadowed heat.

'Thalia, *mia*, we shouldn't be like this in your own house,' he muttered roughly. But she felt his hands clasp tight to her hips, pressing her back against the door. Maybe he felt that irresistible pull, just as she did. That wild need to be together, to touch, to kiss.

A quicksilver thrill shot through her at the thought, the wondrous possibility that he needed her just as she needed him. She went up on tiptoe, looping her arms around his neck. 'It's only for a few minutes,' she whispered. 'I had to be alone with you, to be away from the party. All that silly conversation, everyone watching…'

'Away from Domenico de Lucca? I am sorry he showed up, Thalia. I don't know what the fool was thinking.'

'You won't really duel with him, will you?' Thalia said, suddenly cold at the thought of him wounded. Bleeding. Dying.

'It might be the best way to make him be quiet. Hotheaded, drunken *alloco*.'

'Oh, yes. I certainly don't know any other hot-headed Italian, set on their own course.'

'I am only a hothead around *you*,' he said, and she could hear the grin in his voice.

'Is that so?' she teased. She slid her foot from its slipper, running it up his leg. 'Like now? Or did you like it better when I touched you under the table?'

Marco groaned, his lips swooping down to claim hers in the dark. She met him open-mouthed, eager.

'Or maybe,' she whispered, as his kiss slid to her ear, the arch of her throat, 'you like it when I do *this*.'

She moved her caress down his taut back, pressing to the curve of his buttock beneath the thin wool breeches. His erection leaped against her hip, iron-hard even through her skirts.

'I think maybe you do,' she said, feeling a rush of glorious power. This must be what it was like to be Aphrodite, then!

'*Maledetto*, but you are a fast learner,' he muttered.

'I have an excellent teacher.'

He kissed her again, and any thoughts, any words, shattered and flew away in a hundred shining fragments. She was surrounded by the heat and scent of him, and he was all she knew. All she wanted.

She drove her fingers into his hair, holding tight as their tongues clashed, their hungry mouths mingled. Pressing back against the door, she wrapped her legs around his hips, moulding her body to his until there was not even a breath of air between them.

Through the shimmering mist of desire, she felt him lift her away from the wall, twirling her around until he found her bed in the darkness. She fell back onto the mattress, pulling him down with her.

'*Scusa,*' he gasped. '*Amare*, I'm sorry, but I need you. I need…'

'I need you, too,' she managed to whisper, her breath tight in her throat. She spread her legs as her skirts foamed back, arching to meet him. Her hands fumbled eagerly for the fastening of his breeches.

He pushed her skirts above her waist, his caress skimming over her bare thighs above her stockings. One finger slid slowly inside her wet folds, a hot friction that made her gasp. Her head whirled in a sudden rush of delirious pleasure.

'Do you like it when I touch you here?' he murmured against her ear.

'Yes!' she gasped.

He reached around her with his other hand, pulling up her buttocks as he drove into her body. Binding them together as one.

This time there was no pain at all, only the well-remembered pleasure. The memory of how their bodies fitted, how it felt for him to be with her so completely. She closed her eyes tightly, bracing her feet against the bed as she drove upwards, taking him in even deeper.

He drew back and plunged forwards, every thrust making her sure this was right. This was meant to be.

'Marco!' she cried, as she felt that bubble of pressure deep inside shatter, felt the hot ecstasy fall down on her like a cascade of stars. Like—like…

Fireworks. All white and red, burning hot. Searing away all she had been before, when there was no Marco.

He collapsed on the bed beside her, holding her as the stars faded. As her heartbeat, so frantic, slowed, and a glorious lassitude stole over her.

Thalia reached out in the dark, tracing her trembling fingertips over his brow, his cheek, the taut line of his jaw. Her thumb swept along his damp lips, and his mouth opened, drawing it in deep as he nipped at her fingertip.

She shivered. 'You *won't* duel, will you?' she whispered.

Marco gave a hoarse laugh. '*Cara*, if you intend to stop me fighting like this, I must threaten to duel every day.'

'Marco!' She gave him a shake. 'Tell me.'

'I will not duel. It would accomplish nothing. But if he intends to keep me away from the silver, if he goes on insulting you and your family—I must take action.'

Thalia sat up, shaking her skirts down over her legs. 'You think he is somehow in league with Lady Riverton?'

'I don't know what he is about,' Marco said. She felt him sit up beside her, fastening his breeches and smoothing his no-doubt mangled cravat. 'But I intend to find out.'

'At the fireworks gala?'

'Perhaps. It will be an excellent opportunity, with everyone distracted by the spectacle.'

Thalia knelt down, feeling around on the floor until she found her lost slipper. She slid it on to her foot, smiling secretly. 'Then I can't wait. You do have a way of making parties so much more interesting, Marco.'

'Funny, *bella*,' he answered. 'I was just thinking the same about you.'

Chapter Twenty

Thalia had walked with Marco many times in Sydney Gardens, including the most memorable occasion of their first kiss in the Labyrinth. But now it was so completely transformed she would not have known it. She felt as if she had stepped into a fairyland.

An orchestra played in one of the half-circle stone pavilions, the arches all hung with coloured lanterns that glinted on the gravel walkways and sparkled through the trees. A dance set was forming in the cleared space nearby. Screens decorated with transparencies of various Roman gods stood behind refreshment tables and grotto-like alcoves. Fountains ran generously with wine.

Thalia followed Calliope and Cameron as they made their way to their own seats, greeting all their acquaintances along the way. Everyone was clad in their finest silks and muslins, seemingly in high spirits as the festive atmosphere sparkled in the night sky around them. Even Calliope seemed entirely restored to health, her cheeks rosy again to match her fine Indian cashmere shawl.

'I confess I did not think I would ever enjoy Bath so much!' Calliope said. 'But now I will be sorry to leave it behind when we go back to London next month.'

'We have certainly met with good friends here,' Thalia agreed.

'More than that for you, I think, sister,' Calliope teased. 'For you have found your own future husband! Speaking of which, where is the Count? It does not seem like him to miss a party.'

'Perhaps he is emptying the last of Bath's florists of their wares,' Cameron said, escorting them into their alcove. 'I think there may have been one or two he did not reach this morning.'

Calliope laughed merrily as footmen stepped forwards to pour wine. 'Indeed, we could hardly move in the corridors or the drawing room for all the bouquets he sent! And he had only been apart from Thalia for a few hours. Perhaps you have made a good choice after all, dearest.'

Thalia just smiled at her, sipping at her sweet wine. Yes, she *had* made a good choice—if only she could make it a partnership in truth! Perhaps the flowers were a good sign, but she had heard nothing more of the caves. Of what she could do to help. Her plan to impress Marco, to persuade him to make their betrothal real, did not seem to be going so very well.

As the footmen laid out platters of delicacies for

them, she studied the passing crowd for a glimpse of Marco, or of Lady Riverton or Signor de Lucca. She half-listened as Calliope and her husband laughed tenderly, perfectly contented in their time together.

'Ah, good evening to you, Lord and Lady Westwood, Miss Chase!' Lord Knowleton said, as he and his wife paused by their alcove in the midst of the great promenade.

'Good evening, Lord Knowleton,' Calliope answered. 'Won't you join us for a glass of wine? We did not have time at our card party to get caught up on all the doings of the Antiquities Society.'

'Indeed, it has been too long since you were all with us in town,' Lady Knowleton said, as everyone shifted to make room.

'It has been delightful to see you here in Bath,' Calliope said. 'Though I hope it is not because of ill health that you are here.'

'Indeed not,' Lord Knowleton said. 'I have come on an errand for the Society, though I fear there is not much yet to tell of it.'

'It has been a secret even from me!' Lady Knowleton said with a laugh. 'Though I have enjoyed the chance to take the waters. Perhaps you will join us for tea tomorrow, Lady Westwood? Miss Chase?'

'We would be delighted, wouldn't we, Thalia?' Calliope said.

'Oh, of course,' Thalia said, her mind racing. Was Lord Knowleton's 'errand' something to do with the silver? Hopefully she would be able to discover more tomorrow, discover something that would be of use to Marco.

But she did not have long to scheme. They were interrupted by Domenico de Lucca, who stopped to bow next to their alcove.

'Lord and Lady Westwood, Miss Chase,' he said, with a charming smile. 'Please, you must allow me to apologise for my behaviour at your party. I have no excuse, except that your English wine is stronger than I expected! I hope you will let me make amends.'

Calliope frowned at him doubtfully. 'Certainly I accept your apology, *signor*. But it was my *sister's* betrothal party.'

Domenico turned to Thalia with another bow. 'Then I hope that you will do me the great honour of dancing with me, Signorina Chase,' he said, with that bright, guileless smile. 'To show that we are truly friends now. That there are no—how do you say?—hard feelings.'

Thalia hesitated, glancing past him to the crowd of dancers. She still did not like Domenico de Lucca; he alternated far too easily between hotheaded revolutionary and smooth social charmer. She could read nothing from his smile, from the cool surface of his handsome blue eyes.

On the other hand, it seemed he was friends with Lady Riverton now. He might know something useful she could possibly glean from him. Or perhaps he could at least tell her more of Marco's life in Italy. Of his home, his friends, his work—his women. All the things he hid from her behind his charming smiles.

'Of course,' she said, rising from her chair. 'I would not wish to quarrel with an old friend of my fiancé. If my sister can spare me for a few moments.'

Calliope gave her an uncertain look, clearly torn between playing stern chaperon and conversing further with the Knowletons. 'Of course, my dear, if you would like to dance. Just remember supper will be served soon.'

'I will.' Thalia stepped out of the alcove to take Domenico's proffered arm. His muscles were tense beneath her light touch, and up close she could see the taut lines at the edge of his smile. A few moist beads dotted his brow, despite the mild evening.

It made her feel tense, as well, and she looked around in hopes of glimpsing Marco at last. But he was still nowhere to be seen, and neither was Lady Riverton. The whole garden seemed suddenly dark, the glisten of the lamps dismal, the trees and whimsically shaped hedges encroaching on the brilliant gathering like a green-black net.

As they took their places in the new set, she took a deep breath and said, 'I understand you have become good friends with Viscountess Riverton, *signor*.'

He smiled at her, that strange, taut, too-bright smile. 'She is well known in my country as a great patron of the arts.'

A patron. Well, that was one way of looking at it, Thalia supposed. The first strains of the music sounded, and she curtsied before stepping forwards to take his hand. 'Did you know her before you came to Bath?'

'Only by reputation.'

'And do you find that she lives up to that—reputation?'

He shot her a puzzled glance. 'Most assuredly. Her appreciation for antiquities is unparalleled. Except, of course, for your own family.'

'My family?'

'The Chase Muses are known throughout Italy, *signorina*, surely you know that.'

'I did not know that,' Thalia said. 'It is certainly gratifying, though also rather mystifying.'

'There is nothing mysterious about it. Beautiful young ladies who are also great scholars—it is a rarity. And now that I have met you and Lady Westwood, I see the stories were not at all exaggerated. The Count is a most fortunate man.'

They were separated by the figures of the dance, other couples swirling between them. When they joined hands again, Thalia said, 'You have known the Count a long time, I understand.'

His jaw twitched, yet still he went on smiling. Just as she did. Smiling until she was sure her face would crack. 'Since we were schoolboys. We have always had much in common, though he was always a greater scholar than I. I've always wanted to *do*, and he wanted to read! To think.'

'Yet which will serve better in the end?' Thalia murmured. 'Learning, or bloodshed?'

She thought she could not be heard over the music, but he gave her an angry glance, quickly covered by that smile. 'That is for you to decide, *signorina*, for is the Count not to be your husband now? But I hope that you, with all your own learning, can persuade him to be true to his country. To his great heritage.'

'I believe that his "heritage" is always uppermost in Marco's thoughts,' she answered. 'He wants what is best for his home, for his people. Surely you know that, being of long acquaintance with him?'

'Once, I did think I knew him well enough. I even thought he might marry my cousin, Maria, another young lady of learning and spirit. Much like you, Signorina Chase.'

'What?' Thalia whispered. Marco had been betrothed before? Had loved a young lady, an Italian lady, before? And was this mysterious Maria one of the sources of the quarrel between Marco and Domenico?

It was just one more thing she did not really know about him.

'He was engaged to your cousin?' she said.

'I fear it did not have time to go so far as that. Maria died most tragically, when she was still quite young.' He smiled at her sadly as they turned in the dance. 'So, my old friend is most fortunate to find you now, *signorina*. He seems very fond of you.'

Fond. Such a tepid little word for what happened between them in the secret darkness of the night. For what she felt for him, hidden deep in her own heart.

But was all that enough? Enough to turn a false betrothal into a real one at last?

'We are looking forward to a long future together,' was all she said.

'A future in Florence?' he said. 'Or perhaps Marco now plans to stay here in England. A trained Italian lapdog for your family.'

An edge of steel had invaded Domenico's polite tone at last. Thalia glanced at him, startled, to find that those blue eyes had taken on a strange new glow.

'I doubt anyone could make a lapdog of Marco,' she said slowly.

'Ah, I think you underestimate your own charms, Signorina Chase,' he answered. 'I think you could very easily make him forget all he owes his own country.'

The music ended with a flourish, and Thalia quickly turned to leave the dance floor. He grabbed her arm in a tight, implacable grasp, holding her fast. The tiny, cold needle of jealousy she had felt when he had told her of the lost Maria turned to an icy flood of frozen apprehension. She felt suddenly foolish for agreeing to dance with him, to listen to him at all.

She tugged at her arm, but he held fast, dragging her closer to him as he drew her to the edge of the crowd.

'Indeed, I think we have *both* underestimated the hold you have over him,' Domenico muttered. 'I should have seen it all before.'

'Let go of me!' she cried. She tried to kick out at him, but her silk skirts wrapped around her legs, hampering her.

And then she felt a sharp prick against the bare skin of her arm, just above the top edge of her glove. She glanced down to see he held a small but lethal-looking dagger, the point of it pressed tight against her.

'Come now, Signorina Chase, do not make such a fuss,' he muttered. 'Come along with me, and I promise you no one will be hurt. I only want Marco to listen to reason. Once he does that, you will be safely back with your family.' He tugged hard again on her arm, throwing her off balance and dangerously near that blade. 'A family that includes a little baby, *si*? Babies can be so very vulnerable.'

Thalia gaped at him in mounting fury and—and fear. 'Are you threatening my niece?'

'*Signorina*! I, unlike the many brutal invaders of my country, would not harm innocent *bambinas*. But so much peril awaits those who are unwary in the world. And those who do not co-operate when it is in their best interests. My English is not so good, Signorina Chase, but I do hope I have made my point.'

He had made it all too well. Come with him, be bait for Marco, or this wild-eyed crazy man would hurt her niece.

In a hot panic, Thalia looked back, but they had gone too far from the bright crowd. She could see no one, nothing, at all.

There was a sudden explosion overhead, the promised fireworks shattering in a thousand glittering red-and-green pieces. As everyone's awed attention swung upwards, Domenico dragged her away into the cover of the trees.

Thalia tore off her necklace, an Etruscan gold-

and-garnet pendant on a gold chain that had once been her mother's. It pained her to leave it behind, but she forced herself to drop it at the edge of the gravel walkway. Hopefully Marco or her sister would find it, would know she had not gone willingly.

Once they were off the pathway, she dropped the matching bracelet and, a little way further, stepped on the white satin flounce on her hem, tearing part of it away.

'You are too damnably slow,' Domenico growled. He pulled so hard on her arm that Thalia cried out, certain it was wrenched from its socket.

'I can hardly run!' she protested. 'I am wearing dancing slippers.'

'Maledetto!' He swung around, and Thalia saw his fist come up in an arc towards her jaw.

It was the very last thing she saw before she collapsed into darkness.

Chapter Twenty-One

The fireworks display had already begun when Marco arrived at Sydney Gardens. He had intended to be much earlier, to dance with Thalia, snatch a quiet moment to talk to her about all that had happened in the last few momentous days. But a packet of long-delayed letters had arrived from Florence as he was leaving, claiming his attention.

It seemed an armed uprising was not a figment of Domenico de Lucca's fevered imagination, but a fact. The garrison at Naples was making plans—plans that would surely set his own hard work back for years. He had to return to Naples, as soon as possible.

And he could not take Thalia with him, not now. It was far too dangerous, even for an intrepid soul like her. But perhaps, if he was persuasive, he could ask her to wait for him.

Those were the thoughts that lay on him so heavily as he hurried through the Gardens. The orchestra played a rousing chorus as the fireworks arced overhead, their explosions deafening as blossoms and stars and dragons of green, gold, and fiery red took form and dispersed in a puff of smoke. The faces of the crowd were turned upwards in awed contemplation, the lights gleaming off their diamonds and pearls, their fine silks.

But Thalia was not among them. Marco glimpsed her sister sitting in one of the alcoves, and he turned his steps toward her.

That was when he saw Lady Riverton. She stood in the shadows of another alcove, one tucked away from the glow of the transparencies, but the tall white plumes of her ever-present turban were unmistakable.

She was talking to a tall, heavyset man whose dark clothes helped him blend more effectively with the night. Marco might not have seen him at all if not for the pale glow of his gloved hand reaching out to touch Lady Riverton's arm. Her face was solemn as she nodded at whatever he was saying.

Marco crept closer to the alcove, straining to hear their words above the boom of the fireworks. They spoke too softly, but he saw to his surprise that her companion was none other than the eminently respectable Lord Knowleton, the leader of the Antiquities Society.

What was she doing with him, of all people? Lord Knowleton and the Antiquities Society had the highest reputation among collectors and scholars, a defender of learning, of proper excavation and importation.

The Chases were prominent members of the Society themselves, as was Clio's new husband, the Duke of Averton. None of them could be involved in Lady Riverton's criminal ring, surely.

But then again, Marco feared he could no longer be surprised by anything at all. Not when it involved human greed.

'…do not know,' he heard Lady Riverton say as he edged closer. 'If you say that he does not…'

An especially loud explosion snapped overhead, distracting the two of them from their conversation. And Marco suddenly glimpsed Lady Westwood hurrying through the crowd, glancing about as if frantically searching for something. Or someone.

Marco abandoned the alcove, hurrying towards Lady Westwood as Lord Knowleton, too, slipped out and melted into the crowd.

'Lady Westwood,' Marco said with a bow. 'May I be of assistance?'

'Count di Fabrizzi!' she answered, turning to him with anxious eyes. 'I am so very glad to see you. Have you by any chance seen Thalia since your arrival?'

'I fear not,' he said with a frown. 'I have only just arrived, and I was hoping to find her with you.'

'She went to dance with Signor de Lucca. I should not have let her after his terrible behaviour at our card party, yet he did seem to be apologetic! So eager to make amends.'

Marco froze. 'She went off to dance with de Lucca?'

Lady Westwood nodded. 'And I fear she has not

come back, even though the dance is long ended. My husband has gone to search for her.'

'And he has found nothing of her at all?' Marco asked intently. The whole brilliant gathering, the letters he had received earlier, everything faded away and the world sharpened to one single point. Thalia. His darling, his love.

And the fact that she was gone. Vanished—after dancing with Domenico de Lucca.

For an instant, he wanted to shake her sister, to demand to know how she could have let Thalia be with such a man for even a moment! Yet he knew such anger could accomplish nothing at all. Lady Westwood knew nothing about Domenico, about the past. It was he, Marco, who should have been guarding Thalia.

'My husband did find this,' she said shakily, holding out her hand. On her gloved palm was an antique gold-and-garnet pendant on a broken chain. 'It was our mother's. Thalia was wearing it tonight.'

'Where did he find it?' Marco said, staring down at the necklace, at the broken gold links that looked as if they had been violently snapped. In the lamplight, the garnets gleamed dully, like fresh blood.

'Over there, where the gravel walkways disappear into the trees.'

'And what else was she wearing?'

Lady Westwood blinked hard, as if her mind was too full of mounting fear to remember such mundanities. Then she shook her head, and the fierceness he remembered from long ago in Yorkshire shone through. 'A pink silk gown with white satin flounces. A gold bandeau in her hair. And a bracelet that matches the pendant. But she has no warm shawl with her, and only thin dancing slippers. What if…?'

Marco nodded grimly. What if indeed. A cold calm overtook his mind, and he knew what he had to do. He reached out and gently closed her fingers over the broken necklace.

'Go home, *signora*, and see if Thalia has returned there,' he said gently. 'Soon, a man will come to keep watch by your door. He will look rough, but please do not be alarmed. Let him know at once if you have word of Thalia, or if your husband finds anything else.' He lightly touched her hand. 'And keep a close eye on your daughter.'

'On Psyche?' she gasped. 'What is happening here? Do you know where my sister is?'

'I soon will. And I promise you, I will keep her safe.'

Lady Westwood's eyes narrowed as she held the necklace tightly in her fist. 'I knew she was not safe with you at all! I let myself be persuaded by her own feelings for you, but after Yorkshire…'

'Lady Westwood, *favore*!' Marco took her by the arms, giving her a gentle shake. 'You can hate me all you like—later. Right now, I need your help. Domenico de Lucca is an unpredictable man, I must find Thalia as quickly as possible. Please, go home now and watch for her.'

She looked very much as if she longed to argue with him, to demand he do as *she* said. It was obvious that fiery stubbornness was a Chase family trait. But at last she gave an abrupt nod, backing away from him.

'I will do as you ask,' she said, 'but only because you obviously know far more about all this than I do, and time is of the essence. If something happens to my sister, though, there will be no corner of the world where you can hide from me!'

He gave her a bow, then spun around and strode towards the spot where the necklace had been found. If something happened to Thalia, there was no place where he could hide from *himself*. He had put her in danger, like a selfish fool who was too besotted to stay away. But he would get her out, send her safely back to her family…

And then leave her alone, even if it cost him his own reckless heart.

Calliope paced the length of the drawing room floor and back again, Psyche held tightly in her arms. Outside the windows, where Marco's guard lurked, the night seemed very black indeed, thick and ominous. Even the baby was quiet, her tiny fingers in her mouth as she stared at her mother solemnly.

'Oh, my darling,' Calliope murmured. 'I hope that when you are older I am a far better chaperon!'

Just the thought of her beautiful, dark-haired baby being a beautiful young woman, going out into the world, gave her a terrible pang. All the dangers that waited for her, just as they had for Calliope and her sisters.

Especially, it seemed, for beautiful, impulsive, generous-hearted Thalia.

'I should have been more careful,' Calliope whispered. She had sensed when she talked with Marco that there was more going on here in Bath than met the eye, that he was involved in some scheme, just as in Yorkshire between him and Clio. But she also sensed that he truly cared for Thalia. And she *knew* Thalia cared about him. Too much.

Whenever Thalia talked about Marco, Calliope remembered herself when she fell in love with Cameron de Vere. She had known back then that Cam meant trouble, that he would entirely overset her tidy little world, but she hadn't stayed away from him. She couldn't. Now, they had a wonderful life together with their little girl. Not even the bumpy path of their courtship, or the terrible time she had giving birth to Psyche, could take that away. She and Cam were always meant to be together.

And Thalia's eyes shone when she spoke of Marco di Fabrizzi. She always lit up when he came into the room. Calliope couldn't take that from her sister, not when she and all the Chases feared Thalia would never meet her match.

But Calliope had underestimated the dangers. She had failed to thoroughly investigate Marco, to find out what he had been doing since Yorkshire. Had given in too soon to Thalia's pleading. Now her sister was paying the price.

Outside the windows a light drizzle of rain started

to come down, a cold patter against the glass. The stars overhead were completely obscured by dark clouds. Somewhere out there, in the chilly damp, her sister and her husband wandered.

'Please, let them be safe,' Calliope whispered. 'Let them be safe, and I vow I will be the strictest chaperon that ever was seen!'

Psyche squealed in protest, and Calliope bounced her against her shoulder, not even noticing the mess on her satin gown.

'That is right, my darling daughter,' she said. 'You will feel the effects of Mama's new-found caution. You will never be alone with a man until you are married! Your aunt thinks I never noticed her sneaking off in the middle of parties and such. There will be none of that for *you*.'

Psyche's little face crinkled, as if she was preparing for one of her already-legendary tantrums. But then she just grabbed Calliope's necklace of jade beads and popped it into her mouth.

As Calliope turned back to the window, she glimpsed a swirl of movement in the gloom. She frowned, peering closer. A man in a dark greatcoat and hat, and a woman enveloped in a cloak approached the house, stopped by Marco's guard. It seemed they had some business here, for he let them pass to the front door.

She spun away from the window, clutching Psyche as she dashed to the drawing-room door. She hurried on to the landing just as the butler answered the knock.

'Lord Knowleton and Lady Riverton to see Lady Westwood,' said the man in the greatcoat. 'It is most urgent.'

Calliope stared at them in shock. Lord Knowleton, her father's old friend—and Lady Riverton? The head of the Antiquities Society and the woman Clio had written from Sicily to warn her about? It was a topsy-turvy night indeed. She hardly knew what to think or do any longer, a first in her responsible life as the eldest Chase Muse.

She longed to shout out to them, to demand any news they had of Thalia. But the footmen and maids were hanging about the edges of the foyer, waiting eagerly for any titbits of gossip. She went back to the drawing room to wait for them, ringing the bell to summon Psyche's nurse.

The woman came to take the baby just as Lord Knowleton and Lady Riverton were shown in. Calliope waited until her daughter was gone before rounding on them.

'What is happening here?' she demanded. 'I know that you, Lady Riverton, are friends with Signor de Lucca. Why has he taken my sister? What scheme are you involved in?'

'Please, my dear Lady Westwood,' Lord Knowleton said. 'Please hear us out.'

He looked in silence to Lady Riverton, who slowly folded back her hood. Every time Calliope had seen her in Bath, she had had a merry, brittle smile on her face, a determined social sparkle and flirtatious demeanor. Not to mention some sort of young, handsome, inappropriate escort.

But now she had changed her silk gown and jewels, her feathered turban, for a plain wool walking dress and cloak, her hair brushed smooth into a grey-streaked brown knot. She looked very serious, and every bit her age.

'We think, Lady Westwood,' she said slowly, 'that de Lucca has taken your sister to force Count di Fabrizzi to join in an armed uprising in Naples. Or perhaps in retaliation for the Count's refusal to engage in such foolhardy actions.'

'What!' Calliope cried. 'An armed uprising?' This was even worse than she feared.

'My dear, do not be alarmed,' Lord Knowleton said hastily. 'We have many people out searching for Miss Chase. She will certainly be found very soon.'

'And unharmed,' Lady Riverton added. 'It would not be in de Lucca's interest to harm her. If he does, the Count will most certainly kill him, and that will be two less soldiers for their army.'

'I ask you again,' Calliope demanded, 'what do you know of all this? My sister has written to me of what happened in Santa Lucia. Why should I believe what you say?'

'Lady Riverton works for the Antiquities Society,' Lord Knowleton said gently. 'She has for many years now, helping us to retrieve lost artefacts of the most important and sensitive nature.'

'My latest task has been to retrieve a Hellenistic

silver altar set,' Lady Riverton said. 'Perhaps your sister has told you of it.'

Calliope sat down hard on the nearest couch, her head spinning. Soldiers, uprisings? Lady Riverton secretly an agent of the Antiquities Society? It was a great deal to absorb in only a few moments.

'I have heard something of it, yes,' she murmured. 'But perhaps you had best start at the beginning.'

Lady Riverton sat down beside her. 'I did so hate deceiving your family in Santa Lucia. They were so very concerned about the silver, rightly so. But the local *tombaroli*, not to mention the English collectors, were utterly ruthless. If they had even a hint that I had an ulterior motive in trying to buy the artefacts from them—it would have all been over.'

'Not even your brother-in-law the Duke could know about her when she went to Sicily,' Lord Knowleton said.

'My late husband used to work for the Society in Naples,' said Lady Riverton. 'I wanted to continue his cause, and the guise of greedy collector has served me very well.' She gave a harsh laugh. 'I fear it has rather hurt my popularity with the Viscount's old friends, though!'

Calliope bit her lip, thinking of all the harsh things she and her sisters had said about Lady Riverton. 'What does this have to do with Thalia?'

'I am not the only one who wants the silver,' Lady Riverton said. 'Fabrizzi and de Lucca, too, are after it for their own ends. Not to mention those thugs back in Santa Lucia and their Neapolitan cohorts. It seemed safest to hide it here in Bath, until it could be taken to the Antiquities Society and safely locked up. But Marco was quite unceasing in his efforts to unmask me—and twice as bad with your sister on his side! I see the Chase spirit is not overrated.'

Calliope had to smile at that. 'Thalia is the most spirited of all, I fear.'

'Spirited enough to provoke de Lucca to violence?' Lord Knowleton asked.

'Probably,' Calliope said. 'She is certainly not one to go meekly to her fate.'

'Then we must find her,' Lady Riverton said grimly. 'Soon.'

Chapter Twenty-Two

Thalia slowly blinked her eyes open. They felt gritty, as if glued shut with sand. Her mouth was dry, and her head throbbed. Surely she had not been drinking to such excess! What had she been doing last night, anyway? And why was her bed so hard?

She sat up gingerly, holding her head between her hands. To her shock, she was not in her own room at all. She was stretched out on a hard stone floor, her silk gown tattered and dirty, her gloves gone and her bare arms bumpy with cold and aching with bruises.

Then, like a burst of the party fireworks, she remembered. Domenico de Lucca had kidnapped her from the gala! He had knocked her out, and brought her—where?

She rubbed hard at her eyes, looking around cautiously. It was very dark, but gradually she saw that she was in a limestone cave. Probably the same one where she and Marco had found the artefacts, though now it was bare of crates. Bare of anything at all save one flickering torch.

And, far away, that tall pillar of rough stone that rose up in the middle of the cold space. No doubt it was that witch, turned into limestone for her wicked deeds yet still able to cast terrible spells. Gain awful revenge.

Thalia hardly dared to breathe. What if Domenico waited in those shadows, ready to pounce on her and pound her senseless again? Or, almost worse, what if she was all alone, with no way out of this terrible place?

A bubble of panic rose up inside of her, but she forced it back down. Mindless panic would get her nowhere now, and certainly it wouldn't get her out of the cave. She had to stay calm, to assess the situation in a rational manner, as her sisters surely would.

Even if her first instinct *was* to dash away shrieking like a pantomime *ingénue*.

She pushed herself slowly to her feet, ignoring the painful twinges of those bruises, the ache of lying too long on a cold stone floor. Her hair fell in tangled curls over her shoulders, her bandeau and pins gone along with her gloves. But she still wore her mother's Etruscan earrings, and she remembered leaving the necklace and bracelet behind.

'Oh, Marco, I do hope you found them,' she whispered. 'And I hope they lead you here. Soon.'

And that Domenico was not coming back. Perhaps he had just stashed her in the cave before going off to find more villainy elsewhere. Or maybe he had gone to meet Lady Riverton, so the two of them could have a fine laugh over their evil deeds before coupling like rabbits.

The repulsive thought somehow gave Thalia a renewed burst of strength. She turned toward a faint gleam of light down a short, narrow corridor, hoping it was the cave's entrance. She took one careful step in front of the other on the uneven floor. Her thin slippers were not made for rough stone, but the more she moved the less she ached. Her steps grew surer, quicker, carrying her toward that faint light.

Until she found her exit blocked by Domenico.

He sat on an empty crate by the wall, beyond the witch's pillar and near the narrow entrance, calmly smoking a cigar, as if he kidnapped ladies every day. His cravat and coat were gone, his shirt and waistcoat streaked with dirt, his pale hair tousled. A long scratch marred his cheek, left there when he had tussled with Thalia in the Gardens. She couldn't help but feel a bit of pride at that.

He smiled at her, and she braced her feet solidly to the floor as if she could fight him off.

'My dear Signorina Chase,' he said. 'I see that you are awake at last.'

'I don't know what you hope to accomplish by kidnapping me,' she said, crossing her arms. It was even chillier here near the entrance, the wind sharp through her battered silk gown. But even more, she was frozen by the dead, flat expression in Domenico's eyes. Like a winter lake. He cared not what he did, or who got hurt. He was seized in the vise of his fanatical cause.

'We will soon be followed here,' she said.

'Oh, I am counting on that!' he said cheerfully. 'That is exactly why I brought you here. To make Marco come here, far from the distractions of town, and listen to me. He is making a great fool of himself over you, *signorina*, but perhaps you do have your uses after all.'

'Like Lady Riverton? All women have their uses, so you latch on to a share of her villainy.'

He frowned at her through the silvery smoke of his cigar, as if puzzled by her words. 'Riverton? She has taken me into society, that is all. If you English define villainy as going to parties…'

Thalia shook her head. Lady Riverton hardly mattered at the moment. One lunatic to deal with at a time was quite enough.

'Then what is it you want Marco to hear so much?' she asked. She sat down on a nearby boulder, suddenly weary and aching again. She had to get out of here soon, before she fell over!

Domenico's frown deepened, and he ground out the cigar. 'We were once friends, of one mind on the only important thing in life.'

'To get the Austrians out of Italy?'

'To see our country free of *all* you plague of foreigners! Even people like your family, Signorina Chase.'

'My family? What have they ever done to you, except work to preserve history?'

'They swoop in like beasts, carrying off vases and statues, bits of a culture that does not belong to them!'

'And Marco writes pamphlets about such things, bringing your country many staunch allies—like my father. Marco has hardly abandoned you.'

'Of course he has. He has become like a cautious old man. Once, he would have joined in battle in an instant, anything to see our cause fulfilled. Now he calls me wild, hotheaded. A fool.'

'Do anything—such as kidnap an innocent woman?'

'You are hardly innocent, *signorina*. You and your plague of sisters, meddling in things that do not concern you. Writing, digging in the dirt in Sicily, when you should be tending your house. It is your fault Marco has turned his back on us when we need him most.'

'I refuse to listen to your blathering for a moment longer,' Thalia said, jumping to her feet. 'You are the one who will not see reality! You belong in Bedlam, not among rational people. And you are not fit to wipe Marco's boots. I think you know that, and *that* is the problem.'

She ran toward the entrance, her whole body aching, her feet on fire, hoping against hope she could somehow make it past him. Make it out into the darkness of the night where he could not find her.

But he grabbed her before she could even set foot outside, his arms like steel around her waist, swinging her off her feet. Thalia screamed as loud as she could, twisting around to pull at his hair, claw at his eyes, try to reopen that old scratch. Anything to get him to let her go.

'Fattucchiera!' he shouted in raw fury. He dropped her to the hard floor.

For an instant, all the breath was knocked from Thalia's lungs, and she couldn't see from the white flash of pain. But she tried to roll away, to curl herself into a defensive ball.

Domenico threw himself on top of her, pinning one of her wrists to the stone like a vise. He reached for her other hand, but growing up running around the countryside with a wild pack of sisters had taught her something of fighting. She grabbed on to a thick lock of his hair, pulling hard as she raised her knee towards his groin.

Growling in anger, he evaded her jab and pinned down her other wrist. His weight held her flat to the cold floor, and she was sure she would suffocate. Drown in the acrid scent of sweat and insanity.

'You will pay for that,' he said. 'For everything.'

Thalia tossed her head to the side, closing her eyes tightly as she tried frantically to think. To get out of that sticky web of fear.

Suddenly, Domenico was gone from atop her, the cold night air rushing over her body. Her eyes flew open. For a moment, she saw only a blurry haze. Then the light came back, and she saw that Marco had dragged her attacker away.

'Porca vacca!' Marco shouted, his fists raining a hailstorm of fierce blows down on to Domenico.

Thalia scrambled to her feet, running to the edge of the cave where once they had spied on Lady

Riverton. Now, Marco and Domenico were locked in mortal combat, like a pair of ancient wrestlers on a Grecian vase.

Yet this was not some ritual of combat, distant and beautiful on a smooth pottery vase or fresco. This was all too real, ugly and furious, the smell of sweat and blood thick in the air. Thalia glanced around desperately for a weapon of her own, something to bash Domenico over the head with, but there was nothing at all. Just that one torch in its sconce.

Lady Riverton and her cohorts had cleaned up all too well.

She pressed herself hard against the wall, staring in growing horror at the scene before her.

'I will never let you hurt another woman,' Marco said roughly in Italian, pinning one of Domenico's arms behind his back. 'Never come near Thalia again!'

'*Maledetto!* She is not important, she never was. I would rather they were all dead! All cursed Englishwomen. Though after feeling her tits against me, I can see where she has some use—'

A sickening crunch ended his coarse words abruptly. He collapsed forwards to the floor, coughing weakly before lying very still.

Marco straightened away from him, his face streaked with blood from a deep gash on his forehead. He looked at Thalia, breathing heavily.

'*Cara,*' he said, 'are you hurt?'

Thalia mutely shook her head. Everything seemed to vibrate in the sudden silence. 'You—you…' she said.

But she could say nothing more. Domenico rose with a great roar, lunging towards Marco. Startled, Marco ducked to one side, fists raised. Domenico tumbled past him, falling headfirst into the witch's limestone pillar.

This time when he fell, he did not rise again. A thick swath of blood stained the rock—the witch's vengeance at last, on the man who hated all women. Or maybe just Englishwomen.

Marco knelt beside him, pressing his fingers to Domenico's outflung wrist. *'Scusa,'* he muttered, shaking his head.

Thalia's breath, which she had been holding so tightly, escaped in a great rush. She dashed towards Marco, throwing herself into his arms, sobbing.

'You found me!' she said, kissing his cheek, his lips. Holding on to him as if he were a beautiful dream sure to slip away.

'I found you,' he whispered, cradling her against him. *'Grazie, grazie.'* He drew back, holding her face between his hands as he studied her closely. He gently traced her cheekbone with his thumb, as lightly as if she were rare porcelain. 'But you *are* hurt. This bruise…'

'It doesn't matter, not one whit,' Thalia said, turning her face to kiss his palm. 'You're here now. We're together, we're safe.'

'Safe?' he muttered. 'I should take you home, *bella*. You need to see a doctor, and your sister will be frantic with worry. As I was.'

'Poor Cal.' Thalia suddenly remembered Domenico's ugly threats, and a cold bolt of fear shot through her. 'Psyche!'

'They are all well, I promise. Come, let us go. We should find the other searchers nearby.'

She nodded, suddenly so very weak and exhausted. And why did she keep shivering so? It was ridiculous, now that she was safe!

Marco hastily removed his coat and wrapped it close around her. Even torn and dusty, it was deliciously warm, its superfine folds smelling of *him*. He swept her up into his arms, carrying her out of that terrible place.

At the entrance, she started to glance back. 'No, *cara*,' he said, gentle but firm. 'Don't look. Don't even think about it ever again.'

Thalia buried her face against his shoulder. She did not look, and yet it was all still there in her mind. The terrible suffocation of Domenico's body on hers; his corpse crumpled on to the stone floor. The coppery smell of blood and fear.

Would she ever be free of it again?

Marco cradled Thalia close in his arms as he carried her carefully along the rocky path. She had fallen into an exhausted sleep, her head on his shoulder. She was alive, safe. But his heart was far from at peace.

Thalia was the bravest woman—nay, the bravest person he had ever met. She stood up for what she believed, for what she loved, even in the face of danger. She had a valiant heart, a warrior spirit, and he loved that about her with a passion that grew and grew every time he saw her.

He loved *her*. Loved her in a way he had never thought possible. She brought a light into his life he had never had, and his heart was full of her. He was complete whenever she smiled at him.

Marco kissed her brow gently, and she sighed and shifted in his arms. She was his angel—he had known that from the first time he had seen her in Santa Lucia, though he fought hard against it now.

Now he saw, once again, that he was right to fight against those feelings. His life, his work, had put her in danger tonight. When he saw her being brutalised by Domenico de Lucca, a burning, hellish fury had overcome him! And also a cold fear.

What would his life be without Thalia? It would be not worth even a single breath. And that was why he had to take care of her now. To let her go, as he had resolved before.

Near the bottom of the hill, he saw the glow of torches through the trees. The rescue party, waiting to take Thalia back into her own safe world.

Marco kissed her again, one last time. 'I love you, *bella*,' he whispered. Even if it was far better for her he never said it aloud.

Chapter Twenty-Three

'I can scarcely believe it!' Thalia cried. 'Are you quite sure, Cal?'

'Oh, yes,' Calliope answered, tucking the bedclothes closer around Thalia. 'Lord Knowleton came here with her himself and explained it all.'

'Oh, my. Well, then, it seems Lady Riverton has quite missed her true calling. She should be treading the boards at Drury Lane.' Thalia leaned back against her pillows, her head spinning at the revelation that Lady Riverton had been working for the Antiquities Society the whole time, even in Santa Lucia. 'I was completely fooled by her.'

'I think Clio was, too, and *she* is definitely not someone to be easily taken in.'

Thalia laughed. 'Unlike poor, gullible me?'

'Certainly not! I don't think our parents raised us to be fools, do you?'

'Never. But I suppose we do sometimes tend to see what we want to see.'

'And once we have an idea in our heads, it is nearly impossible to shake it out again,' Calliope said. 'Such great stubbornness nearly ruined my romance with Cam before it even started!'

'That would have been terrible indeed,' Thalia said. 'You two are so obviously made for each other.'

'Perhaps we are. No one else would put up with either one of us.' Calliope paused, carefully smoothing the edge of the blanket. 'Is that how it is between you and Count di Fabrizzi, Thalia?'

'I think…' Thalia sighed. She hardly knew how it was now. It seemed her efforts to make their betrothal real had failed in a spectacular fashion. She didn't know what to do next. 'I thought so once. I thought he was exactly what I was waiting for, someone so intelligent and exciting.'

'Someone handsome beyond belief?'

Thalia laughed with her sister. 'That, too, of course. But he seemed to truly understand me, as no one ever had, or ever even tried to. And I understood him. I—well, I thought we could make a life together. A good one, where we could work together for a common cause.'

'And now?'

'Now I simply do not know. It's been two days since the caves, and I have not seen him again since he brought me home.'

'He sends flowers every day,' Calliope said, gesturing to a bouquet of white roses on the bedside table.

'Flowers with no letter.'

'Perhaps he does not know what to say, and he doesn't want to hurt you any more.'

Something in Calliope's tone made Thalia glance at her sharply. 'Why would he think that? The fact that Domenico de Lucca was insane was scarcely Marco's fault. I know *he* would never hurt me!'

'Dearest Thalia, just the fact that he believes in the causes he does will bring him into contact with fanatics like de Lucca. Even though he himself is a scholar…'

'A great scholar! Even Clio and Father admire him.'

'Of course. I am only saying that perhaps this terrible incident has made him want to protect you.'

'By staying away?' Thalia said. 'But that only hurts me further.'

'I know, dearest. Men are—strange.'

'To say the least,' Thalia muttered. Marco was the strangest of all! She could not read him at all.

Calliope reached for her hand. 'Thalia, none of us want to see you in danger again.'

'I won't be. I assure you, Cal, I have learned caution from all of this. I will not be fooled by the likes of de Lucca again, and not by Lady Riverton, either. The only thing that could possibly hurt me would be if Marco leaves. He can't turn his back on all we have, he simply can't!'

'I see, then. You do love him.'

'I do. So very much. He is perfect for me! Just as

you love Cameron, or Clio loves the Duke. I would a million times rather face danger with him than sit safely here by myself.' If only he would give her that chance. If she could make him see!

Calliope nodded thoughtfully. 'And danger can come even then.'

'Yes,' Thalia murmured, thinking of Calliope's pale face after Psyche was born. And of how her sister would never trade her family to be 'safe'. 'But we will always have each other to see us through. That's the most important thing.'

'Oh, my dear. You are certainly a Chase Muse.' Calliope kissed Thalia's forehead, rising from her seat by the bed. 'I have some errands to see to. You will rest now, yes?'

'I am tired of resting. I have done nothing *but* rest for two days!'

'And the doctor said you must not get up until Friday at the earliest. Then you can go and take the waters, it will do you good.'

Thalia laughed. 'Or finish me off for certain.'

'I will send up some tea instead of water, then. If you promise to rest.'

'Very well. For you, Cal.'

Calliope kissed her again and hurried out of the room, leaving Thalia alone in her bed. She slid down under the bedclothes, rolling over onto her side in the silence. The house was *too* quiet; it seemed Psyche even held her tongue in deference to Thalia's 'illness'. Everyone tiptoed about as if she were an elderly invalid.

The fact was, the scrapes and bruises were fading, and she hardly ached at all now. It was that dratted quiet that was driving her crazy. All that time to think. To remember the dank cave, the terror of it all.

Time to ponder what Marco was thinking now. Why he stayed away. What she had done wrong.

After a while, she heard the carriage draw up on the street below. Thalia wondered where Calliope was off to, the Pump Room or the shops, and wished she could go with her. Anything to escape the quiet.

She must have drifted into sleep, for when she opened her eyes again the light at the window was a deep amber, mellow and fading. Almost sunset, nightfall.

And she was not alone. She heard nothing, not even a sigh of breath, but she could sense the weight of someone watching her. She rolled over to find Marco sitting beside her bed.

For a moment, she was sure she was dreaming. That all her thoughts of him had conjured him out of thin air once again. How very handsome he was, just like in those dreams, his glossy black hair brushed back, his eyes so dark and unreadable. A stark white bandage stood out against his olive-complected brow.

And how solemn he was, watching her so carefully, unsmiling.

Thalia pushed herself up against her pillows, not daring to take her gaze from him for fear he would vanish.

'It is quite improper for you to be here in my bedchamber,' she said.

A tiny smile touched his lips. The merest whisper to break up his solemnity, but Thalia rejoiced in it. Her Marco was in there, somewhere.

'I have seen it before, *signorina*, if you will recall,' he said. 'And this time your sister let me in. So, I think we are safe for the time being.'

'Calliope let you in?'

'*Si.* In fact, she summoned me here. I feared at first that her note meant you were feeling worse, but I see that is not so.'

Thalia shook her head, still dazed by the fact that he was here, that her sister had sent for him. 'I am quite recovered.'

'And I am glad to see that. Would you care for some tea?'

She nodded, watching as he poured out a cup from the tray left on her table. She examined him over the gold rim as she sipped. 'You look rather well yourself, aside from that bandage. Have you been terribly busy?'

'Quite busy, yes. We are preparing to take the silver on a bit of a voyage, to tour the Italian cities.'

'We?'

'Your Antiquities Society. They seem quite excited at the prospect, and I know my countrymen will love to see it.'

'Oh, yes.' Thalia gazed down into her cup. 'I was rather surprised to hear of Lady Riverton's involvement with the Society.'

Marco laughed ruefully. 'Not nearly as surprised as I, I am sure.'

'Has she been helping you to establish this tour?'

'No. I understand she has left on a new task, to Greece this time. With young Mr Dashwood as escort.'

'Lady Billingsfield's nephew?' Thalia said in surprise. 'My, my. How very busy *everyone* is these days. And you yourself must be departing very soon.'

'I hope to. It has been too long since I was at home, and there is work to be done.'

Thalia carefully set the cup down on the tray, not sure what she should say next. What she should do. Ordinarily, she would just do whatever wild thing came into her head. Her every instinct urged her to throw herself into Marco's arms, to hold on to him and beg him not to leave her. Not to let go of what they had found together.

But what she had told her sister was true. She had learned caution, or her own version of it anyway. If Marco did not feel as she did, if it had all been a mad interlude, she should just let him go. Even if it made her miserable.

Even if it went against everything she was.

'I suppose then we should put the word about that our engagement is ended, since that was our arrangement,' she said slowly. The arrangement he had made clear he wanted. 'There is probably much speculation anyway. Bath is such a gossip-ridden place.'

'No one knows of what really happened in the caves,' Marco said. 'You need not worry about gossip.'

Thalia laughed. 'Oh, Marco. The Chase Muses never worry about such things. Do I seem to you like someone who worries about gossip?'

He laughed, too, a deep, rich sound that warmed her to her very toes. 'Not at all. It is one of the many delightful things about you.'

'Do you think I'm "delightful", Marco? Really?' At his words, Thalia felt the dim room brighten just a bit. Had her hard work not been for naught after all? Or was she just being foolishly romantic again?

'How could anyone not?'

'Well, there are those who see me as too—impulsive,' she said.

'No,' he said decidedly. 'It is only because you are so passionate about what you believe in. What you care about.'

'As are you.'

'*Si*. It seems we are two of a kind in that, *cara*.'

Two of a kind. If only she could persuade him of the truth of that. But, for once in her life, she had no words.

'I must tell you of something, *bella*,' he said slowly. 'Once, long ago, when I was young and foolish, I thought I was in love. Her name was Maria, and she had the loveliest dark eyes, the brightest laugh. We would walk in the back streets of Florence together, and read poetry by the Arno.'

Thalia went very still. Was this the mysterious Maria at last? 'She was Domenico's cousin?'

'So you know of her?'

'I—a little. He said you loved her, that you could never love anyone else.'

'I did love her, as only an ardent young man could! I loved her too much, as she did me. When I left for the army, she followed secretly. We hoped to marry, but before we could…'

Thalia swallowed hard. 'Yes?'

Marco gave her a sad smile. 'Before we could, she was killed by a stray bullet when she came to watch the battle with the other wives. It was my fault that she was there, and I vowed then and there that I would never put a woman in such danger again. That I would never love again. But, *cara*, I could not keep that vow.'

'Oh, Marco!' Thalia cried, her heart breaking at his old sorrow. At the way he had walled up his heart from pain. *That* was why he had tried to make her think he did not want her, did not want their betrothal to be true. She kissed his hand, holding it tightly in hers. 'I am not Maria, and you are not that young man now. I have the sense to stay out of danger.'

He laughed ruefully, his fingers tightening on hers. 'Oh, yes? And so what was that in the caves?'

'Oh, very well, so sometimes I *do* run into danger. But I can extricate myself from it, too. I want to help you, Marco, to be a part of your work. I trust you. Do you trust me now?'

'Of course I do.'

'So, then, what of our engagement? Shall I have Cameron send an announcement to the papers saying we have ended it?' she said bravely, hoping against hope he would say no. That he would see that the past was gone, and they had only a future. *Their* future.

His smile widened, and he kissed her hand softly. 'If that is what you want. But I think I have an alternative to propose.'

Against her will, a small, beautiful bud of hope bloomed, just the merest amount, in Thalia's heart. She took a deep breath and said, 'An alternative?'

'Yes.' He reached inside his coat and brought out a tiny box, opening it to reveal a ring. A perfect, deep blue sapphire surrounded by shimmering pearls. 'Thalia Chase, will you marry me? In truth this time.'

Thalia stared down at the ring, its facets blurred by a sudden rush of tears. She pressed her hand to her mouth. That ring, and all it stood for, was everything she wanted. Everything she longed for. And yet…

'Is it because you feel—obligated?' she whispered. 'Because of what has happened between us?'

'Thalia, *cara mia*. Surely you never thought me a cad who would make love to a lady and then abandon her?'

'But I wanted it! I never did that to trap you, to make you—'

'Thalia!' He took her hand tightly in his, stilling her flood of words. 'You have not trapped me. What we have is beautiful; I would not demean it. I feared that I had put you in danger because I selfishly could not stay away from you. I resolved, after the cave, to go away and not make your life worse.'

'Worse?' Thalia cried. 'The only thing that could make my life terrible would be to never see you again.'

'And mine would be the same. All the sunlight would vanish for ever if you were not there, Thalia. You are my whole heart.'

The tears flowed free at his words, those sweet, sweet words that echoed all she felt herself. 'Yet you still resolved to leave me?'

'I could not truly love you if I did not put your happiness first. I was sure after what happened that you wouldn't want to see me again.'

'But what changed your mind? What made you come here today?'

'Your sister brought me something.' He reached under his chair and brought out a thick sheaf of parchment, bound up in string.

'My play?' Thalia said, confused.

'The Dark Castle of Duke Orlando,' he said. 'A tale of a mysterious count and his adventurous wife. The Duke tries to protect her, but his efforts only lead to more deceit, more heartbreak. There must always be honesty between them, for they are soulmates.'

'Yes, that is exactly what must be! But I fear there is no ending yet to their story. I have not been able to craft one.'

'Perhaps that is because their adventure together will be never-ending,' Marco said. 'They will just continue on life's path with each other, wherever it takes them.'

'Because no danger is too great when they face it together.'

'Will you, Thalia? Will you face the rest of our lives with me? With a man who loves you beyond all reason?'

Thalia nodded. 'Of course I will, Marco. For I love you, too. With my whole heart.'

He slipped the ring on to her finger, and its clear blue light gleamed there like a beacon of promise. Like the light of a love that was always meant to be.

Epilogue

From the *London Post*:

Sir Walter Chase announces the marriage of his daughter Miss Thalia Chase to the Count di Fabrizzi on Saturday last at Chase Lodge. In attendance were Sir Walter and Lady Chase, the Earl and Countess of Westwood, the Duke and Duchess of Averton—who were newly arrived back in England after an extensive honeymoon voyage—and the bride's younger sister and niece. A waltzing party followed, with cake and champagne served and dancing through the night.

The Count and Contessa di Fabrizzi will make their home in Florence, after a tour of the Continent observing sites of antiquity.

Author's Note

I've loved getting to know the Chase Muses as they find their true loves! When I was growing up, I always wanted a sister—or several!—yet my parents only gave me a little brother. That ended up all for the best—I love my brother dearly, and he never stole my lipstick or insisted I take him with me to the mall!—but I've enjoyed writing my old dreams with the Chases. Perhaps I'll revisit them again the future. I have the feeling Cory has more to say, and even Psyche, once she grows up into a Victorian lady…

I also enjoyed researching the history of Bath for this book. A few sources I found that were invaluable included several guidebooks I picked up on a visit to the city a few years ago—such as the ones from the Assembly Rooms and from Number One Royal Crescent, the inspiration for Calliope's house; Pierce Egan's 1819 volume *Walks Through Bath*—especially great for Sydney Gardens and the various events held there; R.S. Neale's *Bath 1680-1850, A Social History*; William Lowndes's *The Theatre Royal at Bath*; and *The History of Sulis Minerva at Bath*—the museum where Thalia and Marco met, the Bath Society of Antiquities, is of my own invention, but the artefacts they see there are real.

The silver altar set is based on the famous 'Morgantina Silver', a fifteen-piece cache of third-century BC Hellenistic silver. It is currently in the Metropolitan Museum, but is due to be returned to the Aidone Archaeological Museum in 2010. For more of the silver's amazing journey, take a look at the book *The Medici Conspiracy: The Illicit Journey of Looted Antiquities* by Peter Watson and Cecilia Todeschini.

The armed uprising Domenico de Lucca planned at Naples is also based on historical fact. In July 1820, there was an insurrection there led by army officers, which then spread throughout southern Italy. It eventually led to Ferdinand I, King of the Two Sicilies, conceding a constitution—before revoking it again. The 'Risorgimento'—Rediscovery—of Italian identity led to eventual unification in 1861. No doubt people like the children and grandchildren of the Count and Contessa di Fabrizzi were there to see it.

1109/04a